THESE
NAMELESS
THINGS

BOOKS BY SHAWN SMUCKER

The Day the Angels Fell
The Edge of Over There
Light from Distant Stars
These Nameless Things

Once We Were Strangers

THESE NAMELESS THINGS

SHAWN SMUCKER

Revell

a division of Baker Publishing Group
Grand Rapids, Michigan

Published by Revell
a division of Baker Publishing Group
PO Box 6287, Grand Rapids, MI 49516-6287
www.revellbooks.com

Printed in the United States of America

Library of Congress Cataloging-in-Publication Data
Names: Smucker, Shawn, author.
Title: These nameless things / Shawn Smucker.
Description: Grand Rapids, Michigan : Revell, [2020]
Identifiers: LCCN 2019056024 | ISBN 9780800735302 (paperback) | ISBN 9780800738631 (hardback)
Subjects: GSAFD: Christian fiction.
Classification: LCC PS3619.M83 T47 2020 | DDC 813/.6—dc23
LC record available at https://lccn.loc.gov/2019056024

20 21 22 23 24 25 26   7 6 5 4 3 2 1

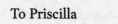
To Priscilla

"The undiscovered country, from whose bourn
No traveler returns, puzzles the will."

Shakespeare, *Hamlet*

"Why do we let our guilt consume us so?"

Dante Alighieri, *The Divine Comedy*

"Be grateful for whoever comes,
because each has been sent as a guide from beyond."

Rumi

PROLOGUE

A Confession

WE MOVE IN a loose group, winding through the trees. We are more people than you can even imagine, yet there is hardly a word spoken. We smell like exhaustion, like miles piled on top of miles, like time when it has already run out. Yet somehow we also sound like hope, like fresh water washing through the reeds. We discreetly share food with each other, nearly all of us strangers, nodding politely, and in spite of our condition, we cannot keep the inexplicable hope from showing in our eyes.

This is our first day out from under the shadow of the mountain. Which sounds exactly like something he would have said in that deep, rich voice of his, if he was here with us. And he would have smiled—how happy he would have been, saying those words!

Then he would have laughed, and the thought of him laughing is too much for me right now. It brings up an ache that makes it hard to breathe. I shake my head and try to laugh it off, but my grin falters, and any kind of sound I might make lodges somewhere in my throat.

It's my fault he's not with us. There's no way around it.

How could I let him go back on his own?

It's more an accusation than a question, and now the aching wells up behind my eyes. I squeeze them shut. I stop walking and think about turning around. It's the guilt that threatens to consume me.

The path goes up and up and up, and everyone is so tired, but the old fears are fresh enough to keep us walking, to keep us moving through this heavy weariness. I reluctantly rejoin the movement up the mountain. Nearly everyone stares at the ground in front of their feet. Maybe that's all that matters right now. One step after the other. Moving farther up. Moving farther in, away from her. Hoping she won't find us, won't convince us to go back.

Up ahead and to the left, I notice that the trees clear along the edge of the cliff, and I find myself walking faster, faster, stumbling over my own feet, pushing between this person and that person, mumbling my apologies, my voice strange in the voiceless woods. I get to the clearing and it is what I hoped it would be: an overlook. A cold wind blows up from the valley, rushes through that open space, agitating the leaves behind me into the wild rustling sound of secrets. I climb a kind of stone platform, and the rock is gritty under my fingers. There's no snow up here, but the rock is cold. Everything feels present and real.

Have you ever, for a flash of time, understood the significance of being? The miracle of existing? That's what I feel now, climbing up onto the ledge: the particular roughness of the rocks under my knees, the chill of the wind on my face. The unique expression of my existence, here, as I stand.

I look out over that huge expanse of miles that all of us walked through, and I scan the valley. I hold one hand up, shield my eyes from the glare of those bright clouds, and hope to see nothing out there except empty plains.

At first I'm relieved and my shoulders relax because all I see is the undulating ground stretching to the west, as far as the horizon. The wind continues to whip up around me, and I draw my arms closer to my chest, duck my chin down, and try to find warmth in my body. It is there somewhere inside of me, that warmth, that fire. I can sense the rustling of all the people hiking, moving up the mountain behind me. I can feel them glancing at my back as they pass, taking in my silhouette on the overlook, probably wondering why I would stop, why I would look back. This makes me angry. I want to turn and answer them, answer all of their unasked questions.

I knew him.

I loved him.

Do you have any idea what our freedom cost?

But I keep looking out over the plains, and finally I see something like two ants wandering along a dusty pile. I sigh. All the way down there in the valley, where we began the climb up this mountain, through the trees, those two small specks walk away, walk west. Their progress is barely visible, but there is nothing to stop them, not as far as the eye can see. We will soon be separated by this great chasm. Every-thing has fallen into a stark, dazzling white, the light glaring off endless miles of glittering frost. I can smell snow, but none is falling.

He is going with her.

I hoped that he might be among the last of the crowd, that he could possibly be tagging along at the back, that he would come up and surprise me. We would hug and I would laugh out loud—my first real laugh in a long time—and he would explain how he got out of going back and that all the wrong I had done was magically undone.

But he couldn't do it. He couldn't reverse my mistakes, couldn't easily untie my deceptions, and the only option was for someone to go back. He is doing it. I strain my eyes toward the horizon, but even from that height, I can't see the mountain we came from, the one whose shadow we have finally escaped. I don't think I'd want to see it, but I search that far-off horizon anyway.

"Do you see him?" she asks, walking up behind me. Not long ago, she would have wrapped her arms around my body, moved in close and held me. I would have felt her warmth against my back. But not now. Not after everything that has happened.

I close my eyes, imagining. I shiver and nod. "I can't believe he has to go back." Unspoken are the words, *It's my fault.*

We stand there in those words, the wind whipping them around us, catching on them, sailing away with them. She doesn't offer any kind of consolation.

"It was here all along," she says, a lining of amazement in her voice. "This mountain was here, waiting for us."

"Are you . . ." I begin, then start over. My voice is hoarse, and I clear it against the dry, cold air. "Do you . . . remember?"

"Everything. It's all coming back to me."

"Even before?"

"Even before."

"Me too," I whisper.

How is it that a mind can contain so many memories? Where does it all fit? Into what nooks and crannies do we place these recollections of love and sadness, horror and joy? Into what tiny space of our minds do we put a person we met long ago, or a disappointment, or a lie? And where do memories go when we forget, and how is it that they can come rushing back, unbidden?

I am embarrassed by what I did, the choices I made. There are things I would rather forget, but because I can think of nothing else to say, a confession emerges: "I'm such a liar. You know that by now, right? How many things I said that weren't true?"

She is still as a fence post. It almost seems like she's holding her breath.

"You know, I would lie for the fun of it," I whisper, "even when there was nothing in it. Just because. I don't even know why. What's wrong with a person who lies for no reason?"

I don't realize she is crying until I hear her try to stifle a sob, like a hiccup. She moves closer but we're still not touching, and we remain there for a time, watching the two people down on the plain. We cry together. She sighs a trembling sigh, and when she speaks I can tell she is trying to lift our spirits.

"The rumor coming back from the front is that the higher you go, the warmer it gets."

"Then we should keep walking," I say, but I don't move. A great silence falls on us as the last people pass by behind us. He is not among them. I knew he wouldn't be, was positive of this after seeing the two far-off figures walking away, but I had still allowed myself to hope.

"There they go." She steps away, as if she can't stay too close or she'll give in to old impulses like hugging me or pulling me close. "He saved all of us," she says, and I can hear the tears in her voice. "And now he's going back."

I nod again, the tears flowing. I wipe them away hastily with the back of my hand. They're embarrassing, those tears. They make me feel small.

"Dan," she says. "It's time. He'll find her, and he'll follow us over."

I look over at her for the first time since she came up behind me. "Will he? Will he find her? Will he find us?"

She doesn't answer.

"Will he find me?" I ask, my voice tiny and quivering.

Wordlessly, we climb down the rock and turn toward the top of this new mountain, this fresh start, this beginning. We can see the tail end of the procession of people moving up the trail. We will soon be back among them, or maybe we'll stay back a bit, find our own pace.

"I wonder," I say quietly.

"Wonder?" she asks, falling into step beside me. I want to take her hand again, but those days are long gone. "Wonder what?"

My response is a whisper. I can't imagine she even hears me. "Can he really cross from there to us? Or is he lost? Forever?"

The breeze snatches my words and throws them out into the void, but she hears them. And she smiles. "He'll find us."

So childlike. So trusting. I want to question her. I want to raise my flag of doubt, but before I can, she says it again.

"He'll find us."

PART ONE

1 THE LIE

MONTHS BEFORE I stood on that overlook and searched for
any sight of him, on the opposite side of the endless plains
and under the shadow of the western mountain, the three
of us laughed together—Miho and Abe and me. Miho was
nearly crying, she was laughing so hard, shaking her head
and trying to stop but then starting right up again, her body
bobbing up and down. She waved a weak hand at us: *Stop it!*
Abe and I grinned at each other, huge, sappy grins. We didn't
know what to do in the face of such laughter. When she did
that, when she leaned back and laughed like that, I could sit
and watch her for days. I felt lighter in that moment than I
had in a long time, released, like a balloon untied and rising.

Miho caught her breath and sighed, and I was filled with
something close to pure joy. What were we laughing about?
I don't know. I can't remember, because there was a pause,
and Abe said those three words, and everything we were
laughing about melted away. They stared at me to see how I
would handle the news, Abe with his steady gaze trained on
my face, and Miho, her eyes dancing nervously from me to
the sky to the plains and back to me again. I realized that's
why they had come up to my house: to share this news, to see
how I would take it, and to talk me off the ledge if needed.

Mary is leaving.

We ended up sitting against the back wall of my house. I went from joyful to exhausted. We looked out over the plains, absorbing the gentle breeze, not saying a word. There was the smell of fresh green grass and wet earth coming toward us from off in the distance, and rain on the way. The breeze was cool and weightless, but I felt the heaviness of nameless things.

The horizon seemed impossibly far off, the clouds low, and I experienced a kind of dizziness, a spinning, an inability to determine what was up and what was down, and then a low-grade panic. Air was suddenly in short supply, and I wondered if this was what it was like to hyperventilate. I rested my head against the wall and stared into the slits of blue sky peeking through. But that didn't help, so I closed my eyes completely.

"Are you sure, Abe?" I asked, and even though my question was aimed at him, I hoped Miho would chime in and tell me it wasn't true, it was all just a joke. I watched a small speck drift across the red horizon inside my eyelids.

Please, Miho, I thought. *Tell me it's not true.*

"She'd like to leave tonight," Abe admitted. The deep, quiet sound of his voice stayed with me even when he stopped talking. His voice was like the earth, solid beneath the long, soft grass. If Mary left, would everyone else leave too? Even Miho? Even Abe? The thought of living there in town alone made me sick. I couldn't keep waiting, not by myself.

"We haven't lost anyone for years," I said. "Why is she leaving now?"

"We're not losing her, Dan," Miho said, the tiniest exasperation in her voice. "Everyone will leave sooner or later. You know that. There's nothing lost. Everyone will leave, eventually."

She paused, and I could tell she was trying to decide if she should keep talking.

"Even you," she added.

I opened my eyes and looked at her, took in her short, black-rooted, dyed-blonde hair rustling in the wind. Her eyes softened when our gazes met, and she surrendered a small smile that showed only at the corners of her mouth and the slopes of her temples. It was an expression as far removed from the minutes-ago mirth as I could imagine, but it was full of compassion. She had a triangle tattoo below the corner of one eye, like a tear. Another, much larger swirling tattoo filled with lines and shapes and blocks made its way up her neck, touched her jaw below her ear, extended up along her temple, and edged her hairline like a kind of border.

I remembered when she had received those tattoos, and why—she had been so sad, trying to cover up the marks of what had happened to her in the mountain. We had all tried to cover up our scars, most of us through distraction or busyness or work or fun. Some of us used tattoos. Some of us, eventually, tried to escape the horror by simply leaving, walking east. I had held her hand while Lou filled in the dark lines. How tightly she had squeezed my fingers, until the tattoo was hurting both of us. Lou had left town soon after that, headed east over the plains. No more tattoos, not after he was gone.

That was long ago.

"It's only Mary St. Clair," she said quietly. "It's only Mary." As if to say, *It's not me. I'm not leaving you.*

Abe gave her a sideways glance, a kind of reproach, but he didn't say a word.

Maybe today it's "only" Mary, but who will it be tomorrow? There are only nine of us left in town. Eight after Mary goes. What will I do when everyone is gone?

But I didn't have to say anything. They knew what I was thinking. They knew my concerns.

"Maybe we should leave with her?" Miho suggested, her voice timid as the breeze, her long, slender fingers finding mine in the depths of the cool grass. "Maybe now is the time?"

"You can go anytime you want," I said, and the words escaped without emotion. She didn't remove her hand from mine, but I felt her stiffen. Why was I always pushing her away?

"Dan," Abe said, and he could have gone a thousand different ways.

That wasn't a nice thing to say.

You will have to go sometime too.

Your brother is never coming over that mountain.

But he said none of those things. He was the kindest man I knew, the kindest I had ever known.

"Dan," he started again, "I am not leaving without you. Do you hear me? Miho is not leaving without you. You know that. We'll wait. We're in no hurry. Mary's leaving doesn't change any of that."

I did know it, but in the way you can know something with your head and not your heart, the way you can know a calculation is correct but still feel you've not done the work quite right. I was always second-guessing myself, always wondering why.

The breeze shifted direction, now blowing out into the plains, away from us, and it was suddenly cooler. There was an ominous feeling in the dropping temperature, the shifting of the wind. I might have suspected there was more change on the way than simply Mary's leaving.

I should have seen it coming.

The wind was trying to tell me.

The air charged around the house in gusting swirls. The long grass panicked, spinning, and out on the plains it billowed and rolled like waves in the sea, flashing white when it bent over and dark green when it stood up again. The movement was hypnotic.

I wanted to say something to ease the tension, something like, "I'm sorry" or "I know" or "Of course, you're right." I didn't want to spoil Mary's upcoming departure, and I didn't want her leaving to change anything about us or the village. It had been a long time since anyone left—I had begun to believe no one else would go, that the nine of us would spend eternity here, together.

I gently pulled my hand out from under Miho's and stood up. I stared out at the plains again, and the breeze burst around the house, this time colder and carrying drizzle. I pushed my hand back through my wet hair and it stood on end. I imagined I was a wild man setting out. The wind ripped at my shirt.

"What if he never comes over the mountain, Abe?" My voice felt empty, and the two of them felt far away. "What if I wait and wait, and he never comes?"

It was a hard question, one I ignored most days. But not on that day, and the question tied the knot inside of me tighter and tighter until my breath was hard to find.

"Did I ever tell you the one memory I still have of him, from when we were boys?" I asked. I had, many times. But they didn't stop me. "Adam and I were standing beside the creek bank, looking out over the water. The creek was swollen and fast after days of spring rain. He started climbing one of the trees—you know, the kind with branches that hung out over the water? And I pleaded with him to come down. But he didn't listen. I don't think he ever listened to me."

I stopped, and I sensed it approaching again, the anxiety.

"He kept climbing out over the water, grinning back at me the whole time, laughing at my concern. I have a feeling he did that often. And then the branch he was on broke, and he disappeared down into the water, branch and all, and was swept away." My voice trailed off. "I ran along the creek, screaming, 'Adam! Adam!' I tripped over rocks, branches scratching my face. He popped up to the surface, still holding on to the broken branch. When I saw him, I shouted his name even louder, and when he heard me, he looked over at me. And he grinned. He was being swept away, and he was still grinning."

I shook my head in amazement. "I remember pulling him to shore, pulling the branch and him and everything else. I never knew I could be that strong. I pulled him up out of the water and we sat there together, soaking wet. He was breathing hard, and I was crying and angry and relieved. I didn't know what to say to him. He scared me so bad. I think he did that a lot too. I don't know. It's hard to tell, but that's how it feels."

But it was all a lie.

I didn't have any memories of my brother apart from knowing he existed. None of us in town remembered anything of consequence about our lives before the horror of the mountain. I mean, we each had a few minor facts to lean on, maybe the existence of a family member or two, the image of a place, but the stories of our lives had been erased from our minds by what had happened to us in that forsaken range.

Abe had tears in his eyes. "The three of us, we've been here for a long time." His old voice wavered. Miho made a sound of assent, a quiet sound, and Abe continued. "I was here long before either of you escaped to this place. I've seen a lot of people come over that mountain, and I've seen a lot of people leave us, head east over the plains. This village will be here as long as you need it to be." He grunted, as if completely convinced by what he had just said.

"What if no one's left in the mountain?" I asked, agitated and shaken. "What if Adam already came over and I missed him? Or what if he's still in there but he can't leave on his own? What if they won't let him leave?"

They. I shuddered at the thought of the ones who had kept us there, flinched involuntarily as if I could feel it all again.

Miho reached up and moved her finger in a line along the tattoo on her forehead. "We're not leaving without you," she insisted. "Not even if it's only the three of us left here. Abe and I, we'll wait with you."

I turned a short circle, not knowing where to walk. We

were all getting good and wet now in the rain. I felt like I was losing my mind. Maybe sleep would help.

"Are you sure Mary's going to go through with it?" I asked. "It's a long walk. Maybe she'll change her mind."

Abe nodded. "She's leaving tonight."

"In the rain?" I asked.

"I expect if the storm comes, she'll wait until tomorrow. Don't blame her, Dan. It's her time. When it's time, it's time."

I bit my lip, nodded. A round of thunder rolled down toward us from the mountain. "And if it's still raining tomorrow evening?" I asked, feeling petulant and angry. I wanted to argue with someone. I wanted to irritate everyone close to me. I knew it wasn't Abe's fault, but I had to take my disappointment out on someone.

"She's leaving," Miho said in a soothing tone. "I talked to her too, after Abe told me. I went to her house, Dan. Trust me. She's leaving. All her stuff is bundled up and ready. Tonight, or tomorrow night, or the next. As soon as the weather's good, she's walking."

I nodded curtly. I didn't want to talk about it anymore. "Feels like the rain's going to get heavy," I said, and they glanced at each other, took the hint.

Abe stood slowly, the way an older man stands when he has been sitting on the ground for too long—a stiff unfolding, a pause when it appeared for a moment that he might sit back down. But he pushed through, stood up, and Miho rose beside him with ease.

"Shall we take our leave, my lord?" she asked Abe in a formal voice with an unrecognizable accent, as if she was a royal lady from some bygone era. She waved her arms in a flourish and bowed in his direction, extending one of her pale hands to him.

I loved her for this, her ability to lighten the mood. I smiled, and she caught my gaze out of the corner of her eye and winked at me.

Abe grinned, sheepish. His black skin had a matte finish to it, a flat sort of richness, and his smile pulled all of that back, stretched it so that he was young again. His face became bright white teeth and flashing eyes, and I could see for a moment what he had probably been like as a boy: mischievous, foolhardy. But not as lovely as he was in that moment. That would not have been possible. What had I ever done to deserve his lavish friendship?

"Yes, ma'am," he said in his low voice.

On the other side of the house, the side that faced the mountain, thunder trembled again, louder, with sharp edges and a crackling that lingered and spread its fingers through the air. Abe took Miho's arm and I felt a small pang of jealousy, even though it was Abe and it was Miho and I had nothing to be jealous about. I followed them around the corner of the house to the front, and the breeze was a chilled wind that raced down the mountainside.

The mountain. There it was, rising only a few hundred yards from the front of my house, tall and terrible and crowned with a realm of dark gray clouds that boiled nearly green around the edges. There was snow up at the peaks—I knew this not because I could see it, but because I knew those mountains the same way I knew my own face in a mirror. It was a constant in my dreams, my nightmares. The shadow of it haunted each of our faces, in the shallow space under our eyes or the dark of our mouths when they hung open while we slept. I felt, not for the first time, that the mountain might collapse on all of us.

I wondered how many remained in that pit in the mountain, how many at that moment were tortured or chased, how many were fleeing. How many were hungry and hiding and moving through the shadows, trying to find their way out, trying to find their way to us.

I glanced over toward the sliver of the canyon that split the face of one of the cliffs, two hundred yards up the hill from my house, the only break in that long line of sheer rock and crumbling rubble. The only way through. I lost myself staring up at the mountain, thinking about that thin canyon, the only way.

When I finally turned to say goodbye to Miho and Abe, they were halfway down the hill, clinging to each other. There was a long gap between my house and the group of houses that made up the rest of the town. The narrow, grassy road we called the greenway traveled from the mouth of the canyon, passed by where I stood, and meandered down to the forty or fifty houses scattered like seeds, mostly empty. Once upon a time, that green path comforted regular arrivals from the other side of the mountain, used so often by those escaping that the grass had been flattened and there had been bare patches, streaking paths of brown. But now the greenway had grown thick and lush, used only by the few of us who still lived here.

"Goodbye!" I shouted, regretting how I had turned the visit sour. They had only wanted to let me know what was happening, and I had made them feel bad. I lived in perpetual guilt about one thing or another.

They disregarded the rain—it was warm and easy to idle through. Miho waved without looking, her hair wet and flat against her head. But Abe turned halfway around, lifted his free arm, and smiled at me. It was a mischievous grin, and I could tell he liked being escorted down the greenway by a beautiful woman.

His face grew serious. His voice barely reached me before being blown back away from the mountain and swept out over the plains.

"Better get inside!" he shouted. "There's a storm comin'!"

2 THROUGH ME, THE WAY

LIGHTNING STRUCK AND I flinched. The rain came down in hard pellets, but I kept watching Abe and Miho as they drifted away. I waited until they disappeared into town before I walked inside my house, dripping wet. The sound of the storm was a steady roar on the cedar shingles above me, but the stone walls, silent and still, filled me with a sense of safety. I didn't light any lamps, and the gray afternoon filtered in through the windows.

There was a small open area inside the front door of my house. To the left, a fireplace along the outside wall. To the right was a rather long, galley-style kitchen, and at the end of it a narrow space where I ate and wrote and spent time thinking. The wide double doors that faced out the back were open, but they were sheltered by the eaves of the house so the water wasn't coming in. I stared at the plains sweeping away in a graceful downhill for a long, long way, covered in a dense curtain of rain that hit the ground before rising in a ghostly mist.

I went into my bedroom, the only separate space in the house, and changed into dry clothes. I tried to think of other things, but my mind kept coming back around to the conversation I had with Abe and Miho.

Mary was leaving.
Mary was leaving.
Mary was leaving.

After she left, it would only be Abe and Miho and me, plus Miss B, John, Misha, Circe, Po . . . was that everyone? I ran through the names again in my mind as I walked to where my desk was pushed up under the large window facing the mountain. I thought back through a handful of the people who had left a long time ago, and it filled me with a deep melancholy.

I sat there at my desk and watched the rain run in rivulets down the glass, pooling above each mullion, dripping down to the next pane. The wind came and went, rattling the wooden frames. Lightning flashed and thunder followed. It was a good afternoon to be alone.

I pulled one of my many journals from the back corner of the desk. I picked up a pen and played with it, ran it over my fingers, took off the cap and put it back on again. It was still dark in the house except for the gray light, and I didn't write anything. I thought of my brother. I wondered where he was in that moment, if it was raining on him too, in the mountain. I wondered if he was alone. I hoped he was alone. I couldn't remember much from my time there, but I did remember wanting solitude, and the terror that came when those who were in charge paid you any attention.

My house was so close to the mountain that when I was inside, I could barely see the top of the steep range through the windows. My eyes drifted over to the left, to the mouth of the canyon, the place from which all of us had emerged at some point.

And I saw something move.

I stood, stared harder through the rain. What was it? Could it be . . . someone was coming out of the mountain? I leaned closer to the glass, held my breath, willed the rain to stop.

There, I saw the movement again.

A hunched form stooped and leaned against one of the last boulders barely outside the canyon. They stopped right beside the wooden sign someone had posted next to the canyon opening a long, long time ago. I had read it many times, because I often walked to the canyon mouth and willed my brother to appear.

THROUGH ME THE WAY INTO THE SUFFERING CITY
THROUGH ME THE WAY TO THE ETERNAL PAIN
THROUGH ME THE WAY THAT RUNS AMONG THE LOST

And then a few lines that were no longer legible, faded as they were, followed by one final line at the bottom:

ABANDON EVERY HOPE, WHO ENTER HERE

Why would anyone ever enter there? Why would anyone ever go back?

The person who had just come through the canyon tried to take a step forward, but they tripped, fell onto all fours. They crawled a few feet and lay down in the rain.

Could it be Adam? A flutter of hope tried to rise in me, but I shoved it down. I stood, willed the person to keep coming, but I didn't move from my spot. It wasn't worth trying to help them yet—they had to find their own way at first, like a newborn calf finding its footing. I remembered coming through that gap and seeing the plains and the small stone houses and feeling like I could finally breathe again. I had wept and cried in agony and crawled down the grassy path when I could no longer walk. Abe had welcomed me.

Yes, it had been Abe. The memory came up from some deep place. It had been Abe. I would tell him that the next time I saw him, that I remembered it had been him welcoming me, helping me down from the canyon to his own house in the village.

This strange, unexpected person crawled down the greenway, and I could see now that the form was a woman. A stabbing sense of sadness moved through me—*This is not my brother*—and I no longer held my breath. She was all knobby bones and stretched, naked skin, typical of those who came out. There was so little food in the mountain, and no spare clothes were ever handed out, at least not that I remembered. She was covered only by her own long black hair draping over her torso. She got to her feet, shaking. She walked like a toddler, one unsteady foot in front of the other, and came closer. Closer. After what seemed like an eternity, she reached the part of the greenway that ran directly in front of my house.

She stopped.

She was a pillar of pale skin and jet-black hair, and I couldn't see her face. She turned off the grassy lane toward my front door, wobbling with each step, and disappeared into that area close to the front door that I couldn't see through the window. I heard a weak knock.

It had been so long since someone had come out of the mountain. I hesitated.

I knew I should immediately lead her down to Abe's house—this was my main responsibility in the village, to keep watch for refugees who came down out of the mountain. Abe could assess her, help her decide what to do next, where to go, where to live if she wanted to stay. But all of that came later. First, I needed to take her to Abe.

But I felt a hesitancy I had never felt before, and it was strange, this reluctance. It scared me. She needed to go to Abe. So why did I want to keep her at the house with me? Where was this hesitation coming from?

I opened the door with a shaking hand, and the roaring sound of the rain surrounded me through both the front and back doors. Small spits of it swirled into the shadows, small as the eye of a needle, then rose back up in the confused air. And there she was, waiting, her arms hanging helplessly at her sides. Thick black hair draped over her upper half. She raised her arms and clutched her sides, shivering, trying to cover herself. I noticed that the water where it left her feet was tinted red, blood still washing off.

"Come in, please," I said quietly. A subtle terror rose in me, and confusion beside it. Why was I inviting her in? Where did those words come from?

And why was I afraid of this helpless woman?

I should have been walking her down to Abe's, rain or no rain. But I turned and grabbed a small blanket from the rocking chair, moved toward her, and offered it to her. She shrank from my approach, seemed to be as scared of me as I was unsettled by her. As the blanket came to rest around her shoulders, her head tilted back, one hand pushed a part in the curtain of her hair, and she looked through. Her irises were dark like unlit tunnels, and the whites of her eyes were bloodshot, streaked with lightning-shaped capillaries. There were cuts on her face, red and swollen so that I couldn't easily recognize her features. She shivered, not the gentle movement of someone slightly cold, but the deep, convulsive shuddering of someone hypothermic. Her knees locked and unlocked, jerking her body this way and that like a marionette in an unwitting dance.

She opened her mouth to speak. I wanted to help her, but it was important that I let her process this new place. When I had first started welcoming people from the other side, I tried too hard to make it easy on them, and they fought me or balked from the help I offered. I learned to wait. I shouldn't have given her the blanket—even that small interference could have caused her to veer into hysterics—but she had seemed so cold and disoriented by her own nakedness. Still, I should have waited. I knew this, even now, but I couldn't take the blanket back from her.

Mary St. Clair. I remembered again that she was leaving, and I remembered when it had been her crawling down the grassy lane, the first words she said, how her name tripped its way out from between cracked lips, how her nose bled down into her mouth as she stuttered, "Mmm . . . Mmm . . . Mary. Mary Say-Say-Say. Mary Say-Saint. Clair."

I'd always had a soft spot for Mary.

But this woman couldn't even speak, and my fear died a little inside of me. Sounds simply wouldn't come out. She closed her mouth and stared hard at the ground, then met my gaze again and opened her lips. I found myself nodding slightly, coaxing her to speak. It was like watching a baby chick break out of its own egg. I wanted to reach in and help, but it wasn't time. Not yet.

"Go ahead," I whispered, not able to help myself. I reached out and touched her elbow.

That's when I blacked out.

HUGE BOULDERS SIT along the walls of a gorge. Unrest fills the space, along with crushed rocks and sparse bits of crabgrass and tall cedars that are nothing more than spindly trunks sprouting dead, snapped-off branches. They stretch up forty, fifty, sixty feet to the top of the gorge where green needles dust their uppermost limbs. Through all of this, a woman comes walking, the same dark-haired woman I welcomed into my house. She's in pain. A lot of pain.

She looks broken, like the stones. She holds herself in a perpetual hug as she walks, her forearms self-consciously covering her chest. Her long black hair falls down all around her naked form, covering her arms and back, tangled and matted with something that looks like tar or dried blood. Because her hair is so long and thick, she almost looks armless.

A small dove watches the stumbling woman's progress, hopping along the top of the gorge. It flies ahead of her, following each of her steps with interest, its head cocked to one side or the other. Gradually she passes under the gaze of the bird and walks farther ahead, only for the bird to dance along the top of the gorge, catching up. But as the woman approaches the opening where the gorge spills out into the valley, out from the mountain, the dove suddenly stops, pecks two or three times at a red vein in a silver rock, then flies away, disappearing in the cliffs.

The black-haired woman limps out through a fracture in the mountain, and as she turns the corner, finally coming out from the canyon, there is the village and a home. My village. My home. This is the woman who came to my house, and I am watching her approach, but from the canyon.

What is going on? I stir, but I cannot escape. I see a leopard creep along the edge of the gorge. A hungry lion bends over its prey, hidden among the boulders. A pregnant she-wolf, lean and starving, collapses onto her side, moaning in the shadows.

I cry out.

I WOKE UP, opened my eyes. I was covered in sweat. Somehow, I was sitting in the armchair facing the still-open back doors, facing the plains. I couldn't shake the eeriness of the . . . what was it? Dream? Vision? Memory? The house was darker than it had been before, but not as cold. Everything was completely still—the rain had stopped, and the silence left behind was like its own sound. I could feel my pulse fluttering, and a chill spread through my body, not from the cool breeze but from something else, something deeper inside of me.

I heard a sound behind me, at the front door. A moan. I jumped out of my chair, still woozy from the dream, and turned. The front door remained wide open. There was a puddle of water on the threshold. The dark-haired woman was on the floor in the water, under the blanket I had given her, unconscious.

I took a step in her direction but stopped. I turned around, went to the back doors, and closed them. The house grew even darker. I made my way back to the woman, slowly, slowly. She still hadn't moved. I reached down to shake her shoulder, perhaps push her hair back, but that deep fear returned, made my hand tremble, and I didn't touch her.

That's when I saw it on the floor, barely outside the reach of one of her extended hands. A skeleton key, the kind used in old houses, with a small circle at the top, a long shaft, and uneven teeth at the other end. I reached for it. Her fingers were so close. I took the key and lifted it without a sound, stared at it, and slipped it into my pocket.

I had to tell Abe about this.

I eased my way around the woman's body, my eyes on her the whole time. I justified my decision to leave her by telling myself she would be fine. She wouldn't regain consciousness while I was away. I went through the front door and closed it gently behind me. The air outside was fresh and cool and the greenway grass was all bent over, heavy with moisture that soaked my shoes and the bottom of my trousers. I didn't run. But I wanted to.

There were dozens of houses in the village, including mine, and nearly all of them were empty, but we kept even the empty ones tidy, at least on the outside. There were flowers in the window boxes that we transplanted from various spots on the plains, and we swept the dust from the eaves, but there was no denying the emptiness of shades always drawn and footpaths overgrown. The tall grass from the plains had begun encroaching on our small town, growing high where the walking of so many people, so many old friends, used to keep it low.

As I walked down to the homes, all the doors were closed, blinds drawn. Dusk approached and the light dimmed. We didn't visit with each other as much as we used to. I had to admit that it seemed we were growing apart.

Miss B opened her door as I walked past, and the loud sound of the latch made me jump.

"Hello, Dan," she said in her rich voice, her dark freckles dancing, her dreadlocked hair pulled up in a massive knot above her head. She seemed to be as old as Abe, but she didn't take things as seriously as he did. She floated along, rarely offering an opinion or criticism of any kind.

"Miss B, hi." I turned toward her, slowing but not stopping. "Everything okay?"

"Where you off to? You think you're going to pass on by without giving me a hug?"

I smiled, laughed to myself, and it felt good. I took a deep breath, turned around, and approached Miss B on the short path that led off the greenway to her front door. She was a large woman, and she gathered me in. She was warm and smelled of lavender.

I returned the hug and took a step back. "Have you seen Abe?" I asked, trying not to sound worried.

"I think he went all the way down to Miho's," she said, slow and steady. "You heard about Mary?"

I nodded, started to walk away.

"Finally leaving, our dear Mary," she said in a singsong voice, and I could tell she thought it was just about the best thing, miraculous even. And maybe it was. Maybe it was the miracle we'd all been waiting for. But it was hard for me to see it that way.

"I'll see you soon," I said.

"That was quite a storm," she said as I walked away. I waved again over my shoulder, but then a strange thing happened.

"Dan," Miss B said, and her voice was different. Completely different. Before, she had sounded airy, light, as if nothing about the day could go wrong. But in that whispered word, everything had changed. Her voice was strained. Her shoulders were slumped, and she was using a broom to hold herself up.

"Dan," she said again.

"Miss B?" I jogged back over to her and took hold of one of her large arms, wrapped it around my shoulders. "Miss B. Are you okay?"

"Help me down. Here's fine." She motioned to the thick grass beside the front door of her house. "Oh, yes, that's good. That's good."

I brought her down and nestled her into a spot, her back against the wall of her house, both of her hands planted into the ground beside her.

"Mmm-mmm," she exclaimed. "That came on fast."

"Are you okay?" I asked again. "Maybe I should go get Abe." I wanted to leave. I wanted to get away from her. I had never seen Miss B like that before, and it made my stomach churn. Her sudden weakness reminded me too much of the woman lying in my entryway, how that woman had made me feel.

Miss B kneaded her hands, as if trying to rub out the anxiety, and swayed forward and back. "No, no," she said in the breathless voice of someone who had run a marathon. "I'll mosey on over to Abe's a little later. He'll want to know."

"Know what, Miss B?"

As soon as the words came out of my mouth, I wanted them back. I wanted to swallow them and walk away. There was too much going on—what was happening? I wanted to keep everything as it was, nothing new. But it was too late. Mary was leaving and there was a strange woman lying on the floor in my house and Miss B was having some kind of a breakdown, emotional or physical or both.

"I really think I should go get Abe," I insisted, trying to backtrack from my question.

"I remember now," she said, and I realized that what I had mistaken for weariness in her voice was actually a kind of bliss.

Miss B was enraptured.

"I remember what happened," she said, amazement in her voice.

3 THE STORM

MISS B AND I sat in the foot-long grass that leaned up against her house, and only after we sat did I remember that the ground was wet. I could feel the water soaking into my clothes.

"Dan, Dan, Dan," she whispered, and her voice was filled with amazement at her own recollection. "I remember it now. I remember all of it! It's been coming back to me in pieces these last days, but this morning I had almost all of it right there, just outside of my mind's grasp, and then something you did, something you said . . . You hugged me." She sighed and shook her head. "Something." She lifted up her hand and stared at her palm as if looking for a line to interpret, and I could see the wet slickness there from the grass.

"What, Miss B?" I asked. I wanted to know even though I was afraid.

"No, wait," she said, curiosity in her voice. When she spoke, it was a strange mix of words, some meant for me, some meant for herself. "It wasn't something you did. I'll be. It was something I said. 'Quite a storm.' Remember how I said that? That was the phrase. 'Quite a storm.'" She paused. "I'll be," she said, wonder in her voice. "Brought it all back. All of it."

She shook her head, and at first I thought she wasn't going to tell me.

"It was one of those beautiful days after the rain, like today. The night before, there had been quite a storm." She smiled. "Quite a storm. But that day, heavens, that golden light streamed in the windows. I looked out into the flower beds and the summer flowers were up, beaming at me, like stars that fell to earth, like solid pieces of a broken rainbow. Mmm-mmm! What a sight."

I knew she was going to tell me everything, and I felt myself tensing up, the way you might when you're reading a book and the woman is about to open the door and inadvertently let the killer inside. It's a book you've read before, long ago, and you can't remember all the details or exactly when all the frightening things happen, but you have a distant premonition. And you don't like it.

"My husband's name was Carl Bird." She let out a young laugh, the laugh of a teenager flirting with the boy who is about to become her first kiss. "Carl Bird. Dan, it feels so sweet to finally remember his name. I knew it was there. I knew he was there all along. Where he is now, only heaven knows." Tears pooled in her soft brown eyes. "He was a good man. I remember that now too. The kind everyone else thinks is too good to be true. But he wasn't. He was just good. It aches me even worse now, the missing."

She wept, and I looked around to see if anyone else was close by, someone who could console her better than me, but there was no one. Only the surrounding empty houses and the greenway and the mountain behind us, although I couldn't see it now. I wished one of the other women would come out of her house, Circe or Misha. But they didn't, so I reached over and touched her hand sympathetically. She didn't let my hand come and go—she grabbed on to it, and she wept some more before gathering herself. She squeezed my fingers as she talked, and it made me feel claustrophobic.

"Maybe I should go get Misha," I suggested, but she plowed ahead.

"That morning was a normal morning, but it was also a rapture, and that's because we had recently moved out of the city into a middle-of-nowhere place. It was our Eden, Dan. And it was all for me. We did it for me. It was my choice for us to move all the way out there. But Carl loved it too, though he tried to pretend and gave me a hard time. He called me his mountain woman." Her great frame shook with barely held laughter. "Mountain woman. Psh! He didn't know nothing about mountain women. He wishes! But he moved there with me, and he flew in this tiny plane back to work, back to the town we had moved away from."

When she said the words "tiny plane," a shock wave moved through me. Like déjà vu.

"Three days a week he took that flight. Three days a week he was gone from me, Dan, flying in that tiny buzzing plane over the mountain. Three long, stretched-thin days every single week, three short flights, and I waited until long after dark on those days, begging his headlights to come dragging up the lane, through the trees."

I stared at the empty house across the greenway. These empty houses had always felt like nothing more than empty space to me, just parts of the past of the town, parts that were left behind every time someone left. But as I heard

Miss B's story, as she told me more and I could see where it was going, the house across the way started to feel menacing. That's the only word that fit. Like that old house wasn't completely innocent, like it was hiding things.

Were all of us hiding things? Miss B had these memories hidden in her like the rest of us had other memories hidden away. Secrets? I had a woman in my house that no one else knew about yet. It seemed suddenly possible that even Miho or Abe were keeping things from me.

The windows in the empty house pulsated with a strange, living darkness. The eaves concealed crucial things. I imagined the attic under the thatched roof was coated in some kind of mold, something eating away at the inside of it. I wondered if maybe some of the people who we thought had gone east across the plains had actually doubled back at night and slipped into their old houses, where they now watched us through the dark panes and plotted our end.

I shook my head. Where were these thoughts coming from?

"Even though he left me in the morning, the headlights of my husband's car returned every night, Dan. They did. I sat in a chair by the window in the bedroom, and when I saw him coming, I quickly climbed into bed and got under the covers so he wouldn't know I was worried. Sometimes I pretended to be asleep, although I don't know why, now that I think back on it. Sometimes I welcomed him home, and we lay quietly in the bed for a long time, listening to each other breathe, wondering if it was too good to be true, this Eden we had created away from everyone. Everyone."

Her voice went flat. "Then came the day he left me."

The void that had found its way inside her voice scared me.

"Quite a storm."

She was empty.

"Quite a storm."

I would have run for Abe if she hadn't been holding my hand so tight it hurt.

"I knew he was in the air already, and I hoped that storm would leave him be. What could he have that the storm would want? Leave him be. Leave him be! And behind the storm, the quietest sort of peace you've ever seen or heard."

We sat there as if she was trying to re-create that stillness. The cool air rushed around us. I heard a door open and close somewhere else in town, and a voice shouted to someone else, but I couldn't tell who it was or what they said. The sounds in our empty town were often lonely, few and far between, always distant and fleeting.

"After the storm, all day the phone was ringing. I mean, all day, ringing off the hook. And you know? I knew something was wrong. I knew someone was trying to call me about Carl, to tell me he was gone, and I couldn't make myself answer that phone. I wouldn't answer it, not for anything, because as long as I didn't answer it, nothing bad had happened. Does that make any sense to you?"

I nodded without looking over at her. It did. It made perfect sense.

"I even went outside for the rest of the day and found things to do—picked weeds, put together some more plantings, tilled a new flower bed. That night I lay in bed, staring at the ceiling, my eyes wide open, but no matter how late it got, his headlights never shone through the woods. Never lit up the window and slid that square of light along the wall like he usually did. Never came back to me. That was a dark night, Dan. A dark, dark night."

She pulled her hands into her lap like a child burned. She held them there still as stones, and her face went flat. She stared into the empty windows of the house across the greenway. My own hand ached from where she had squeezed it.

"I remember now, Dan. I remember what happened to my Carl. That's why I'm still here, why I never left. And now I don't know what I'll do."

She didn't know what she would do? What did she mean by that?

"I'm sorry, Miss B," I said, and she nodded. I stood up, but I didn't go. It was like her memory clung to me, a web holding me in place.

"What is this place, Dan?" she asked, lifting her palms and motioning around her. "What is this place? This town? This plain?"

Her voice stumbled as if she had used up all her words. But there was something else too. Something came to me, some strange knowledge, and I couldn't tell if it came from Miss B or the story she had told. Something resonated with me.

I knew her story already, somehow.

I knew it before she even told it to me, or at least certain parts of it. That's why the part about the plane had jolted through me. I was connected to it in some long-ago way. I wondered if she knew it too, if she sensed this connection I had to her new memory, the part I played in it. Maybe that's why she had grown quiet. I didn't want to press her. I didn't know what to do. So I stepped back, away from her.

"I'll talk to you a little later, Miss B," I said in a gentle voice, and she nodded again. "Let me know if you need anything." Her eyes were empty like the house across the greenway. Miss B had never been anything but grins and light, breezy sentences. Nothing but cookies and fresh bread and deep, comfortable hugs. This Miss B was different.

I walked down the greenway to the other side of the village, all the way to Miho's house. It usually took less than ten minutes to walk to her place from mine. I didn't see anyone else, but smoke rose from John's chimney, and I could hear Misha singing in her house at the edge of the village, her voice far-off and melancholy. I thought I recognized the tune.

Miho's place was the last house in the village before the greenway ended. The town's expansive garden stretched out behind her house, out into the plains. Her house was also the closest to the large oak at the edge of town with its massive, spreading branches that reached up into the now-clear sky.

I knocked on Miho's door but didn't wait for a response before walking in. Her place was bright on the inside, partially because of the fire always burning in the fireplace, but also because she kept her windows wide open and curtains pulled back. Her wood floors shone, a much lighter color than mine. I closed the door quietly behind me, still pondering the memory Miss B had shared, but I soon realized I wasn't the only one there.

There were three of them sitting at the dining room table that was partially covered in baskets of different sizes, all holding vegetables. Abe, Miho, and Mary St. Clair. I remembered again greeting Mary when she'd come over the mountain. She had moved into a house tucked in the second row off the greenway. In those days, she had a few neighbors, but now the houses in that part of town were empty. And she was leaving us. Sadness filled me again, and this time it wasn't a selfish sadness, the kind that came when I considered being left alone. No, this sadness came from knowing how much we would all miss her. Our village would be less without her. There would be only eight.

"Hi," I said quietly, frozen in place. "Hi, Mary."

"Hi, Dan," she whispered, giving me a sad smile.

The four of us remained there, no one knowing what to say, and finally Abe cleared his throat. "We're making preparations." He tried to sound upbeat and beckoned to an empty chair at the table. "You're welcome to join us. Give us your two cents."

Miho smiled.

My mouth went dry. I cleared my throat. "Of course," I mumbled. "Preparations."

"What's wrong, Dan?" Miho asked. She knew me better than anyone. She knew something was going on. I wouldn't have come down at dusk, only hours after seeing her and Abe, unless there was something I needed to tell them. For the first time since Miss B's story, I remembered the woman in my house. The woman I should have brought with me and relinquished to Abe. I squeezed the key in my pocket so hard it bit into my hand.

But I put on a dim smile. "No, no. Fine," my voice said, skipping words, a record player out of groove. "Everything's fine."

"Mary is leaving after dark, in just a few hours," Abe said, and I didn't know why he was telling me this again. Didn't everyone already know?

An irrational irritation rose inside of me. I tried to speak, tried to say, "Yes, I know," or something else along those lines, but the words had burrs on them, and they stuck in my throat.

"Would you mind gathering the firewood for the ceremony?" Abe asked. "You might have to go out to the second or third tree. I haven't seen much wood around the mountain, and this tree out here is picked clean."

I nodded, numb. "Sure." The three of them stared at me. I felt like I should say something else, something that would explain my coming. "I had a word with Miss B."

"Good," Abe said, appearing a little confused as to why that was noteworthy.

"You should go talk to her. She had a memory."

"Is that so?" Abe sounded interested, as if he might ask me more, but I was already backing away.

I clumsily opened the door, spilled out onto the greenway, and returned through the village, toward the mountain, toward my house. I waited for one of them to come out and shout in my direction, ask me why I was going back to my house and not out toward the long line of oaks to collect wood for the ceremony. If they wondered where I was going, no one said anything. No one came after me.

After walking for a bit, I realized I could breathe again. Again I pictured the woman lying on the floor inside my front door, and I stopped. I was torn. I thought about going back to tell Abe. I had to tell him what was going on.

But something else pulled me onward, pulled me home.

My walk turned into a jog, and when I passed Miss B's house, there she sat, not having moved from where I left her a few minutes before. She was staring down at her hands, as if her fingers were squeezing into fists on their own, without her permission, and she was trying to figure out how to undo the knots they had become.

I didn't slow down, and I didn't let go of the key. I ran faster when I reached the gap between the town and my own house, the heavy grass swishing with each step. And the fear was there too, that inexplicable fear, growing until it sat in my gut like a throbbing mass.

I opened the door to my house, breathing hard. The puddle was still there, sending up a glass reflection. The gray light was still there too, as the afternoon died off and darkness approached. The back doors remained closed.

But the woman wasn't lying there anymore. She was gone.

4 THE WOMAN

AN UNBEARABLE STILLNESS settled on the house and made its way inside of me. I stepped in and stood in the puddle where she had been, my feet momentarily stirring the water, and the dying light that came in from outside reflected off the rippling surface. I felt like a foreigner in my own house, but in an unlikely act of bravery, I pulled the door closed behind me. I turned the lock. I couldn't remember the last time I had locked the door, but the metal slid home in a clean motion.

"Hello?" I said, my voice husky and fading. The air quivered around that one word, but there was nothing that came out in response—no sound, no movement. I stepped out of the puddle, kicked off my shoes, and opened the back doors, looking through them at the sky and the plains and the heavy, after-rain air. It wouldn't be long before night fell. I breathed deep. I closed the doors and locked them too, and again I wondered why. Was I locking someone out? Or locking myself in? Either way, it felt too late, an afterthought.

I walked through the kitchen to my desk, searching the mountain for any sign of the woman. Did she go back? Maybe. I'd seen it happen before, people shocked by the freedom, the cool breeze, the fresh air, turning and stumbling back into the mountain. She couldn't have gone through the village and followed the greenway east or I would have noticed, unless she had hidden among the houses and waited for me to pass, which seemed unlikely in her condition. The thought of her hidden among the empty houses made my skin crawl. She couldn't have meandered out into the plains or I would still be able to see her from my back doors. It would take a long, long time to walk out of sight in that direction. I stared at the canyon, but everything around it was as motionless as the inside of my house.

What if she hadn't left?

I moved to the closed bedroom door, stared at the knob and my warped reflection in it, held on with one clammy hand. My eye twitched at the corner, and I rubbed it with the back of my other hand. I was tired. Why was I so tired?

I pushed open the door and it swung without a sound. There, lying in my bed, small beneath the down comforter, her form barely enough to create any kind of topography, was the woman, asleep. For a moment the fear dimmed, replaced by a warming sense of concern. She was like a broken animal, something harmless, an injured bird or a lost kitten, and I wanted to take care of her, to nurse her to health. I could do that. I could help.

I walked over and sat in the chair beside the bed. I didn't want to wake her—I only wanted to watch her, to take her in. By then, I had already pushed away the vision that had overwhelmed me when I touched her arm, the strangeness of her arrival, the fear I had felt before. I only wanted to sit there and stare at her.

Her breathing was so peaceful, so gentle. Why had I been afraid of her? I couldn't remember. Was she a tangible re- minder of what it was like to live on the other side of the mountain, the terror of what went on over there? Was it because she was a secret I shouldn't be keeping?

"Are you awake?" I asked quietly, my words barely above a whisper.

She tugged the covers down so that her eyes peeked out at me. She nodded slowly.

"Are you okay?"

Her head moved slightly, uncertainly. It could have been a yes or a no.

"Are you hurting anywhere?"

She paused, seemed to shrug. I waited before asking the next question, not wanting to force her memory back to the other side of the mountain too soon, but I couldn't resist. Even in that moment, even in the face of someone gravely injured, I still had to ask about my brother.

"Was there anyone else left? Did you see anyone else? On the other side of the mountain?"

Her eyes rolled back and I thought she might pass out again. But instead she nodded, barely moving her head. She squinted in pain.

"Good, good," I said encouragingly, like a parent to a small child, wanting to coax more out of her. I paused, but the words came out before I could stop them. "A man?"

She nodded again. I felt a surge of adrenaline or emotion, and my hands shook. I wanted to stand up and clap, or shout out a hoot. But tears formed in her eyes, shimmering, welling up, and streaking along her skin.

"Yes," she whispered.

She could speak!

"Was he still alive?"

She nodded once more, and her eyes dropped below the line of the blankets still pulled up to her face. Could it be? Could this person she had seen actually be my brother? I stood up and paced around the room, feeling caged, trapped. Why was he still there? Why wasn't he coming out of that place? What were they doing to him to keep him there?

"Where?" I asked. "Where?"

She pulled the covers down even farther, down below her chin. There were wet spots on the sheet from her fingers, a damp halo around her head on the pillowcase. There were also dried brown stains in random places from mud and blood and drool. Already some of the cuts on her face had begun to soften around the edges—this was how it was on our side of the mountain. Inexplicable, really, how quickly we had all healed after arriving. How completely. Maybe it was the air. Maybe it was the grass, or the rain, or the food.

I sat down in the chair again so that my knees were against the bed. I put my palms on the edge of the mattress, consciously keeping my hands away. I was scared of the vision that had come to me the last time I touched her.

"Where?" I asked for a third time, trying to sound calm and gentle, even though I wanted to press her. I wanted to lift her by her shoulders and shake her, demand information, details. But she looked so fragile. It was like negotiating with someone on the edge, someone preparing to jump.

"The very bottom," she said, barely moving her mouth.

I sat back and shook my head. The bottom. I had so few memories of that place, but an image flashed in my mind when she said those words: a mile-wide funnel, like a pit dug into the heart of the mountain, and the road that made

53

its way down, hugging the edge, dropping into the darkness. The bottom of that? I didn't remember seeing the bottom. I had been in there somewhere, but I couldn't imagine a bottom. It seemed endless.

What was I going to do?

"Was there anyone else?" I asked her. "Anyone?"

She looked at me as if she didn't know what I meant.

I reworded the question. "How many people did you see over there before you came here? How many people do they still have over there?"

A subtle rustling began under the blanket, the smallest of movements, and I realized she was pulling her hand up. She moved it out from under the cover in a tight fist, and one finger slowly uncurled.

"One person? He's the last person there?"

She nodded.

"How do you know?"

"Emptiness," she whispered. "Silence."

I held my face in my hands and tried to stop the tears from coming. "Are you sure?"

She nodded, her eyes closed, and she fell asleep, but there was still that one finger above the blanket, now slightly bent. One finger. One person left.

My brother. It had to be him.

DUSK GREW DARKER, leaned toward night, and I watched it happen from the comfort of my armchair, facing out over the empty plains. I couldn't look at the mountain anymore, knowing my brother was there, alone. Sadness hung around me like a fog, and loneliness, and that new companion, fear. So I pretended the mountain wasn't rising just outside my house, and I stared through the wide-open double doors in the opposite direction.

I should have been going for wood for Mary's sending off. I should have been telling Abe any number of things, either about the woman in my bed or the memory Miss B had told me or that my brother was the last one in the mountain. But I said nothing. I did nothing. I sat there and watched the darkness drift in on us all.

There had been no sound from the bedroom since I left her there sleeping, and there were no windows in that room, so it wasn't like she could escape without me knowing about it. But I did feel like I was guarding the door. Why? What was I guarding against? Her coming out, or me going in? Or something else?

I didn't know.

It started to rain again, a steady, soaking rain, and relief washed over me because I knew without being told that Mary wouldn't leave, at least not on that night. A spark of hope murmured inside of me, the thought that perhaps she would change her mind. But as quick as that thought came to me, I knew it wasn't true. I knew she would leave as soon as there was a clear evening. And then there would be eight of us left. Nine if I counted the woman in my bedroom, but she didn't seem to count. She seemed somehow separate.

I stood up and walked forward to lean against the frame of the back door. From there I could see down the gentle slope, to the left and into the village. The houses were quiet in the settling darkness, but I could smell a wood fire burning, and I wondered if it came from John's or Miss B's or Miho's. Miss B's house was the coziest one in town, and she was constantly bringing out fresh bread or cookies or something else she had made. I wondered if anyone else was there with her. I wondered if she had told anyone else about her new memory. I doubted it—after she had finished telling me, and when I had passed her on my way back home, I had this sense that she regretted the sharing. This is the way of secrets, an always present desire to share them and a pervading guilt after we do.

I watched Misha and Circe walk out into the rain, making a wide circle through the knee-high grass. I could barely see them in the dark. They stopped at one point and looked up in my direction. I gave them a wave, but I didn't think they saw me because they didn't wave back. Maybe they were looking up at the mountain. Maybe they couldn't see me in the darkness of the doorway. They turned, kept walking, and hugged each other at one point. The darkness got thicker and they drifted out of eyesight. Did they plan on leaving too? The town wouldn't be the same without either one of them.

I was surprised when I heard a knock at the door. A ball of anxiety rose up in my throat when I remembered the woman in my bedroom. The woman I hadn't told anyone about. I convinced myself it wasn't the worst secret in the world, but it would have been awkward explaining her presence, especially to Miho, so I was a little relieved when I unlocked the door, opened it, and found Abe standing there, getting wet as the new band of rain became steadier.

"Come in, come in," I said. "Get out of the rain, Abe."

He came in and sort of shook himself off, like a dog emerging from a lake. We both laughed.

"Let me get you a towel," I said, moving toward the bedroom. But I remembered the woman, so I veered into the kitchen and grabbed him a small dishcloth. "Sorry." I shrugged. "Best I can do."

He waved off my apology and, while his face was covered with the cloth, asked, "You locking your doors these days?"

I swallowed hard and turned away, pretending to be busy with something in the kitchen.

I sighed. "I don't know. I guess." With that simple answer a kind of oppressiveness pushed down on me. I stared at the floor while Abe wiped off the rest of his head, his face, his arms. His hands. I stared at them as he handed the small cloth back to me. I knew where the feeling of oppressiveness was coming from: I was lying to Abe about the woman, and I was going to keep lying to him. I wasn't going to tell him about her. I couldn't see any way out of it.

When I took the cloth from him, I wanted to cover my face with it, hide my shame, but instead I carried it back into the kitchen and draped it over the counter where it could dry. I lit the lamps in the house and carried one into the sitting room, hung it on the hook in the ceiling. The flames danced and the shadows in the corners of the house came to life.

"I guess you know why I'm here," he said quietly, still standing inside the door.

"Come in, Abe. Come in," I said, motioning for him to come with me to the armchair. "Have a seat."

"You sit there," he said. "I know that's your spot."

"Abe," I said, taking a serious tone. "Sit."

He grumbled something about not getting any respect. I laughed and tried to shake off that sense of letting him down that comes with lying to someone you trust.

I sat with my back toward the back door. Cool, damp air lingered there. It had become too dark to see the plains, or the rain, or even the village, although a bit of lamplight glowed from various windows.

There had been a day when the village lit up at night. When all the windows were alight and people gathered around fires built outside of town, when the sound of laughter made its way up to where I sat. Everyone else seemed to think that people leaving indicated progress, that going east was what we were all supposed to do eventually, but I missed the old days. I wished them back, and I didn't know what was wrong with that. They had been good days. Very good days.

"So," he began again.

"Yeah. I know why you're here."

He looked at me with a question in his eyes, asking me to prove it.

"You're here because we're postponing the ceremony. The weather is too wet, so Mary will leave tomorrow evening. Or whenever this rain finally clears."

"So, you do know," he said, giving me a wry grin. His face went serious before he said, "One more day."

"One more day," I echoed, resigned. "Abe, why does it bother me so much that Mary is leaving us?"

"It's a hard thing, isn't it? This town has been good to all of us."

I could tell it bothered him too, and in some strange way that was a comfort to me, seeing that I wasn't alone. "Why do we have to go? What could possibly be better about any other place?"

He leaned his head back in the chair and stared up at the lamp. The whites of his eyes seemed especially white in the dimly lit room, in the flickering lamplight, and his mouth worked this way and that while he thought.

"You know, this is a wonderful place. I'll give you that. The friendships, the time we've had together. The way we helped each other recover from . . . over there. It's a special thing, this kind of community. No doubt about that. But can't you feel the sameness of it, Dan? Do you ever get the sense that time stands still here, that it's nothing but a place for waiting?"

I hated to admit it, but he was right. We kept ourselves busy. We grew our own food from seeds the previous harvest had left us. We gathered wood from the base of the mountain and the oak trees that stretched a straight line into the plains. We slept and talked, and the night was followed by the morning. But he was right—nothing ever progressed. If that woman hadn't stumbled out of the canyon and gone to sleep in my own bedroom, I would have even gone so far as to say nothing ever happened.

But something had happened. She had arrived. I was hiding her. Miss B had a memory. Something new was taking place. Were things changing? And if they were, why couldn't Abe feel it too?

"Yeah," was all I said. "Yeah, I hear you."

He stood up.

"You don't have to go, Abe," I said, although his leaving was a relief to me. I kept waiting for the woman to make a sound.

"Thanks. But I have a lot to do to get ready for tomorrow. I'm rather relieved Mary's been delayed. It's been a while since anyone left." He said this with a mischievous look in his eye. "And I'm not sure I remember all my lines."

"Who was the last to go?" I asked him. "I'm drawing a blank."

"You don't remember?" he asked. He even looked as if my forgetfulness was slightly alarming.

I shook my head, shrugging. "I can't. I've been thinking about it all afternoon."

"I can't believe you don't remember," he said, laughing to himself. "What a curious thing, all of this forgetting."

And all of this remembering, I thought. "At least give me a hint."

He turned to me with a glint in his eye, and his voice changed into a high squeak. "Danny! Oh, Danny! Can I come up and pick out a book to read again?"

"Oh, wow," I said, my eyes widening. "I forgot all about her. But I still can't remember her name." It was strange to me that I couldn't remember. Had it been that long?

"Does the name Moira ring a bell?" he asked.

Moira. How could I forget Moira? The woman had practically tried to move into my house with me. She had been up at my place all the time, driving both me and Miho crazy. She always wanted to peruse my books, running her pale index finger along the spines, mumbling the title names and authors to herself. She pretended she had read every book

I owned—whenever I mentioned something about a book, any book, she replied with the same all-knowing words. "Ah yes," she would say. "Of course."

"Moira," I said, more to myself than to Abe. "How could I possibly forget Moira?"

Abe looked at me over his shoulder, his hand on the front door, and his face was serious again. "It's this place, Dan. It's not made for remembering. It's not a settling kind of place—it's an in-between place. This town has always been that. I know why you're here and why you're waiting. Everyone else knows too, and we understand. You want to see your brother again. Everyone else here is waiting for something too. And that's okay. But don't forget, you can't stay here forever."

"Have you talked to Miss B?" I blurted out, and he froze in place.

He turned toward me again. "Yes," he said, and I knew he was wondering how much she had told me.

"She shared her memory with me," I said. "I'm guessing you know about it too."

He nodded in a guarded sort of way. "How much did she tell you?"

I gave him the summary. He listened. After I finished, we stood there in silence.

"Seems strange," I said. "All of this in a place not made for remembering."

He gave an absent-sounding chuckle, and I could tell his mind was elsewhere. He mumbled a half-hearted goodbye, never completely returning to that place, that moment, and he was back out in the light rain, disappearing in the darkness. I desperately wanted it to be day again—I was tired of people disappearing. I was tired of standing by and being left behind.

A cold wind blew through the house while the front door was open, swept in through the frame and out the back. It felt like even the wind longed for the east.

That was the night when everything was set in motion, the night I could have told Abe but didn't. The night I could have gone down and spent a final evening with Mary. But I didn't.

That was also the night I started to remember. Not made-up memories. Real ones.

I promise. This part is true.

5 REMEMBERING

I WISH I could adequately explain how strange this all was—for a long, long time, I had lived in the village and nothing out of the ordinary had happened. Not one thing. I mean, in the early days, people were always coming over from the other side, so I would run down to Abe's and we would tend to them and help them get acclimated. Every so often someone would leave and head east, so we'd have a little ceremony and some of us would cry, and then we'd return to the same old routine.

But most days were normal days. Most days I woke up. Ate breakfast. Listened to the wind in the grass. Wrote in my journal. Read. Watched the rain. Walked down to the village and helped in the garden. Shared lunch with someone. Went home and took a nap. Stared at the mountain. Wished my brother would come through the canyon. Met up at someone's house for dinner. Sat by a fire and told stories or went home and sat in the darkness, staring out over the plains, listening to people sing down among the houses. Fell asleep.

That was it.

But then, this strange sequence of days: Mary preparing to leave, Miss B sharing her memory, and the woman asleep in my bedroom.

That was the night I started to remember things.

I was in and out of sleep. I thought I was dreaming, the kind of dream I came back to as soon as I drifted off again. I saw scenes from when I was a baby, things you wouldn't normally remember because you would be too young. But there it was, like a show in my mind: I saw me, and I saw my brother. Both of us. And in that moment, I remembered it had always been both of us. We were twins.

How could I have forgotten? I was beginning to realize how much the mountain had taken from me. The trauma I had experienced in that abyss had robbed me of any memory of the life that had come before it. In the village, we had always assumed this to be the case, that we had each had a life before the terror of what had happened in the mountain. But none of us could remember. Or if we did, the memories were brief, shallow, and inconsequential.

On that night, the memory that came back to me was dripping with detail. I saw the moment when my brother was born, and I saw my birth right after his, and even though we looked exactly alike, I could tell which one was me and which one was him. There was something wrong with me because all the nurses were crouched around the narrow table I was on, poking at me and prodding my limp arms and fastening a tiny oxygen mask to my face.

All this time, my brother was in my father's arms. My mom looked like she had passed out with exhaustion, and I guess because something was wrong with me, they had bundled up Adam and handed him to my dad. My dad stared down into Adam's eyes, stared hard, as if Adam was the only thing in the whole world, and he kept getting closer and closer until their eyes were only inches apart.

My dad. I suddenly remembered him too. He was a rough man, wild around the edges. His hands and fingers were thick, and even though they made him wash his hands before he held me, the creases around his knuckles were black from oil. He was a long-haul trucker as well as a mechanic in his spare time.

Of course, I thought. *How could I have forgotten?*

My dad wore a T-shirt, tight around his barrel chest, and his biceps were huge. His face was all blunt edges and flat surfaces. His eyes were dull and young, a strange combination. When he smiled, it looked like his teeth hurt.

My mother's beauty was disarming, to the point that men couldn't look her in the eye and women found her to be either their favorite person in the world or completely insufferable. Her attractive face was placid, like still water. Her hair was blonde, almost white, and her skin the color of milk. Her lips were a rose-petal pink. Her mouth was exquisite.

She was so still she might have been dying. Or dead. Wait, was that what happened? Was this a memory of my mother's death?

But I saw her coming back from darkness, and the movement started around her mouth. She licked her lips. Barely. She moaned. A nurse moved to her side again, and she emerged up into this painful exhaustion. I must have been doing better because some of the nurses cleared off while one wrapped me in a blanket, wrapped me tight. My mom cried as they handed me to her, and she couldn't stop nodding as they entrusted my small being into her love. And she did love me, fiercely. I could see it there, in her face, her tears. It was so obvious. She loved me.

The memory started to fade, and I clung desperately to it. It was mine now. I could keep it.

At the end, I saw an image of my father holding Adam and my mother holding me, and a thousand subtle memories returned, not in sharp images or clear pictures like this one, but in insinuations and deductions. This was how it always was, how it always would be. My mother and me. My father and Adam. Two separate teams in a single family, two sides to every problem. I never had my father, not even from day one, but I always had my mom. Adam and I were left to fend for ourselves across those clear lines, even from a young age, and we sometimes crossed them, but always as representatives seeking some kind of temporary treaty.

I woke up feeling woozy, drugged. I had slept in my clothes and was still in the armchair. The back doors were wide open, had been open all night. Cool, damp air mingled around the house. I rubbed my eyes and sat up straight. It was nearly morning, and a soft light caressed the plains, the easiest blue, the simplest ivory. The grass was rustling as far as I could see, and I wanted to walk out into it.

I thought of the woman in my bedroom. I rose up and stretched and listened for her, for any sound coming from the room. But all I heard was the roof creaking in the wind and the rush of air through the grass. It was a lonely, quiet sound. I moved to my bedroom and leaned in, put my ear to the crack where the door met the wall.

Complete silence.

I turned the knob carefully and pushed the door open, willed it not to make a sound. I peered into the room. There she was, lying on the bed, as still as ever. Was she dead? I walked in practically on the tips of my toes, trying not to make a sound. I waited beside the bed for what felt like a long time, staring at her face, the angle of her eyes, the depth of her dark hair. If I concentrated on the blanket, I could see it moving up and down ever so slightly with her breathing.

At least I thought so. I couldn't be sure. I convinced myself everything was okay. She was okay and the town would be okay, and though Mary would leave, everything would stay as it was. Which was proof that everything would remain okay, because no one else was leaving.

I leaned over the woman, put my ear right up to her mouth, and only then could I hear her breath coming and going. In and out.

"Dan," she whispered.

I jumped back.

She smiled. "Did I scare you?"

"Your breathing was so quiet."

"You take good care of me," she said in a sleepy voice. "Thank you for letting me stay here."

I looked up at the ceiling, let my gaze wander around the four walls of the room. The floor creaked as I sat down and shifted my weight in the chair. "I need to go check on some things," I murmured. "I have to go out. I'll be back soon."

"Oh, Dan," she said, and her voice startled me, because there was a kind of barely revealed longing in it.

"Yeah?"

"I've lost something."

I could feel my heart beating. I reached up and rubbed my chest, trying to hide it. I could feel the muscles tense up in my face. "Yeah?" I asked again.

"A key. I had a key when I arrived here, but I can't seem to find it."

The key was in my pocket. I wondered if she could see it, if there was any sign of its presence. I nearly reached down to hold it, but I managed to keep my hand away from it.

"I'll keep my eye out," I said. "Actually, I'll walk up to the canyon later. Maybe you dropped it when you came through?"

"Thank you, Dan." Her voice was smooth, easy to take in, like sunshine.

I stood and walked toward the door, but before I got there I turned. "Don't make any sounds if someone comes into the house. You shouldn't be here. I should have told someone."

She raised one pale finger and pressed it against her lips as if she was saying, "Shhhh."

A chill spread down my back. I couldn't remember if at any point she had asked me not to tell anyone that she was there, but it seemed important whether or not she had made this request. I didn't think she had. This was a slight relief to me. But I couldn't be sure.

I left the room. I paced around the kitchen, stared up at the mountain, paced around the living room. I stared out into the plains and listened for anything coming from the bedroom that might break the silence. The grass was inviting, so I walked out the back doors, my head no longer hazy from sleep. I was tense. Aware. I needed to talk to Abe. I wanted to tell him everything about my memory and the arrival of this woman. I didn't know if I would go through with it. But I could try.

On second thought, I went back inside the house and

looked over my bookshelves. If I was down in the village all day, I would need something to give to Mary when she left that night. I scanned the shelves for a particular title. There it was, the pocket edition of a book Mary had always enjoyed. I looked at it for a moment, and then I walked out, leaving the back doors open.

I DIDN'T REALIZE it had gotten so late in the morning, but as I walked down to the village I could see that a few of the others were already out and about. Miss B trimmed the long grass around her house and the neighboring houses, waving absentmindedly to me when I passed, as if nothing had happened the previous day. John was repairing something on his roof, too busy to look up as I passed by. Po sat on his front stoop, smoking a pipe, staring at me. I waved. He nodded in reply and let out a long stream of smoke that clouded around his head. But he didn't stop staring at me.

I nearly turned toward Abe's place situated in the very center of the town, a little bit off the greenway toward the mountain, but I wondered if Miho was outside, so I kept walking, all the way down. I could hear her around back, behind her house. There was a rustling of tall grass, the sound of a basket being dragged along the dirt, and humming. Whenever I found her by herself, she was always humming.

Miho took me in without her normal smile. There was a strange look on her face, as if she was seeing me for the first time. "Rough night?" she asked, looking back down at the ground.

I reached up and tried to flatten my hair, realized it was sticking up in every direction. Maybe that's why Po had given me that strange stare. I shrugged. "Slept in the armchair."

"The armchair? Someone kick you out of bed?"

Fortunately, she wasn't looking at me, because I could feel the crimson rising in my face. I walked over to where she was working and joined her. For someone who avoided the truth as often as I did, I was pretty terrible at it.

She pulled green beans from a series of large, round bushes. The beans were hard to see since they were the same color as the rest of the plant, but if you bumped the fragile stalks lightly, the beans danced and moved in a way that differentiated them from the rest of the plant. I reached in and grabbed one of the larger ones, chewed the end off.

"Everything okay?" I asked.

"You going to help or eat?" she asked without looking up. She smiled to herself, but there was sadness in it, and that brought all kinds of questions to my mind.

"You sleep okay?" I asked.

She shrugged, standing up straight and wiping her face with the back of her hand. I wanted to tell her what the strange woman had told me, that Adam was on the other side of the mountain, that she had seen him, that he was the last person there, that we had to do something.

She hesitated, then blurted out, "I had some strange dreams."

I kept picking beans, hoping she'd continue. I wasn't sure if I was ready to share my own. When she didn't say anything, I tried to encourage her a bit. "And?"

"And," she said, drawing out the word so that it pulled

her voice higher, "I'm not sure if I'm ready to talk about it. I woke up early and drew some pictures of what I saw. I came out here to try to work it out."

"Work what out?"

She stopped moving—no bean picking, no wiping her face, no dragging the basket. Just her standing there, still. "I'm trying to work out if it was only a dream or if it was a memory."

"You know the difference," I said.

"What's that supposed to mean?" She arched her back in a stretch, staring at me.

"You know." I smiled, trying to lighten the mood. "It means you know whether you had a dream or are remembering things. And if you're pretending not to know, it's probably because you know it's a memory you don't want to be true." By the end of my little speech, I wasn't smiling anymore.

She stared at me for a moment, as if trying to decide whether to laugh me off or accept my wisdom. The flat line of her mouth wrenched to the side in reluctant agreement. "Yeah. You're right."

I nodded. Now I really wanted to hear about it. I decided asking wasn't going to get me anywhere, so I stooped down beside her and kept working. Kept trying to find those invisible beans.

The garden was one of my favorite things about the village. We called it a garden, but that didn't do it justice. It stretched the entire width of the town and at least fifty yards into the plains. By that point, we didn't use nearly the entire space anymore, not all at once. When the village had been full, there were fifteen or twenty people out there working every day, tilling up the ground and planting and weeding and harvesting. But as the village dwindled down to the nine of us, we no longer needed the entire space. Pretty much everyone helped from time to time, even Miss B, although she found it slower going.

I loved the garden because it reminded me of us, of how we were making our way on our own, how we didn't need anyone else. It was a picture of this new life we had created outside of the mountain. I didn't know why anyone would ever want to leave the garden, the food, the space that was so entirely ours.

I stuck another bean in my mouth, then coughed and spit it out. "That one doesn't taste right." It had a bitterness to it, an underlying wrongness to the flavor.

Miho was troubled, and at first I thought she was still dwelling on her memory, but there was something else. "Something's strange about the plants," she said, clearly puzzled.

"Strange? What do you mean?"

"Look around. The newest batch of pepper plants hasn't been growing properly, and the tomatoes aren't ripening." She pointed at a line of plants where the tomatoes had emerged from the blossoms, but they were tiny and pale green. She pointed at the bean plants. "Same with these. And the corn is a total loss."

"A total loss?" I asked.

She nodded and wiped sweat from her forehead, leaving a streak of brown dirt. "The plants grew okay, but there are no ears on the stalks."

I walked over and held out my hand so the stalks tickled my palms. A wind rushed through and set them whispering. She was right. There were no ears growing, at least none that I could see.

The sense of premonition that had been low-grade bothering me ever since I welcomed that woman into my home simmered into questions. And there was the welling up of fear again, like indigestion. I pushed it down, walking back over to Miho. I reached up and wiped the dirt from her forehead. She stood patiently while I did it, even closing her eyes slightly.

"I need to go talk to Abe," I said in a quiet voice.

"Everything okay?"

"Yeah." I paused. "I had a strange dream too."

She gave a wry smile. "A dream or a memory?"

I chuckled and admitted, "A memory."

"About your brother?"

I nodded. She took in a deep breath. Sighed. But she didn't say anything.

"I'm going." I spun around on my heel in the dirt, looking over my shoulder to see if she had changed her mind, if we could swap tales of what life was like for each of us before the mountain.

But she only replied, "Okay," picking more beans and dropping them in the basket, then dragging the basket farther along the row.

I picked my way carefully out of the garden and back to the houses.

I had to talk to Abe, but there were so many things to discuss I didn't know where I would start.

6 MORE SECRETS

I WENT BACK up onto the greenway, walked along it for a short distance before cutting between the houses toward Abe's. The previous night's rain had left everything feeling very green and fresh and new, and anything in the shadows was still wet. I could almost make myself believe that Mary wasn't actually leaving, that nothing was changing, that today was like any other day since I had come from the mountain. It was a short walk to Abe's house, tucked away as it was among a thick cluster of now-empty houses, but even in that short distance I made a lot of progress in self-deception.

Mary will change her mind.

She's not going to leave.

Nothing is going to change.

In front of me was a house that looked more like a small compound, as if three or four cottages had somehow been pushed together into one. Each section was made of a different material—stucco and brick and wood and stone—while the roof was one long stretch of thatch, the color of slate and brittle as brush ready to be burned.

Even though the after-storm weather was cool, all of Abe's windows were open. I smelled coffee brewing, and I knew there would be a whisper of a breeze moving around inside the house. If the breeze made the house too cool, he'd start the fire rather than close the windows. I glanced up at the chimney but didn't see any smoke. I wondered if he was home, and a kind of relief filled me at the thought of walking away without talking about any of these new developments.

But voices murmured through the open windows. Should I knock on the door and interrupt the conversation? Should I go away and come back later? I stood there for a moment, feeling the breeze, taking in the blue sky and the shadows cast by all the little houses around me. Carefully, quietly, I walked over to the side of Abe's house, sat down under one of the windows, and listened.

"It will be sad not having you around," Abe said, his voice deep and comforting.

Silence settled in the house. Had they heard me? My face flushed with embarrassment at even the thought of being caught eavesdropping. No one did this. No one. There was no reason to. If you wanted to know something, to hear something, to talk about something, you simply asked. But I thought about the memories we were recovering, how we were holding things back. Something was different in our town. Something was changing.

"I have one other thing I'd like to talk about," Mary said, so quietly I had to turn my ear up toward the window to catch her words.

"I thought you might," Abe said, and I could imagine the kind smile on his face. He was so receptive that it felt like you could tell him just about anything, confess to any possible sin, any act committed or omitted.

I heard something that sounded like Mary standing up from the couch and walking around the room. When she spoke, her voice had an airy quality to it. The breeze picked up, and all around me the grass bent low and made a gentle whooshing sound, nearly drowning out her voice. But not quite.

"I remembered something a few days ago. And it . . ." She paused. "It helped me. That's why I'm ready to leave. Because of what I remembered."

Abe didn't say anything. He knew when to speak and when to wait.

"It was my father," she said. "I had a memory of my father. He was old in this memory, with white hair and deep wrinkles around his mouth and eyes. They were happy wrinkles, though, the kind that stick around after decades of smiling." She laughed quietly, and I could tell it was laughter mixed with crying. "I haven't had memories of him before. I don't know what he was like when I was a child, but I like to make things up, you know? I like to pretend. But this memory wasn't pretend. This was real. It happened."

I stared up into the sky. My heartbeat quickened. It felt like I was stealing something from Mary, taking something that wasn't mine. But I couldn't tear myself away.

"There's this flash of memory that happened a little before the main part. And in that quick flash I'm driving him to work. He's starting a new job. He's sitting in my passenger seat, and he rolls down the window and holds his hand out in the rushing wind outside the car, like he's arm wrestling the day. The air coming through is warm and feels like summer, and his thin white hair blows around. I remember thinking

76

that he should close the window because it's going to mess up his hair, and he shouldn't show up to his first day of work looking like that."

She laughed at herself. "That's all I remember from the car ride. After that, we're in this huge grocery store, and I realize he's taken a job there stocking shelves. I was still there, but secretly. I didn't tell him I was going to stay. I follow him through the grocery store, peeking around the aisles. I have this intense feeling of wanting to protect him, you know? It was like he was my kid starting his first job." Her voice ended quickly, as if she had choked on the words.

"Oh, Mary." That was all Abe said, though he said it multiple times. "Oh, Mary."

The wind kicked up, and for a moment I couldn't hear anything above its rushing. I felt a sense of panic rising. Now that I had heard the beginning, I needed to hear the rest. I sat up against the house in a kind of crouch, getting as close as I could to the window.

"I was there for a long time. It's kind of embarrassing, admitting that I spent so much time spying on him."

"It's actually quite sweet, Mary," Abe said.

"I guess," she admitted. "But I see him walk toward the front of the store and stand outside the manager's office, and I get worried. Has someone given him a hard time? Did I miss something? Does he hate the job? Is he going to quit on the first day? I'm very worried. I nearly run out and ask him what's wrong, but I don't. It seemed like he had been enjoying himself stocking the shelves, even humming. Anyway, the manager opens the door and they talk for less than a minute. I can't hear what they say, but neither of them seem upset. My dad walks away, and I see him pull something out of his pocket."

Again, the wind kicked up.

"Cigarettes! I didn't even know he smoked! He pulls out a pack of cigarettes and a small book of matches and walks toward the front door. I was shocked. It was the strangest thing seeing this, realizing my dad had this entire life I knew nothing about. How had he hidden it from me? I hated the smell. I would have known. Right? And it wasn't the cigarettes that bothered me, you know? It was this realization that he existed on his own, that he was his own person. An individual. Not 'Mary's father' or my mother's husband, but he was him. He was himself, and he contained many stories I would never know."

Abe chuckled. "That's some wisdom right there. More coffee?"

"No, thank you," Mary replied.

They sat in a long silence, and I thought that might be the end of the story. I gathered myself, getting ready to run off so I wouldn't be seen. But then she continued.

"I watch my dad and decide I'm going to leave. I'll sneak out the other side of the store. There were two large entrances, you know? He goes out one side to smoke and I go out the other, but when I get to the glass doors, I realize it's pouring down rain, a harder rain than I've ever seen. People who had been caught in the rain come in from the parking lot, and they are soaked, like they jumped into a swimming pool. I stand outside the store, under the overhang, and I wait for the storm to clear. The clouds are boiling and dark and

I wonder if there's a tornado warning. I'm literally listening for the sirens. That's when I hear it."

Quite a storm, I thought. I couldn't get Miss B's phrase out of my mind. I was listening so intently to Mary that I lost track of everything going on around me. But the wind came in hard and the rustling grass drowned out her voice.

"It's okay, Mary," was the next thing I heard Abe say. "It's okay."

I heard her crying. What had she said? What had happened to her father? Why did she now feel like she could leave the village?

"I know it might not make sense, but remembering the whole story helps me feel free of it," she said. "And even though I know it was Dan's brother, I can forgive him, and I can leave."

My insides trembled. I couldn't breathe.

My brother?

She can forgive him?

"What do you think you would have done if he had come earlier, before you had this memory?" Abe asked in a soft voice.

Mary paused. "I hated him, Abe." She stopped, and when she spoke again, the words came out reluctantly, in tiny, sharp bursts. "I thought up many ways that I could kill him. Isn't that awful? But not now. Seeing what happened, remembering everything . . . I can forgive him. I can leave. I'm at peace."

My brother's fault? What had Mary remembered? I felt desperate now to know. If it involved my brother, I had to know. I scrambled out from under the window as quietly as

I could, moving like a shadow over to the front walkway. I tried to approach the house as if I was just arriving. I tried to compose myself, tried to pretend I hadn't heard what I had heard. But I needed to know more.

All of that receded in my mind as the door to Abe's house opened in front of me and Mary came out. Her eyes were red, and she rubbed tears away before she saw me standing there.

"Oh, hi, Dan," she said, clearing her throat, hastily wiping her eyes. I could tell in that instant she didn't want me to know what she had been talking about, that it would be pointless to ask.

"Hey, Mary," I replied in a hushed voice.

She looked into my eyes, and it was as if she was reading my mind, as if she could see everything I had been thinking, every worry I had been feeling. Had she needed to forgive me too, in whatever story it was she remembered? Had I been at fault? Would she hate me for what Adam had done? I waited for her anger or her contempt, or even for her to simply dismiss me and walk away.

Instead, she tilted her head to the side, and I felt nothing coming from her except compassion. She genuinely cared for me. It caught me off guard.

Mary took a half step toward me—we were already standing very close—and she gently placed her hand on my shoulder, like a quiet promise, and said, "Oh, Dan."

That was all, those two words. She said them the way you might if you found out that someone had gone through something difficult a long time ago, and you had no idea before why they were who they were or why they did what they did, but now you knew and you wished you would have always known, because it would have changed things.

I couldn't reply. I wanted to talk, wanted to tell her I had heard the story. Mostly, I wanted to ask her what had happened and how my brother had been involved, but I couldn't. The words all stuck in my throat. I was afraid, afraid she might say no, afraid of what she might tell me, afraid of being discovered as an eavesdropper. So I said nothing.

The two of us stood there for a long time looking at each other, and the kindness in her eyes somehow grew even larger. She removed her hand and moved past me, back toward the greenway.

"Dan? Is that you?" Abe called from inside the house, and for a quick moment I considered not answering. But I couldn't walk away from Abe. I had to tell him about the vision I had. Or dream. Or whatever it was.

I walked through the door. Daylight streamed through the windows, and I realized the happy things made me sad. The gray days and the rain kept everything as it was, stopped things from changing, and the sun reminded me that there was nothing I could do to keep Mary from leaving, or anyone else for that matter. They would all leave, and the sunshine reminded me of this. The sunshine made it possible. It's hard to take when the things that used to make you happy start to make you sad.

I found Abe sitting at a small desk tucked up against the wall. "Did you know there's something wrong with the garden?" I asked him.

He nodded, not looking up from the papers he was examining. "So, you've been over there this morning? I don't like it, Dan. We have plenty of food for now, but I've never seen a crop fail in that rich soil."

"Are we overusing it? Maybe we should pick a different site for the garden."

He shook his head, finally looking up at me. "I've tried. I planted crops all over these plains—up by the mountain, among the rocks, on the other side of your house, even out by the fourth tree. Nothing's growing right."

"You were out at the fourth tree?" I asked, surprised. "I've never been out that far. Did you see anything?"

He shrugged and waved his hand dismissively.

"And—wait. How long have you been worried about this? Did you say you've been planting seeds all over the valley? Since when?"

The look on his face told me he felt he had said too much. More secrets.

"I'm sure it will be fine. All will be well and all will be well and all manner of things will be well." He smiled when he said this, as if it was an inside joke he had with himself. "Do you need something?"

I had to think for a moment to remember why I was there. All the things came rushing back, too many things to keep straight. I was becoming mired in the uncertainty of what I could and couldn't talk about. A few days ago, my mind had been a blank slate. But now it felt too complex, filled with knotted threads. There was Mary leaving and Miss B's memory and the woman in my room and the dreams I was having, and now the garden and Miho's dream and the way Po had stared at me and the fact that I had heard Mary's memory but shouldn't have, so I couldn't talk about that.

I couldn't remember what I was trying to keep secret and what was public knowledge.

"I feel strange inside, Abe. I feel like I'm disappearing."

He stood from his desk and gave me a kind smile. But I wanted to weep—at my deception and my brother being the only one left on the other side and the bitterness of green things not growing.

Abe put his hand on my shoulder. "What's wrong, Dan? What's really wrong?"

I stared into his dark eyes and realized we were the same height. I had always thought of Abe as much taller than me, a presence, a force that stretched far beyond me. But there we were, eye to eye. It was a revelation.

"I had a memory last night," I told him, and I was trembling with the strangeness of it. I told him about my birth, my twin brother, my mother holding me in her weakness, and my father far away, distant, unconcerned with me. I told him about the vague knowledge that came along with the memory, the sort of knowing that it brought: the realization of the distance between me and my father, the line down the middle of our family, my mother's devotion.

Abe's eyes were soft, and I nearly told him about the woman, but that was becoming something I could never tell anyone, a secret too deep to unearth. I lied to myself, reasoning that I could keep her from everyone.

He mumbled one word. "Interesting." He said it over and over again, and he was pacing when I finished, like a metronome, back and forth, back and forth. This went on for some time, and when he finished pacing, he collapsed into a different chair, one I hadn't noticed before in all the mess.

There was a silence in his house that reminded me of the silence in my own house. A silence full of nameless things.

I cleared my throat, and Abe came back from wherever his mind had taken him.

"This is all very interesting," he said.

I could tell by the hesitance in his voice that he was weighing his words carefully, trying to decide if he was going to tell me more, if he could tell me more, or if the things he knew were best kept close.

"You will remember more soon." He motioned toward his old gray couch, indicating for me to join him among the books and crates of garden equipment and half-finished carvings. So many carvings. There were crosses that circled in on themselves and walking sticks with curving vines and eerie houses with tall windows and elven doors.

I pushed a few things to the side and sat down. Despite all the things on the cushions, despite the pressing nature of all these unfinished things, Abe's couch was the most comfortable spot in the village. I sank into it and remembered my short night's sleep in the armchair. I wanted to close my eyes.

"How do you know?" I asked.

"It would seem that something is happening," he said in a vague, wandering voice. "Ever since this last storm, that is. Everyone seems to be . . . remembering."

"Remembering?"

"Remembering. Things from life before the mountain."

"Like my memories of my birth?"

"Yes, like that, but not always births. Other memories. Sadness. Joy. Other things. Death." He looked like he was going to say something more, but he shook his head. "Other things. And they're coming quickly now. Hard and fast and not always welcome."

"Has anyone told you? What they're dreaming? What they're seeing?" I tried to ask this innocently. I even had a small hope that he would use my questions as a launching pad to tell me the part of Mary's story I had missed. But I knew he wouldn't. When you told Abe something, it went into a heavy chest with a lock on it, and no one besides you could ever bring it out.

As expected, Abe didn't answer me. He stared at a lamp beside the sofa where I sat, a lamp that also served as a coat hook for various scarves, bags, and woolen hats.

"I can't tell you other people's memories," he said slowly. "I'm sure you understand. Maybe they will share them soon. But something is happening."

"In this place where nothing ever happens?" I asked him, remembering our earlier conversation.

"Yes," he said in a curious voice, as if that was the most alarming part. "Even here. Something is happening."

7 ANOTHER ARRIVAL

I STOPPED AT the corner of Miho's house and lifted the binoculars that hung around my neck, staring out into the plains. It was the middle of the day, but the town remained quiet. Everyone was staying close to home. Maybe they were getting ready for Mary's leaving party. Some days in town were like that, though, so it didn't feel completely out of the ordinary. Some days, we all just wanted to be alone. But I couldn't help wondering if these swirling new memories were driving people into seclusion.

Miho and I had eaten a quiet lunch together, neither of us wanting to ask the other about their dream. She seemed to have softened since our encounter in the garden that morning. She seemed to be more herself. I was still flustered from what I had heard Mary telling Abe. I so badly wanted to tell Miho what Mary had said, ask her what she thought about the story. But that meant I would have to tell her I had been eavesdropping. The secrets piled up inside of me. They hibernated into cocoons, transforming into things that had lives of their own.

Lunch had been earlier. Now, the two of us planned to go looking for firewood for Mary's ceremony.

At first I had trouble finding the oak tree in the binoculars as I scanned along the horizon. I made my way slowly from left to right along that distant line, and there it appeared: massive, thick enough that the trunk could have been carved out and turned into a hut. Where we lived at the edge of the mountain and the plains, the leaves were perpetually green, although we had miniature seasons where the trees faded to something like yellow or darkened into a lush color nearly black. But on that day, the sky was bright, the plains rustling and alive, and the tree's leaves were a lively green. Far beyond the tree, the storm that had come through the night before sat like a blot on the horizon.

Miho stepped in front of the binoculars, basically a huge blob of blurry color, and held up her hand in front of the lenses.

"And then it grew dark," she said in a mysterious voice, laughing.

I shook my head in mock annoyance. "Very funny." I lowered the binoculars and pushed her arm to the side.

"What are you looking for, anyway? You're always staring east."

"I don't know. I'm not really looking for anything specifically. I'm just looking to see if there's anything to see."

"But there never is," she said, smiling again, looking at me as if I was a puzzle.

I ignored her, pretended to be miffed while I folded up a large tan canvas tarp, tied it into a bundle, and carried it under one arm. We started to walk the long path from the tree beside her house to the first tree out at the horizon. When numbering the oaks, we didn't count the one by Miho's house. The first oak tree was the one we could barely see from town.

"Tell me this: have you ever looked through those binoculars and seen something worth seeing?" Miho insisted as we walked through the tall grass.

"Of course I have," I said. "Plenty of things."

"Like what? Name one."

"Well, it's not an object. But I like looking through the binoculars because it makes me feel like I'm out there. Out in the plains. Far from the mountain."

We both walked quietly for a minute.

"What else?" she asked, her voice soft.

"My house is far from the rest of you. I like to keep an eye out, see what you all are up to."

"You spy on us a lot, do you, from up in your high castle?" She swatted playfully at me.

I shrugged. "There's a beautiful woman I have to keep my eye on."

She laughed out loud, a free kind of sound, but it made me feel sad because I remembered everything unsaid between us. She reached over and grabbed my hand, and I glanced at her. Our friendship had grown during our time together. I loved everyone in town, Abe especially, but with Miho it felt different. With her, I felt chosen. I don't know, it doesn't make much sense, but she meant a lot to me.

We got out to the first tree, but as we expected, there was no dead wood for burning. I put my hand against the oak and closed my eyes. What a tree. Its bark was rich with deep grooves. The roots spread into the earth. One side of the tree had a fine layer of moss growing at the base of the trunk. Under the spreading branches lay a thick shade, almost darkness, like an eclipse.

We'd have to go to the next tree.

I raised the binoculars again, looking out to the next tree that had now appeared on the horizon. We couldn't see that second one from the town—it only came into view as we approached the first oak. The plains were empty, so silent and vast. I felt the tug of it, a desire to keep going, one tree after another, leave the village behind without even saying goodbye. But I knew I couldn't. My brother was still over there, behind us, lost in the mountain. The last one. I had to wait for him.

Miho and I kept walking. The grass was taller in some places, reaching to our waists. In others, it was nothing more than short, green stubble barely covering the brown earth. It took us a little while, but we got all the way out to the second tree, almost identical to the first in size and height. I had only been this far from the village a handful of times. It felt like we were on an island in the middle of an endless ocean.

"It always makes me feel funny, being out this far," Miho said, her voice timid and nervous as we gathered kindling.

The storm had brought down a few large, dead branches, and Miho and I broke them up as best we could and piled them onto the tarp. To be honest, there wasn't much, and I considered going out to the next tree, but I didn't know if we'd have enough time. There was a lot to be done before Mary's leaving ceremony that evening.

"Feels really far away," I replied. It was kind of a haunting feeling, like we were the last two people.

"There's something good about it, though, don't you think? It does feel far away, but it also feels nice to get out from under it."

She meant the mountain. She was right.

Once we had the wood arranged, I slid a rope through the eyelets in the tarp and pulled it tight. We could drag it back to the village without too much trouble, but it would take us longer than the walk out.

Despite our need to hurry, I sat down at the base of the oak tree and took a deep breath, facing south. To my left, the plains stretched on, and at the very edge of my vision, at the very edge of the day, I could see the next oak tree. Nothing else. Only the next oak in a long line of trees that Mary would follow, starting tonight when she left the village. When she left us. Going where? To what?

"Do you ever want to walk east?" Miho sat down beside me, breathing heavily from the work, gazing past me in the direction I was looking. "Are you ever tempted to leave your brother and go?"

I nodded. "Sure."

"Really? You never seem that interested."

I thought about that. I thought about Abe's words from the night before. They resonated with me. He had named something I didn't even know I was feeling.

"Everything is standing still here, you know? In the village. It's like time stopped. Leaving seems somehow inevitable. It's about taking that first step."

"Yeah, I feel that way too. And I wouldn't mind getting farther away from the mountain." Miho reached up tentatively and felt along the edge of her hair where the tattoo was. "Do you ever wonder what they're doing over there?"

"What do you mean? What who's doing?"

"The ones who ran that place. In the mountain. If everyone's leaving, escaping, they can't be happy about that."

We sat with that thought for a few minutes. It was an awful thing to think about.

"Do you mean they might come out, come after us?" I asked, my voice flat.

"I don't know," she said. "Probably not. I mean, they would have come before now if they were going to, don't you think?"

"Why do we stick around?" I asked, more to myself than to her.

"I guess we all have reasons for staying." Her voice had a strange tone to it, like she wanted to say more. "But it feels safe, doesn't it?"

She was right. The plains, even at the edge of that terrible mountain, felt safe.

"What do you think is out there?" she asked.

We both stared east, away from town, and I was happy about the change of subject. There was a story, believed in varying degrees depending on who you asked, that if you followed the oak trees all the way across the plains, one after the other, you'd come to a last tree planted at the foot of another mountain, a much different mountain. You'd see an opening that led to a path that would take you up and over, to a different place, a better place. Maybe even a city. I used to believe this story. I used to watch wistfully as friends and neighbors headed east on their way to the far-off place. I used to look forward to the day Adam came over and he and I could head to this new place together.

Now I wasn't so sure what I believed. Another mountain? A city? It all felt so improbable.

"Will you ever leave?" I asked Miho without looking at her.

"Me?" She said the word in a whisper, as if it was caught in her throat.

"Yeah, do you ever want to walk, head east?"

She let out the tiniest of laughs. "Sure." She paused. "But not without you."

It made me feel good when she said things like that. But it also made me nervous.

"I don't know if you should be waiting for me. You know? I might be a while. Besides, I don't know if I'm worth hanging around for."

She didn't answer, simply reached over and took my hand again, and we sat under the oak. I wouldn't have minded if time stood still in that moment, the light of another day cresting before it faded, the mountain comfortably far off in the direction we were not looking. Maybe we should head out, Miho and I, leave our ghost town of a village and the mountain, get out of here. See what we could find. Maybe we wouldn't even have to follow the trees. Maybe we could head north or south and make a new life in the middle of the plains, the two of us in the middle of nowhere.

But . . . Adam.

It always came back to my brother.

I looked to my right, past Miho, in the direction of the village that I knew was there even though I couldn't see it. And the mountain. There was always the mountain. It rose in a grayish purple ridge with pink hues in the midday light. A thin line of white graced the top. Snow. I imagined that I could even see the black line of the canyon that led to the other side of the mountain. The strangest part of all was how beautiful that range was from this far away.

Miho stood and stretched. "We should go."

I took an extra minute before I stood up, gathered the long rope, and pulled it snug. "Back under the shadow of the mountain." I sighed.

As we returned toward the first tree outside the village, Miho glanced back one last time, and I felt a joke rising in me, something about Lot's wife. I wondered where that phrase came from, what long-ago story I couldn't quite remember, but before the words came out, she grabbed my arm. "Dan."

I peered more closely at her, waiting for the joke or one last deep thought about the distance between here and there. But she didn't say anything. Her eyes were wide open, staring east, so I turned.

At first I didn't see anything. The light was strange, the grass blew in a hypnotic dance, and the third tree was barely visible. A strong wind came down from the mountain and blew our clothes tight up against our bodies. It felt like there might be another storm on the way, ready to spill over.

"C'mon, Miho. What are you doing?" I took one step away from her, but she didn't loosen her grip on my arm.

"Dan," she said again. "Look."

An annoyed look crept onto my face and I nearly argued with her about time running short, how we needed to get back. But I gave her the satisfaction of looking one last time toward the east. The tallest branches of the oak tree lashed this way and that in the strong breeze. I dropped the rope. I took a few steps east, passing her, passing the tree, and staring. I lifted the binoculars to my eyes.

Far off in the distance, closer to the next tree than to us, I saw someone.

She was walking in our direction, a girl or a small woman, and she was stumbling with determination but also with uncertainty. A tan cloak covered her, wrapped around her body and head. She pinched it together under her chin, but long hair escaped, billowed around her. She kept looking up as if expecting someone to meet her. I couldn't tell if she could see us or not. She wiped her forehead, stumbled again, leaned hard on a walking stick. She kept coming.

I handed the binoculars to Miho. Her mouth dropped open when she saw the girl. She turned to me with a million questions in her eyes.

"We need to go." I grabbed the rope attached to the tarp and tightened the load.

"What if she needs help?" she asked. "I think it's a girl, maybe a teenager."

The girl wasn't stopping either. I shook my head. "No one has ever come back," I said, my hands shaking so badly I could barely grip the rope. "No one."

We moved as fast as we could, dragging the tarp filled with wood behind us.

8 SOMEONE IS COMING

ABE MET US out beyond the edge of the village. I guess he noticed our urgency from a long way off. I dropped the rope and collapsed onto the grass, taking deep breaths. Miho bent over, hands on her knees, gasping for air.

"What are you two doing?" Abe asked with an uncertain grin. "Is everything okay?"

Still trying to catch my breath, I pointed out toward the first tree. "Someone's. Coming."

"What do you mean?" he asked, looking from me to Miho and back to me again.

Miho stood up straight and held her hands together over her head, trying to make more space for her lungs to work. "Someone's coming, Abe. From the east."

His smile shifted from uncertainty to doubt. He kept looking back and forth between us, as if he was trying to decide which of us would break down and tell him the truth. The fact that we both returned his gaze without hesitation seemed to knock him further off balance.

"You must have seen something that looked like a person. Maybe a branch fell from the next tree?"

"It was a person, Abe," I said. "We saw her in the binoculars."

"But no one ever comes back," he said. "There's no reason to."

It was true. If what waited in the east was so good, why would anyone leave it? Why would anyone return to this mountain?

"I don't know what to say, Abe. We saw what we saw."

"What should we do?" Miho asked.

"I don't know," Abe said, looking away from us. "If someone's coming, we don't have any reason to fear them. But it doesn't make any sense."

The three of us took in the darkening eastern horizon. The first tree faded as evening approached. We certainly couldn't see the second tree, or the third tree, where we had first spotted the person walking. How far could she have gone since we saw her? Was she still able to walk? She had looked like she was nearly collapsing.

"Should we tell everyone?" Miho asked.

"No, not until we're sure," Abe replied.

"We are sure," I said.

"Not until we know more," Abe said.

"Is it right, sending Mary out there," I asked, "if we don't know who or what is coming?"

"I think it was a girl, Dan," Miho said hesitantly. "I don't know that there's anything to be afraid of."

"When someone's ready to leave, to make the long trek east, it's time," Abe said. "No matter what. I don't think we should say anything. Mary's time to leave has come. We should celebrate that."

I didn't know what to say. They knew I didn't want Mary to leave, even before this stranger appeared, so any objections

I raised would feel loaded with ulterior motives. I wished Miho would speak up.

"It doesn't seem right, Abe," she said. "If this person is coming from the east, wouldn't it be better to find out what she knows before sending Mary out there?"

"If it's time, it's time," he reiterated. But there was something in his voice that told me he wasn't completely sure.

"Okay, then let's go out and see what this girl is doing, see what she wants," Miho said quietly. "At least then we'll know what Mary is up against."

"Up against?" Abe asked. "How do we know she's up against anything?" He was thinking again, weighing everything. "Okay," he said to Miho. "Let's go. Dan, keep the preparations going for Mary's departure."

"Did I miss something?" a deep voice called over.

It was John, who lumbered to where we stood.

"The meeting of the minds?" he declared when we didn't reply, his voice bounding out over the plains like a mastiff.

"Just getting ready for tonight," Abe said, the tone of his voice telling Miho and me that now wasn't the time to talk about the stranger approaching. "Would you help Dan get the fire started? Miho and I need to run a quick errand."

"'Course," John said, grabbing the rope and practically lifting the tarp off the ground.

I stared at Abe and Miho, and they both looked at me as if to ask, *What else is there to do?* I turned away because I had no answer for them.

I followed John over to the large outdoor stone patio where we held our community meetings. We piled up the wood, broke off some of the smaller twigs and slices of bark, and stacked it in the iron ring in the middle of the patio.

"Do you have matches?" John asked me.

"No, but I can grab some from Miho's place."

He dusted his hands together, coughed loudly, and watched Miho and Abe as they walked away. "What are they up to?"

"You'll have to ask Abe."

The air grew cooler even though the breeze was gone, and everything stood still. I waved up the greenway when I saw Misha walking leisurely toward us. I noticed Miss B was with her, and even from that distance, I could feel a kind of coldness coming from her, a hesitance, as if she wanted to walk in the other direction. The story she had told me surged back to the front of my mind.

I ducked into Miho's house. It was dark and tidy. I walked straight to one of the drawers in her kitchen and pulled it open, grabbed the matches. I turned to go, but curiosity got the better of me, so I slipped over to the large picture window that faced the plains. The light in the sky had faded, and even the first tree was nothing more than a dark silhouette against a darkening backdrop. I couldn't see Miho or Abe.

A chill shot down my spine as I thought again of the other stranger in the village, the one no one else knew about: the woman in my house. I had this feeling that I should go check on her, see if she was still resting, still there. I couldn't explain the deep desire I had to keep her presence a secret from everyone else. Why didn't I tell them? I squeezed the small box of matches in my hand. The dim gray light that remained fell through the large window and down onto the table where Miho, Abe, and Mary had met the day before.

Unlike the rest of the house, the table was cluttered, covered with papers and pens and pencils and even some paint and brushes. I pushed the papers around a little bit to see what Miho had been up to. Even though we were close, snooping through her stuff seemed inappropriate. I pushed past the discomfort and saw my name peeking out from one of the pages, so I pulled it into the dusky square of light. It was part of a question written in Miho's familiar handwriting, and as I read it, my curiosity and guilt welled up into tangible things.

Am I waiting for Dan's brother?

That was it. A question. But a strange one. Why would Miho be waiting for my brother? She hadn't known him before all of this.

Had she?

The house grew dark, but I was curious. I struck one of the matches and it hissed to life, creating an orb of light right there in my hand, like magic. I pushed a few more of the pages around. There were some beautiful pencil sketches. One of Abe, charcoal dark and shaded perfectly, his eyes looking up into mine, nearly alive and asking me what I was doing looking through my friend's things. Even a drawing of him made me feel guilty, and I flipped the paper upside down so he couldn't watch, so he couldn't ask me questions with his drawn eyes.

There was another pencil sketch under that one. It was less developed than the one of Abe. I didn't recognize the person, a woman about the same age as Abe. I looked closer. I didn't think I knew her, but she had the same almond eyes as Miho and there was something similar in the shape of her mouth. A relative perhaps? Was this the memory she'd referred to when I saw her in the garden that morning? Something about her mother?

The match diminished down toward my fingers, but I didn't notice until it burned me, and I dropped it on the table where it landed in darkness. I told myself I had time for one more. I struck a new one and held it straight up so it burned slower.

I saw the edge of a third sketch, and I pulled it forward. Complete and utter shock left me breathless. The chin and cheek lines were perfect, and the ears were fine in their subtlety. The wiry hair stood in a very specifically unkempt way, the way I suddenly remembered it. The eyes were clear enough to bring tears to my own. It was almost like looking in a mirror, but it wasn't quite me.

It was Adam.

Miho had drawn my brother. I felt like someone had punched me in the stomach. I leaned on the table with one hand and squeezed my eyes tight. A light-headedness threatened to drop me to the floor.

Another memory came to me, precise and unbidden and sharp. I remembered standing beside him, telling him he'd better get out of bed and do what he needed to do. Did I tell him to go? It felt like it. But I was earnest in my appeal. *Go. You have to. If you don't, we're ruined.* I remembered very specifically saying those words.

If you don't, we're ruined.

Miho's drawing was familiar: those same eyes, that same unkempt hair.

He'd shaken his head, and I'd grabbed him by his collar and lifted him and forced him to do what I wanted him to do.

I stepped back from the table. The match burned out, once again on my finger, and I dropped it, cursing. I got down on my knees and searched the floor for the charred end, but I couldn't find it. So many lost things.

What had I made my brother do?

"Yo!" a voice shouted from outside. John's voice. "Yo, Dan, what is taking you so long, my man?"

I left Miho's house, and suddenly I felt like a stranger in the village, like I didn't truly know anyone. Abe had said everyone was having new memories. And Miho, the person I was closest to, wasn't willing to tell me anything, not even when it obviously involved my own brother. What about John or Misha, Circe or Po? What did they know? What had they remembered?

"Found them," I shouted up to John, trying to sound light and carefree but barely succeeding. "I'm coming."

I didn't look up until I got to the stone patio. Everyone was sitting around the edge facing the plains, as they always did whenever we met there, the mountain in the distance behind them. There were houses close to the patio, huddled all around us, fencing us in. Miss B sat on an old chair that John had dragged over for her. Misha and Circe whispered to each other, both giving me a smile when I arrived. Was something else there, in their smiles? Were they hiding something too? Po sat at the end, carving something in one of the sticks meant for firewood. He didn't look up.

"Po," I said, motioning toward the stick we were supposed to be using for firewood. "I walked a long way for that."

He finally made eye contact with me, smiled, and held the wood up to me as if in a toast. "Thank you," he said in his curling accent, his bright red hair seeming to have its own light source in the near dark.

"Is Mary ready?" I asked no one in particular.

"I saw her by her house," Circe said. "She was waiting for the fire."

That's when I noticed Miho and Abe still hadn't returned.

"And Miho and Abe?" I asked.

"They're not back yet," John said, scratching one of the matches against the stone floor. It sputtered to life.

"Back from where?" Po asked without looking up from his carving.

"The plains," John said without fanfare.

"The plains?" Circe and Misha asked simultaneously.

"What are they doing out on the plains? At this time of day?" Miss B asked.

"Don't ask me," I said, trying to deflect all the unwanted attention. "Ask John."

Everyone looked at John.

"What? I don't know."

I wondered if it was possible that even John could be hiding something. I doubted it. I didn't think he had it in him.

Meanwhile, the fire grew, moved up the larger sticks, laid down a foundation of glowing embers, and cast dancing shadows behind the group, shadows that stretched toward the mountain. *Under the shadow of the mountain*, I thought. The early evening seemed even darker once the fire rose up.

I glanced around one more time. "Well, what do you want to do?" I asked. "Should we wait for Miho and Abe or get on with it?"

"Get on with it," a firm voice said from the darkness between two of the nearby houses. It was Mary. "They know I'm leaving," she said. "It's time."

"Okay," I said, uncertain. "I can try to fill in for Abe if you don't mind, although I'm not sure I know all the words." Po grunted, his eyes still on his carving. I took a deep breath. "You sure that's okay with you, Mary?" I asked again, hoping she'd change her mind.

"Yes," came Mary's clear reply. "I'm ready."

"Okay, well, in that case," I said, holding out my arms as if I were going to embrace the entire world, "please stand with me, friends."

I closed my eyes and took a deep breath, feeling nervous and unsure of myself. It had been a long time since anyone had left. I wasn't sure if I could remember the correct order of everything. And while I considered each of them friends, I was also still feeling the uncertainty I had experienced in Miho's house—what memories had they all had? What nameless things were in that circle around the fire?

I could feel the heat from the fire, and the light flickered against my closed eyelids. What was taking Abe and Miho so long? I opened my eyes and began with what I thought were the right words. "Friends! Today we celebrate the leaving of Mary! Today we light the fire of friendship and send her on to the east, where we all will someday go. Do not mourn her passing. Do not weep."

But even as I said those words, I could feel the tears rising in my eyes. Mary entered the circle of firelight, dressed in a plain white dress with a circle of white flowers on her head, flowers that only grew up close to the mountain, hidden among the boulders. I had forgotten—usually anything involving the mountain was my job.

I walked over to Mary while Circe placed a large bowl of warm water on the ground between us. I looked at Mary, our eyes met, and she smiled a kind, sad smile. I wiped my eyes and smiled back, and in that moment, I was overwhelmed with the desire to go with her, to finally leave this village at the edge of the mountain, get out from under its shadow and move on.

But . . . my brother.

I got down in front of Mary, and the stone patio was hard and uneven against my knees. She put one hand on my shoulder for balance, then raised one of her feet over the bowl. I washed her small, very white, dainty foot. Tiny indigo veins wound their way up her ankles. She put the other foot over the bowl, and I washed it as well. The water cooled quickly, as did the day fading into evening, and I could feel the collective gaze of those sitting at the edge of the patio.

"Do not weep!" I said again, my voice cracking. I stood, drying my hands on a towel. "She travels a path we all must travel. Where her washed feet go, so must ours."

I leaned toward Mary. The others were at the other side of the fire. "How am I doing?" I asked with a smile, trying to cut the sadness. I hated feeling sad. I hated feeling like this was the end.

"Wonderfully," she whispered, reaching up and pushing back a strand of her hair. "Dan? Can I tell you something?"

I leaned closer. Her hair smelled like flowers and her skin smelled like spring. She talked so quietly that I was the only one who could hear her.

"I remembered something about your brother. I had a memory."

"My brother?" I tried hard to pretend I hadn't already heard this while eavesdropping outside of Abe's house.

"Yes." She paused and held on to my elbow. Her touch was cool, her fingertips electric. "I've been waiting for your brother too."

"Why?" I asked. If she didn't tell me now, she would leave, and I would never know.

"I didn't realize it until recently. I told only Abe. Your brother . . ." She paused again. "Your brother brought me great pain, Dan, once upon a time. A long time ago."

"You mean in the mountain?"

"Before that. He did something horrible, and I didn't think I could leave this place until I confronted him. I wanted to kill him for what he had done."

"I'm sorry, Mary." I found it hard to breathe. "I don't know what he did, but I'm sorry."

She shook her head, clearing away the past. "It doesn't matter anymore, not to me. I forgave him. I wanted to tell you so that if you ever see him again, and he remembers what happened, you can tell him for me. I forgive him. That's why I'm leaving now. I'm free to go. I can feel it."

I could feel everyone staring at us, their curiosity building.

"Is this going to take all night?" John asked with a loud chuckle. I held up one finger, asking him to wait.

"Care to share with everyone?" Po said, his voice cynical.

But I continued, whispering only to Mary. "You knew my brother back before the mountain?"

She gave me a solemn look. "Our paths crossed."

I waited for a moment, trying to think of what to say, what to do. "Can you tell me what happened, Mary?"

"No," she whispered. "Maybe someday, Dan, if we meet again, but not today. Today, I am leaving."

"Nothing?"

She shook her head in quick jerks, tears filling her eyes. "I'm sorry." She let go of my elbow and took a few steps back. "Today, I leave," she said in a loud, firm voice.

I wanted to stop the ceremony. I wanted to hear how she knew my brother, demand to know what he had done, take this story from her by force if necessary. But I also had a feeling that the memory was coming to me too, that it was on the edge of my mind.

"Tomorrow, we follow," all of us said in response.

Mary left the circle for a moment, and when she returned, she was holding a large sack. I knew that in it was everything she held dear. She put it down at her feet. Everyone walked over to her and gave her a gift, something of their own that was precious, something she would appreciate. I gave her the small book I had brought with me, the one I had put in my pocket that morning. When she saw it, she cried even harder.

Mary picked up the sack and put it in the fire, and the flames grew steadily until they were roaring. She reached down and took each of the gifts one at a time, appreciating them, then looking at the person who gave it to her. Her eyes were full of such thankfulness, and it was with great tenderness that she also put each of the gifts into the fire. It hurt me to see that book burn, I won't lie. I made myself watch it, though. I watched the pages turn brown and swell, the thin cover curling and blackening and rising in smoke. I watched the flames catch.

"You have given up anything that might keep you here," I said, still staring at the book I had given her. I felt certain that I hadn't quite gotten the wording right on that one, but I was somewhere else, my mind circling back again and again to the realization that she had known my brother, that he had done something to her. She had been waiting for him, just like me. Just like Miho too, apparently.

I tried to keep the ceremony moving forward. "Does anyone have the rocks?"

Circe walked over and handed me two rocks, both the size of a small fist. "Where do you think Miho and Abe are?" she asked me quietly, deliberately facing away from the others.

"They'll be here soon, any minute." I nodded with what I hoped was assurance, taking the rocks from her, but I didn't believe my own words. They should have been back by now. Fear for Abe and Miho fluttered inside of me. But I reasoned with myself—she was a small girl. Barely able to walk. What trouble could she have caused?

One of the rocks Circe gave me was white with dark gray veins. The other was black like coal. I handed the two rocks to Mary, and she stared at both of them for a moment. She walked up the hill a short distance, as close to the mountain as she needed to get. I watched her, but the rest of the group didn't face the mountain. Even then, they chose not to look.

Mary threw the black rock up toward the mountain, and it clattered among the shattered boulders, falling at the foot of the cliffs. She held tight to the white rock, and as she turned toward us, we formed two very short lines. I remembered when those lines used to be fifty people long, one hundred people long. But now there were only three of us on each side.

She walked between us, taking the white rock with her. Circe was crying, shoulders shaking. Miss B wiped a tear from her eyes. John kept clearing his throat. Misha nodded, as if someone was telling her something she agreed with in the deepest way. Po stared into the fire.

There was no waving, no goodbyes, no words—those had all been spoken earlier, in private. I wondered who she had met with that day, who she had spoken with. Had she told anyone else about my brother? Did one of them know more than I did?

I wished I would have taken the time to talk to her. I wished we would have sat down together. If I had visited her, would she have told me more?

I watched her walk away from the village, toward the darkness, and I was overwhelmed with anxiety for Adam, for me, for all of us. The village was emptying—how much longer until John or Po or Circe traveled east? Who would say the words for me when it was my time to go? Who would give me a gift to put in the fire or hand me the rocks?

Before Mary disappeared, I saw movement in the shadows. It was Miho and Abe, returning from the plains. And not only them—Abe carried a girl in his arms. The girl we had seen from the second tree. He stumbled at the edge of the light, went down on one knee, and laid her there in the grass.

9 PO'S THEORY

"I CAN'T STAY," Mary said, as much to herself as to us. She had come back to us when Abe appeared with the girl, and now there was a slight twinge of panic at the edge of her voice, as well as a kind of asking for permission. "I can't. I just can't. I made up my mind. I have to go now." She looked around with wild eyes. I couldn't make myself meet her gaze.

We were all looking at Abe and Miho and the girl lying in the grass. She was tiny, curled up in the fetal position, like a fawn that's been delivered too soon. Miho squatted down and placed her hand on the girl's shoulder, felt her neck, stroked her hair, and pushed it back behind one ear. The girl's hooded cloth poncho was disheveled and bunched underneath her, and the rest of her clothes were also a plain tan color. Her bare feet were stained green from the long walk through the plains. I couldn't look away.

Nothing felt stable anymore, nothing felt moored down. What was going on in this place? We had been there for ages, and within the span of two days Mary decided she was leaving, the black-haired woman came out of the mountain, and this girl came back over the plains. And people were remembering things. No one had ever come back. I had never kept things from Abe or Miho. It felt like someone had picked up the puzzle pieces of my life, a puzzle that was nearly assembled, and threw it into the air so that everything was separating and coming undone.

I wanted to tell Mary that she had to stay, at least until we found out what this girl's appearance was all about, that it couldn't possibly be safe out there in the dark, walking east into who knows what. What if there were others? What if this girl was trying to escape trouble? But I knew, coming from me, an appeal to stay would seem insincere.

Before anyone else could make a recommendation either way, Abe spoke up. "You're right, Mary. You need to keep going. Everything will be well. Please. Go. This is your time."

His words jarred me. But Mary nodded, unsteady, and then she walked into the night.

Misha took a few steps after her, and for a minute I thought she was going to leave too, without any fanfare, simply vanish into the darkness with Mary. But she stopped where we could all see her. She watched Mary walk off, and her voice came out tiny, barely a squeak. "Mary?"

"Are you sure Mary should leave?" John asked, but Abe cut him off.

"I need some food and water, right now. Hurry."

Miho slipped into her house and came out with half a loaf of bread and a glass of water. She bent down close to the girl.

"Out of the light," Abe mumbled, and we shifted where we stood so that the dancing firelight made its way down the bank and into the midst of our small gathering. John lumbered back up to the stone patio. I could tell he was miffed at the way Abe had ignored his concern. He threw a few more logs on the fire, sending up a shower of sparks.

Soon the fire roared again, but John didn't come back down. He stood there, staring into the fire, his massive paws fisted on his hips.

I moved closer, staring again at the girl. She had long, light brown hair. Her arms were lean with muscle, and even though she was small, her shoulders were strong. Her face was lined with determination, even when she was unconscious. A deep bag was on the ground beside her. Abe put a hand under her neck and raised her head, and with his other hand he put the glass of water to her cracked lips.

The girl's mouth moved, barely, the way a leaf might flutter when there is no wind, so subtly you could hardly see it. Then her lips moved toward the water, and her tongue flashed between them. Abe tipped the glass a little more so that water trickled into her mouth, and she swallowed, wincing. He went on like that for a long time, giving her small sips, until some kind of relief washed over her. She became less rigid, and her head turned to the side.

Abe bent even closer, whispering in her ear, "You're okay now. We will take care of you."

Her eyes fluttered. Her mouth opened again with a kind of yearning that we all felt and understood. Abe raised the water, and she drank in a thirsty way this time until it was gone. She opened her eyes, looked around at us in confusion, and closed them again.

I stared off into the darkness, looking for Mary, but she was gone. It was night, the traditional time of day for heading east. The great, empty plains had swallowed her. I hoped she could find the first tree in the darkness, but I also knew that if she couldn't, she'd wait for morning and then find her way east, one tree at a time, all the way across the plains. How long would it take her? What waited for her on the other side? There was so much that we didn't know.

"She's awake again," Circe whispered.

"What do you need?" Abe asked the girl.

That's when I noticed she was staring at me. She didn't say anything, but she stared with intensity, as if she knew who I was.

Abe turned to Miho. "Can we keep her in your house for now?"

Miho nodded. The others murmured questions and thoughts to each other, but no one had anything productive to offer. We were all stunned.

The fire dimmed and a log fell by itself, collapsing in the space of things already burned. John hadn't moved. He still stared into the fire. A cloud of ash moved upward in small wisps and sparks. Po had returned to his seat beside the fire not far from John, carving quietly. We had all become stir-crazy. No one wanted to go home and sit in the heavy silence that waited for us.

I walked over and sat beside Po. "What's going on around here?" I asked him, shaking my head. "This is absurd." I thought of the strange looks he had given me earlier that day. It seemed awkward to ask him about that directly, but I thought that maybe if we spoke, some explanation would come out.

John glanced over at us, opened his mouth to speak, then closed it and stared back into the flames. Po peeled away a small slice of wood with his knife, and it dropped to the stone patio, joining a small pile of similar shavings.

"Feels like we're coming to the end," he said without emotion, blowing on the walking stick, eyeing it critically before shaving off another piece.

"The end?" I asked.

He grunted, kept carving, and didn't say anything else for a little while. There was something tender about the way he carved, something intimate, as if he wasn't cutting the wood but coaxing it.

"What do you mean, the end?" I asked again.

He sighed and spoke without looking at me. "Think about it, Dan. What happens when that place empties out?" He motioned with his head back toward the mountain, and returned to his carving.

"You mean what happens once the last person comes out?"

He nodded.

"I haven't given it much thought."

He gave a wry grin. "I don't think anyone has."

"But you have?"

"For years now, as long as we can remember, people came out of the mountain. Right? You've seen them. Beaten down. Tortured. Bloody. You came over, I came over. We can barely remember what happened to us over there, but it's pretty clear it wasn't some kind of party going on. 'Escaped,' we call it. 'Escaped from the other side.'"

I nodded.

"Now, it also seems pretty clear to me that there were some nasty folks running that place over there. Judging by the state of us when we came over. Fair to say?"

I nodded again. "That's fair. From what I can remember,

it's true." I tried to sound like I'd been thinking of this for a long time. Images of some of the worst abuses came to mind, and I squeezed my eyes shut instinctively, trying to push those images back. But they never went anywhere. Not really. I could close my eyes, but I couldn't keep the nightmares at bay. So I opened my eyes and stared into the fire.

"Okay," Po continued, "so put all of that together and then ask yourself, when's the last time anyone came over the mountain?"

He said this as a kind of final point in his argument, but I couldn't help picturing the dark-haired woman who had come over the day before and was lying in my bed. The woman who had told me my brother was still over there alone, that he was the last one.

"It's been a long time," I said, trying to go along with his game, my voice faltering in the lie.

"What if they're running out of people to torment?" Po asked. "What if there's no one left over there? What if they're gathering their forces and preparing to come over the mountain and retrieve us, take us back, use us for whatever it was they were using us for before?" His eyes grew wild and he stopped carving, punctuating his words with his knife, a stab in the air for each question mark.

I sat there as his words sifted through the air. There was no breeze. The fire burned straight up with very few sparks. John stood, walked over to the pile of wood, and threw a few more large pieces on.

"Do you think that's what's going to happen?" I asked Po, my voice low, not wanting to bring John into the conversation. And if that's what he thought, why had he been glaring at me? What did I have to do with any of this?

"Makes sense, doesn't it?"

"So what are you waiting for? Why stay so close to the mountain? Why haven't you headed east yet?"

He looked at me, squinted, and stared back at the walking stick, but he didn't carve. "For a long time, I didn't know why I was staying. But last night, I remembered something."

"Really?" I asked. Po too. Not only me and Miss B and Miho and Mary, but Po was remembering too. "Something about the other side of the mountain? Or before that?"

"Before."

"Really?" I said again, and this time I couldn't keep the fascination out of my voice.

He nodded.

I waited. He was silent.

"Can you tell me?" I asked hesitantly, already knowing what he would say.

He gave out a small laugh. "It's mine. I'm not giving it away, Dan. But that's why I'm still here, why I can't leave. I had a feeling about it for a long time, but that memory confirmed it for me."

"Fair enough," I said, disappointed and feeling spurned. Again.

Miho walked up to the fire. "You guys okay?" she asked.

"Anything new?" My voice came out weak and tired. Po was back into his carving, sitting right there yet also somewhere far from us.

Miho shook her head. "Do you have that book Abe likes to read to people when they first come over?"

It had been a while. I had to think about it. Did I have it, or had I last left it at Abe's?

"Yeah, I think I do," I said.

Po's words still occupied my mind. What if he was right? What if we were moments away from those horrible slave masters coming out of the mountain and hauling us back to that hell?

"I'll run up and get it. Where do you keep it?" she asked.

Po peeled back another long piece of wood and it curled in on itself, fell down onto the stone patio. I was drowning in all the recent realizations—Miho's drawing of Adam and Mary's memories about Adam and Po's theory about those on the other side and the woman's revelation that my brother was the last one.

"It's probably on the first bookshelf by the door, up toward the top. Red spine," I said absentmindedly. I was trying to think through some flaw in Po's theory that would keep me from worrying about it. I'd never been able to visualize our tormentors, but that neither supported nor undermined his idea that they were coming back for us.

Minutes passed before I realized Miho was walking to my house to get the book. She was walking by herself, to my house, where the woman slept in my bed.

I ran after her, wondering what made me think I could ever keep all these lies and half-truths straight in my mind.

10 YOU NEVER TOLD ME YOUR NAME

THE BREEZE RETURNED in the darkness, coming back at us from the plains, and it was sweet and melancholy. It pulled a deep sense of nostalgia from me, a kind of remembering, but not of specific things: nebulous, old memories of tears and great happiness, of devastation and celebrated rebuilding. I wondered if my memories of those old days would ever come back to me, if I would ever remember everything, or if they would always be made available in fits and starts, small pieces here and there.

The grass was nearly dry, and my feet swished along quickly as I ran first through the dark village, then through the short empty space that led to my house, and finally up to my front door. I opened it, breathless, just as Miho came out.

"Oh!" she shouted, jumping.

"I'm sorry," I said, laughing nervously. "I'm sorry." I looked into her eyes to see if she had found anything, to see if she had seen the strange woman in my house.

"What is wrong with you?" she asked with a laugh, raising one hand to her chest as if to slow her heart. "You scared me, Dan."

"I'm sorry," I said again, bending over, still breathing hard. "I . . . I wanted to make sure you could find it."

She held up the book by its spine, her laughter shifting into a small suspicion. "What is going on, Dan? You haven't been yourself lately. What's wrong?"

I couldn't look up into her face or she would have convinced me without saying anything to tell her the truth, so I stayed bent over and stared down, catching my breath. "It's Mary," I said. "Just Mary. And now this girl."

Miho put her hand on my head, a kind of blessing. "Dan," she said in a quiet, breathless voice. "Oh, Dan."

We stood there like that for longer than made sense. The two of us, I knew, were looking for something to connect to, someone to trust. And guilt seeped through my entire being. She was that for me. She was someone to trust. And I was so utterly not.

But the guilt was also compounded by a feeling of indignation that she knew more than she was telling me. I kept seeing in my mind that sketch of my brother on her table. What did she know? And why wasn't she telling me? I felt this growing chasm between us, and I wasn't sure what to do about it.

"I have to go," she said, regret in her voice. "I have to take this down to Abe." She raised the book again. "Do you want me to come back up here? I feel like we need to catch up."

Concern etched itself around her eyes. I felt it too, the distance.

"No," I said, standing up and shifting so that I stood between her and the rest of the house. "That's okay. Just grabbing a few things. I'll be right behind you."

She reached out and touched my arm, gave a small smile I could barely see in the dark, and drifted toward the village, swinging the book by her side while she walked.

I watched her disappear into the darkness. How could she remain so carefree? When I went inside and closed the door quietly, the latch barely made a sound.

I meandered around in the kitchen for a bit, taking out some bread and gnawing on the crust. I walked over to the rear door, opened it, and looked out over the plains. I couldn't see very much in the dark, but the grass rustled in the wind.

I left the back door open and walked to my bedroom, paused for a moment, then went inside.

She was still there, and it looked like she had barely moved since I had left earlier in the day. She was on her side, eyes closed, hand still reaching over toward the chair where I had sat. I walked slowly to it and sat down. Why was I so afraid of her? What could she possibly do to hurt me?

Her eyes opened slowly. They were beautiful eyes. I could see this, finally, since they were healing. The redness had gone out of them. Her dark irises were soft, even inviting.

"What are you going to do?" she asked in a drowsy voice.

"About what?" I replied. There were so many things on my mind. I couldn't narrow them down to what she might be referring to—telling everyone about her? Going east? Trying to find out more about the memories everyone was having and not telling me about? Finding out more about the girl?

"Your brother," she stated.

"I don't know."

"Your brother needs you," she said, and I felt like crying.

What was there to do but wait? I couldn't go back over the mountain, not back into that hellish place. When I thought of it, screams echoed in my mind. Pain frayed my nerves. I didn't think I could bear it, going back in there.

"How did you make it out?" I asked. "Do you remember anything?"

She coughed, moved her hand to cover her mouth.

"Wait, let me get you some water." I walked back to the kitchen and returned with a glass. "Would you like to sit up?"

She shook her head. She leaned to the side and managed to drink some water like a bird, tipping her head back. "I don't remember much. I remember the path going up and up and up. I remember hiding. I don't know how I did it." Her eyes went momentarily wild.

"I wish we knew more about it," I said, more to myself than to her. "I wish I could remember something."

She coughed again. "When I left your brother, he was at the very bottom. The very bottom." The darkness in her eyes shifted to sadness, the way a sunny day can suddenly dim.

I leaned toward her. Again I was taken by her beauty, her vulnerability.

"I wanted to bring him with me," she said. She licked her lips, and they, too, were soft, healing. Tears formed in her eyes. I leaned closer. "But he wouldn't come. He was too afraid."

Something about her courage latched on and stirred up a longing in me. I moved to kiss her cheek at the same moment she turned to look up at me, and our mouths came together. She was warm, and she kissed me back. I felt a rush of confusion and the soft delight of intimacy.

I see him kneeling on a mound of rock, and he looks like he's been there for a hundred years. His clothes are tattered, and when he looks up, his eyes are wild. I wonder if he's sane anymore—there's something about him that looks missing, vacant. I want to walk toward him, but something is between us, something is keeping us apart.

This vision was quick, like a stabbing pain. I leaned back in my chair, shocked, existing on some other plane.

"You should go get him," she whispered. "You could convince him to follow you out."

"I can't go down there on my own," I murmured, trying to catch my breath. My heart was pounding. I wanted to kiss her again but knew I shouldn't. I thought of Miho. What was I doing?

"You wouldn't have to go alone," she said, and her voice was relaxing, mesmerizing, convincing. "You have friends here who would go with you if you asked them. If you all went together, you would be safe."

"I couldn't do that," I said, but I didn't sound convincing, not even to myself. Would they do that? Would they come with me? Maybe the horrible ones waiting on the other side wouldn't expect us. Maybe we could sneak in unobserved and bring back Adam. Safely. All of us together.

My voice emerged empty, distracted. "If you want to get cleaned up, there's a bath in there." I pointed mechanically toward the bathroom no bigger than a closet.

I stood up. I had to get out, take a walk, clear my head. I moved to the door, but when I got there I stopped and turned. "You never told me your name."

But she was already asleep.

"You never told me your name," I said again, this time in a whisper. I stared at her placid face, my hand on the doorknob. I wanted to stay, but I left.

IN THE MIDDLE of that dark night, Miho's house became the new center of our small universe. Misha and Circe sat in the soft grass outside her front door, talking earnestly, quietly. Miss B walked in circles around the stone patio not far away, every so often looking down toward the house. As I walked up, John and Po passed by.

"Where are you guys going?" I asked, worried for a moment that they were leaving too.

"We're going for wood," John said.

"You'll have to go a long way," I warned them. "I was at the second tree and there wasn't much left."

"We'll check it out," Po said dismissively. There was an edge to his voice that seemed unwarranted.

"Everything okay?" I asked their backs as they walked away, but they didn't reply.

"Should they be going out there right now, in the dark?" I asked Misha as she came up beside me. "I can't even see the first tree."

She shrugged. "What can we do?" Her voice was so slight that her words melted away.

I sighed. "Anything new in there?"

"The girl woke up a bit ago," Circe said. She clenched her jaw. "I've been hounding Abe for an update. I'd love to know what they're talking about."

Misha nodded in agreement.

"Why would someone come from the east?" I asked. "After all this time, after all of these people leaving, why come back?"

Could it be there wasn't anything on the other side of the plains? What if the promised haven didn't even exist?

But if there wasn't anything over there, why didn't more people come back, and sooner? Were the people over there sending for help?

Miho's face appeared at the door. "There you are," she said to me in a calm, kind voice. "Thanks for the book. It's helping her relax."

"Is she okay?" Misha asked.

Miho nodded. "She's sleeping now."

Abe came out, walking past Miho. "Why don't you all get some sleep," he suggested. "There's not much else going on here right now. Let's meet at the patio in the morning. We'll give you an update."

"Sleep? Abe . . ." Circe replied, clearly ready to interrogate him about the woman, but he interrupted her with a tired voice.

"Circe, please. We're all tired. Let's talk in the morning."

"Do we have that long?" she asked.

He stared at her for a moment. "In the morning, Circe."

"The guys went out for wood," I told him. "I think they'll have to go out to the third or fourth tree."

"I wish they hadn't done that. Listen, let's all stick together until tomorrow, okay? Stay in the village. Stay together. I'll keep the fire going to make sure John and Po can find their way back."

The women glanced at each other nervously.

"Can I stay with you?" Misha asked Circe.

Circe nodded as Miss B came over.

"Miss B, we're having a slumber party," Misha said, smiling, trying to lighten the mood. "You want to stay with me at Circe's tonight?"

"And sleep on that godforsaken sofa of hers? No thank you, ma'am. I will enjoy my own bed quite well, thank you."

Everyone laughed, and for a moment the air felt more breathable.

"Well," Misha said, "can we at least walk you home?"

"Of course."

The three women walked up the lonely greenway into the darkness. They walked slowly, accommodating Miss B's easy pace. I made a mental list of where everyone was: Miss B at her own house; Misha and Circe at Circe's house; John and Po on an unadvised wood run; Abe and Miho in the house with the girl. Who was I missing? I was convinced I was missing someone.

Oh, of course. Mary. But she was gone, walking east, somewhere in the dark, maybe at the fourth or fifth tree by now if she had walked straight, if she had found her way.

I turned to walk home, wondering if the woman in my house had fallen asleep for the night, but Abe called my name.

I turned around. He motioned for me to come back to Miho's door. "You need to come in. We have to talk."

THREE LAMPS LIT the inside of Miho's house, and their softness caused a seed of homesickness to rise again. I loved our town, and I was heartbroken at how empty it had become. There were times we had picnicked out by the first tree, well over a hundred of us. Maybe even two hundred at one point. People had shared houses in those days. The greenway had always been full of people—barely green, in fact, usually trampled to dust by all of the coming and going, the visiting. There had been the constant sound of laughter and even, sometimes late at night, singing.

I could barely see the girl lying on the small couch against the wall, resting in the shadows. I took a step toward her, but Abe held out his arm like a small barrier. I stopped.

"Wait," he said, motioning toward the table where Miho sat, her face in her hands. She looked up at us, her eyes tired, more tired than I'd ever seen them, and she gave me a sad, uncertain smile. She reached out her hand to me, and I crossed the space and took it with a pang of guilt, remembering how I had kissed the woman in my house. The woman without a name.

Abe pulled out a chair for me and I sat in it. I glanced around the table, but the sketch was gone, as was the note with the question about my brother. How could Miho possibly know what my brother looked like? Why was she waiting for him?

The three of us sat still for a few moments, saying nothing.

Abe broke the silence. "She can't speak," he said quietly, and I could tell he was trying to keep our words from reaching the girl.

"What?" I asked.

"Or won't," he clarified. "Can't or won't."

"This isn't good," Miho whispered to herself, as if it was

the only thing she had been saying since the girl arrived. "This isn't good."

Abe seemed to consider disagreeing, then thought better of it. "We don't know what it means," he said to me.

"But everyone's already freaking out," Miho said. "What will they do when they find out she can't talk? What if she can't talk because of something that happened to her on the other side of the plains?"

I knew immediately what she was implying—that the other mountain, the faraway respite we had heard so much about, might simply be a mirror image of the one we had escaped from. Another place of torment. If that was true, we were trapped in between them, mountains to the east, mountains to the west. Where could we go?

"We don't know anything for sure," Abe said firmly.

"But that's the whole point," I said, anger or cynicism or despair rising in my voice. Or all three. "We don't know anything. She's here, and we still don't know anything. What could be more discouraging than that?"

We sat in the quiet. The lamp in the kitchen burned down too low and winked out, and the shadows that formed in its wake felt like living things drawing closer, predators closing in.

I felt the key in my pocket. I gathered myself. It was time to tell Abe and Miho the truth.

But then I heard a sound from the sofa. The girl was sitting up, staring at me with eyes wide open. She was either terrified of me or surprised to see me, and neither response made any sense.

"Hi," I said to her, glancing nervously over at Abe. He

nodded at me, encouraging me to keep going. I realized he was hoping we might get her to say something, to explain why she had come back.

She didn't reply, so I tried something else. "Are you okay? Would you like something to eat?"

She stood up and limped toward me.

Again I thought of how far she must have come, the toll the journey must have taken on her small body. She moved more fully into the light, and when I saw her face, I felt the tug of familiarity, but it was a flash, here and gone. There were tears in her eyes as she raised her hand to touch my face, but just like that, the light went out of her eyes. Her hand fell back to her side, her mouth closed into a straight line, and her eyebrows furrowed in confusion. She turned and went back to the sofa, curling up under the blanket with her narrow back facing us.

I looked over at Abe and Miho. We stared at each other. No one knew what to say.

What I didn't say was that I had experienced this before. I knew that old familiar feeling of someone looking at me, thinking they recognized me, only to apologize and walk away.

It happens often when you're a twin.

So, she knew my brother. I considered telling Abe and Miho this revelation, but it became another nameless thing.

"Tomorrow morning," Abe said, weariness in his voice, "let's meet up at the patio. We'll tell the others everything we know."

"We don't know anything," Miho replied, but it wasn't a protest of any kind, simply a statement of fact.

"And that's what we'll tell them."

MY HOUSE WAS dark and quiet, and there was an under-current of something I couldn't identify, like a high-pitched sound I heard for an instant and then lost track of. I assumed the woman was still sleeping in my bed, and I felt guilty because of my recent treasons, so I didn't even go back into the room. I didn't trust myself. Why should I? No one should trust me. Not anymore.

I pulled the armchair over to the back doors and opened them, sat in the chair, and stared out over the plains. Since it was night I couldn't see anything, but I could hear the wind moving madly through the grass. It whipped in the door and stirred the air in the house, so I got up, found a blanket, and sat back down.

I fell asleep, drifting into a shallow snooze. I tossed and turned all night. I even watched the sky brighten in fits and starts as I slept and woke up, slept and woke up. Finally, as light took over the morning, I found a place of deep sleep.

When I woke up, I had it. Another memory. One that filled me with dread and a deep, deep sadness.

11 A REAL SHAME

I SAW THE sunlight glaring off the windshield and felt the warm summer air gusting through my passenger-side window. My arm rested on the window ledge and my chin was propped on my forearm. I stared out at the passing fields and it gave me an empty feeling. The wind blew my hair around as we drove through a cloud of dust, the specks rising up and stinging my face and eyes.

I could feel the resentment of my father, who was boiling in the driver's seat of the car. I was old enough to drive, but if he was in the car, he was driving. On that particular trip, he was a tornado of pent-up energy, twitching and biting his fingernails and muttering the beginnings of sentences that never came to fruition. I was sixteen, and he was afraid I was about to let him down.

Finally, he managed to actually say something, real words, and he had to shout to be heard above the wind rushing through the open windows. "I don't care what happened. He's your brother." His words simmered there in the air, spitting hot, before being swept out of the car. We left them behind, or at least I wanted to leave them behind. But words have a way of keeping up.

The car carried us around bends and over bridges, and for

a moment I was a child again and pretended we were launching into space. I closed my eyes and felt the darkness around me, the earth moving away faster and faster, the encroaching stillness of space and the pinpricks of stars all around. I felt like I was floating, and I had to catch my breath when I looked down and saw nothingness for all eternity. The earth became a tiny blue dot, remote, and I felt a great sense of freedom.

But my imagination could only take me a certain distance from reality, and when the car stopped abruptly and my father shut it off, I had to open my eyes. We were at my high school. He pulled violently on the parking brake, even though the car had come to rest on flat ground. I wondered if you could break the parking brake by pulling on it too hard. He might pull the handle right out of the car and carry it with him into the principal's office.

"C'mon," he growled.

As we crawled from the car, I knew a couple of things.

I knew my father believed you should never rat out your brother—never, never, not for any reason.

I knew we were going inside so I could tell a lie.

We crossed the baking pavement. My father treated the handle of the front door much the same as he had treated the parking brake. We entered the air-conditioned lobby, and the cold air clung to the sweat on my forehead, under my arms, on the small of my back. I followed my father as he plunged through door after door, never knocking, never waiting.

Then, the door to Principal Stevens's office.

"How can I—" his assistant began, but my father ignored her and pushed through the door.

I followed, my shoulders hunched over apologetically. I stared at the floor tiles.

"Gentlemen," Principal Stevens said, unfazed by my father's entrance. "Have a seat."

My father paused, as if he was considering the most brazen way to reject any seat ever offered to him by this no-good principal, but he scowled and sat. I sat beside him. In the remaining seat sat a police officer.

Principal Stevens looked across the desk at us. "As you know, Jo Sayers has accused your son of . . ." He hesitated, weighing his words. "Of violating her at a party three months ago."

"Why'd she wait so long?" my father hissed.

"I'm sure we can sort all this out," Principal Stevens said, somehow managing to remain completely removed from my father's spite.

My dad glared over at the officer. "What's he doing here?"

"He's here to collect your son's statement and make sure there are no . . . inconsistencies."

We lived in a small town, one that didn't give too much standing to things like Miranda rights or the right to have an attorney present.

"Boy?" the police officer said, staring at me.

"I was with my brother all night," I said quietly.

"Which night?" the officer asked.

"The night Jo claims he . . . was with her."

"That's right," my father muttered. It was the closest thing to encouraging me that I had ever heard slip from his mouth.

"A few kids say they saw him at the party," the officer said. His voice was neither skeptical nor believing.

I glanced at the principal. I had the sense that this was

a performance they had all created, and all I had to do was play my part.

"I heard there was a lot of alcohol there." I shrugged, staring back at the floor. "Easy mistake to make."

"This isn't just any violation," the officer said, a sternness entering his voice. "This is rape, boy."

I didn't reply.

"Where were you boys, if not at the party?" Principal Stevens asked in a completely unconcerned voice, but he did lean over his desk toward me.

"Camping. Sir. Up at the state park. We left right after school and didn't come back for two nights. I was with him the whole time."

"You sure?" the police officer asked.

I swallowed hard. "Yes, sir."

The principal leaned back, and it was clear he was immensely relieved. "We don't need a good boy to be kept from graduating, not over something like this," he said. "Thank you, Dan. Officer?"

The police officer shrugged. "This clears it up pretty good."

We all stood at the same time. I was amazed at how easy it had been, not only the process but also the telling of the lie. A shiver ran through me, as if I'd swallowed something raw, something not meant to be consumed.

"Why'd that little swine wait to come forward until now?" my father asked as we all shuffled toward the office door.

Principal Stevens shrugged. "No one knows for sure," he said. "Maybe because she's pregnant."

The officer shook his head. "It's a real shame," he said, and the other two men grunted their assent.

I couldn't tell what it was he referred to as being "a real shame"—the fact that she had come forward, the baby, the rape, or the lie we had all agreed on.

IT WAS A quiet morning, and I knew they were probably waiting for me at the stone patio, waiting for me to come down so that all of us could decide what was next. What would we do in the face of so many unexpected things?

But the new memory gave me so much more to think about, and I needed to sit with it a bit. I wondered how I could do that, how I could lie for my brother, but then I remembered the look on my father's face while we drove. The images swirled in my mind—the wind in the window, the anger of my father, the baking pavement as we got out and walked toward the school. The sense that I had to fix what my brother had broken. Anxiety at the impending lie.

I stalled. I woke slowly and rose even slower, weighed down by what I remembered. The day was already there, and it was bright. The grass was still and the air had warmed, now that the storm was two days gone. The horizon formed a line where the deep blue of the sky rested on the rich green of the grass, barely moving. I stood in the doorway, shading my eyes with one hand, staring out into the emptiness.

There was something about the light of a warm day that scattered the fear from the night before. Po's theory, that those who had held us captive were returning for us, had felt so true in the flickering shadows beside the fire, but here? In the daylight? It seemed ludicrous. The valley was too peaceful to imagine some kind of impending invasion.

I heard rustling from my bedroom, a sound that caused nervousness and other feelings to flutter in my gut. The woman. I walked to the door and stood there listening before raising my hand and knocking lightly with two knuckles. "Hello?" I said in a hushed voice no one could possibly hear from the other side of a door.

But she must have heard my tender knock, because her voice called out to me. "Come in."

I pushed the door open. She sat in bed, her back against the headboard. She had combed her long black hair and it was straight and shining. Her dark eyes searched mine. She pulled the covers up around her and sighed.

"Thank you," she said, her voice rich and purring.

"For what?"

"For taking me in. For helping me. For letting me stay here without telling anyone else. I needed this rest. I'm still not ready to be interrogated."

She was a vision sitting there. Stunning.

"Have you found my key?" she asked in a distracted voice, as if it was the last thing on her mind.

"No," I managed to get out, even though the key was right there in my pocket where it always was.

"Have you decided?" she asked me, her eyes wide with curiosity.

"Decided what?"

"Decided what you're going to do."

"About what?"

She smiled, and it was the closest she had come to condescending. It was a smile that said, *You silly boy. What would you do without me?*

"Your brother," she said, and the blanket lowered so that I could see her bare shoulders. "What are you going to do about your brother? You can't leave him there."

"I should probably go find him," I said, looking away from her. My voice was noncommittal, not convincing in the least. In fact, the words surprised me—I could never go back into the mountain and look for him. Where had that come from? Still, it was embarrassing that I hadn't gone for him as soon as she told me where he was.

"To be honest, I don't know if I can do it," I muttered.

"Of course you can! But you can't go alone," she replied, and there was an urgency not quite hidden in her voice. "You need to take them with you. You will need help."

"Them?"

"Your friends. All of your friends who live here with you. They should all go with you."

I nodded, but my words went in a different direction. "I can't ask them to do that. It's too terrible. I can't."

She looked at me as if I had said something very noble, and she nodded at the truth of it—the deep, aching truth. "But you can't go alone," she repeated.

"I know." I wanted to tell her I didn't think I could go back there at all, on my own or with an entire crowd of people, because what was over there was simply too awful.

"It wasn't as bad as you remember it," she said in a soothing voice, looking down and to the side as if she was afraid to make eye contact.

"What?" I asked, confusion all over my face. "Are you kidding?"

There was a sincerity in her face that I couldn't argue with. "I know you have terrible memories of it, but you've made it much worse than it really was."

"You just crawled out of the canyon a couple days ago," I said. My voice sounded like someone else's, someone far away, someone rather silly. "You were bleeding. You could barely stand." Why did I sound silly to myself? I made a resolution not to say anything else.

"What are you talking about?" she asked. "I'm completely fine. Look at me. You found me in the plains and brought me here. Don't you remember?"

She was right. Her skin was like white soap, clear and soft. Her face was untainted by anything. Her eyes were sharp and black, and her hair glowed. I squeezed my eyes shut and shook my head, trying to loosen this grip of confusion. I was getting mixed up between finding her and seeing the girl out by the third tree. How long had this woman been in my house? Where exactly had I found her?

"Dan," she whispered. "It's okay. Look at me." She paused. "Dan, look at me."

I opened my eyes. Her gaze was a deep pool. Her hand moved up my arm until it stopped behind my shoulder. She pulled me down toward her and kissed my cheek, my forehead, and then my mouth. Softly. So softly. I closed my eyes and fell into visions of other times, other places.

But always, at the heart of everything I saw, was my brother, alone.

MY HEART POUNDED when I locked the house and walked down the greenway toward the cluster of houses. I felt all emptied out, turned around, and disheveled. It was like someone had taken my mind, with everything it knew and believed and felt, and shaken it, so that all the papers mixed up, all the files opened, all the pieces jumbled.

The day couldn't have been more beautiful. The air was the perfect temperature, cool on my skin. The sky was blue and clear, and the grass on the plains rippled in gentle waves. I wanted to go lie in it, stare up into the blue, feel the blades of grass against my arms and ears and fingers. I took in a deep breath and let it out, another deep breath, another letting out. Yes, this was it. No matter what else was happening, this was the village I loved.

I walked through the houses. No one was there, and this went beyond the normal quiet of our near-empty town. Even the places where people usually moved around were empty. No one peeked out to say hello, no one invited me in for a chat, no one offered me a drink. The doors were closed and the alleys were empty and the blinds were all drawn. Even Miss B's. Even the women's.

By the time I approached Miho's house, I could hear them. I looked up the small hill to the stone patio, and they all were sitting in a circle, talking in murmurs and whispers, their voices mingling with the breeze that moved through town, stirring the long grass, sounding Circe's wind chime. I felt like a kid late to class.

I walked toward the patio and everyone stopped talking. Now I felt like a defendant entering the courtroom. Their eyes were on me. When I returned John's gaze, he looked down at the ground nervously. Po didn't look away, though. Neither did Circe. Misha swallowed hard. I kept walking toward them and took in each person in the circle. Finally, Miho pulled her mouth up at one side in a kind of apology and started crying softly. Then she pulled her knees to her chest, her feet coming up onto the seat.

"Hey," I said, the one word a question. I stopped walking and stood at the edge of the small circle. The charred remains of the previous night's fire sat black and lifeless.

"Dan," Abe said, standing and motioning to an empty spot right beside him, "where have you been all morning?"

I shook my head slowly, not answering.

I noticed that the girl sat on the other side of Abe. Someone—Miho, I guessed—had brushed her hair and braided it. Her skin was clean. Her eyes seemed cooler in the daylight. She was biting her fingernails, and her eyes kept flitting up, looking at my face, and then looking elsewhere quickly. She didn't say anything.

I walked across the patio, and I had never felt so self-conscious of each step. I was sure I'd catch an edge and trip. But I made it to my seat and sat down.

Abe walked to the other side of the small circle so he could face everyone. But he spoke mostly to me. "Dan, we've all had memories in the last two days that need to be shared."

"I thought we were going to talk about her," I said, motioning toward the girl. "And try to figure out what's going on around here."

"I think it's important that we take some time today and share our memories because, well, as it turns out, they all pertain to you." He paused. "Or your brother."

I couldn't have been more confused. But I thought about Miss B's memory and how I'd had a feeling it was connected to me somehow. And I thought of overhearing Mary's memory. Miho's drawing of my brother. I looked at the rest of them: Circe, John, Po, Misha.

Now what?

"Dan, if you don't mind, we're going to have everyone take turns sharing their new memories."

I was relieved and terrified. Relieved because I would finally know what everyone was thinking about, what everyone else had remembered. Terrified because . . . well, I wasn't sure. What was it about these memories that had anything to do with me?

I had a sense that their stories might change me, make me into something entirely other than what I was. Could stories do that?

12 THE DAUGHTER

I LOOKED ACROSS the circle at Circe. She couldn't hold the connection, and her eyes dropped to the stone patio. The whole time she told her story, she stared at the ground, then at Abe, then back at the ground again. But never at me.

"My daughter used to call me Susie," Circe began, her voice almost apologetic, as if she'd rather not share all of this. "It was just her two-year-old way of squeezing out 'Circe,' and it always made me smile. I don't know why I'm telling you that. I guess it all comes together, doesn't it? It always does.

"The memory that came back to me doesn't have a sharp starting point. It's like trying to remember a dream. There are all these dull edges, things I can't quite see, but up out of those came this memory. It's been right there on the edge of my mind all week. You know how sometimes you can't quite remember a word? That's what it felt like. Then, last night, I was pacing through the house, thinking about all of this, and, *pop!* There it was."

She paused and took a deep breath. She sounded nervous. I leaned forward. I wanted to know now. I was hungry to know.

"I've known for a long time that I was waiting for Dan's

brother, that I couldn't go east until I saw him again, confronted him, whatever. But I didn't know why until this memory came. I still don't know exactly why, but I know it's connected to this somehow.

"It was her birthday. I remember that now. She was turning three, and she loved giraffes. Everything was giraffes. Her curtains, her pillowcases, her blankets. She had a dozen giraffes, anything from stuffed animals to small plastic toys. How strange to remember all of this now. It seems impossible that I ever could have forgotten. I feel guilty for forgetting. I feel guilty that something as selfish as the pain I experienced in the mountain could take her from my mind, could eliminate her from my thinking."

She stopped, and I wasn't sure if she'd be able to continue, but Abe spoke up. "Pain isn't selfish, Circe."

She sniffled, wiped a tear from the end of her nose, and nodded. "What happened to us in the mountain that could have made us forget all of these things?" she asked, and for once she scanned the group, but no one offered any answers.

"Anyway," she continued, "the two of us were at the grocery store picking up a few things. She was only three, but she understood it was her birthday. She was a big fan of birthdays, actually. I guess most kids are. And she was never one to sit in the grocery cart. At this store, they had miniature carts for children, so she would push it along behind me, clipping my heels or knocking things off the shelves. I tried not to get upset, but it always hurt when she caught my heel with her cart, and I think I was a little stern with her about the mess she was making. I wish I wouldn't have been so harsh. I wish it wouldn't have bothered me."

She was crying, but she kept going. "I saw her too, got a really good glimpse of her in this memory. She was so beautiful!" Circe held both hands over her face, and Misha moved to go to her, but Abe held up his hand and shook his head.

"I'm sorry," Circe said. "I'm trying not to get emotional. It's hard and good, seeing her in my mind again. She had wispy blonde hair pulled up in a precious little ponytail. Her eyes were a kind of icy blue, a sharp, piercing blue, and she was sassy! My, she was sassy. She'd fill her cart up, and I had to make a pile at the register of all the things we weren't going to buy." Circe smiled, then laughed. "She'd pull it all from the shelves, anything she could get her hands on, and at the checkout I had to figure out how to get rid of it all."

A few people in the circle chuckled. I felt a slight sense of relief at the idea of her not finishing. I didn't know if I really wanted to know any more, and her silence took away some of the apprehension I was feeling.

"The strangest, most maddening part of the whole thing is that I still can't remember her name. I can't remember my own daughter's name. Not knowing what I named that beautiful little girl is almost the worst part. Almost.

"It was a Tuesday. That much I remember. The exact date, I'm not sure, but it was a Tuesday. The woman at the checkout was so kind to both of us, not making a big deal of all the groceries in my daughter's cart that would have to be put back on the shelves. The woman smiled down at her, asked questions about the things she had chosen, and complimented her on her choice of shirts—it had a cartoon giraffe on it—and the perfection of her ponytail. She looked at me when she said this, and we smiled at each other. I felt a kindred connection with that woman, the two of us going about our daily lives, neither of us having any idea what that morning was about to hand us. And we both laughed when my daughter explained her need for nearly every item. I laughed and laughed, and it felt so good."

She was smiling. I felt strangely happy that something about this memory, which had to do with me, brought that smile to her face. I wished it would be happy all the way to the end, but I knew that wasn't where Circe was going. She wasn't going toward happiness.

"I needed that laugh," she said. "I can't remember why, but there was something about the other parts of my life, something missing or sad, that made that laugh important somehow. That woman helped me to laugh, and it felt like a big glass of ice water on a summer day. What a gift laughter is. I've never thought of it like that before.

"My little girl and I walked outside, and it took me a little while to convince her to leave her cart inside the store. She always wanted to take those things home with us. I think I found some treat or other from the groceries we had actually bought and managed to bribe her with that. When we got outside, I realized the wind was gusting. There was a storm coming, but not a normal storm—the horizon had these swirling green clouds, like boiling water, and the gusts of wind would stop for a moment, then come back harder than before. We had parked far out in the parking lot, so I scooped my daughter up and put her in the cart, preparing to run through that charged air to our car and quickly load up the groceries before the rain came. But we were too late."

She paused.

"We were too late."

Even the mountain seemed to be listening in on her story. It seemed like it might be nearing the middle of the day, maybe even later, and I wondered if I had really stayed in my house for that long. Where was the day going to?

"Lightning struck and the thunder came right after it. Before we even left the shelter of that overhang, the rain came down in buckets, and we stopped where we were. Anyone walking toward the store was drenched in seconds. The sound of it was a roar overhead, and all around us the smell of the steaming pavement rose up as the water pounded down. It was raining so hard that the raindrops were exploding where they landed, creating this misty coating everywhere. I didn't want to take my daughter out in that rain—she'd get soaked in seconds. Why would I do that? Right? And the groceries too. Everything would get soaked. So I thought maybe I could run out quickly to the car and leave her there with the cart. It would just take a moment. Only a minute.

"I looked around for someone who would stay with her while I went for the car. A woman and her elderly mother had come walking in from the parking lot after being caught in the storm, both of them wet through. But they were laughing, pointing at each other's soaked-flat hair. Their eyes were shining.

"'Excuse me?' I said to the woman. 'My name is Circe. This is my daughter. Would you mind watching her and my groceries while I run out to get the car?' Or something like that. I don't know. Was I a terrible parent? Would any of you have done this?"

"Oh, Circe," Misha whispered.

144

"She agreed. She was very kind. Her mother immediately took to my daughter, chatting with her in a very grown-up way. When the next round of thunder rumbled around us, she jumped. But the woman was kind and reassured me that the two of them would watch her and take care of her. How often I thought of those words! How often I cursed myself for leaving her with someone else!"

A breeze made its way down from the mountain, stirring every loose thing: the grass, our clothes, the ash in the fire pit. A gray cloud of it burst out and swirled in a funnel shape before blowing past Miho's house and disappearing in the plains. I looked over at the girl. She was listening intently. A strand of her hair blew into her face, and she pushed it behind her ear.

Circe got a firm look on her face, like she was determined to see this through. "I stared out into the downpour and gathered my courage to run, but then an older man came over and asked if I would like him to go out and get my car. I thought about it, but it was still raining so hard, and I felt bad asking him to do it. He was sort of hunched over, and I didn't want him to get pneumonia or something from getting wet when I was quite capable of getting the car myself. I thanked him and told him I would do it. And I didn't mind. It was warm, and it would only take me a moment.

"He turned, and he smiled real big when he saw my daughter. The mother and daughter who were watching her both sort of squealed when they saw him, and then they were hugging because apparently they were very old friends. As the three of them stood there chatting, the older woman had her hand on the man's shoulder, and he was acting very

145

bashful about it. 'Are you sure you don't mind watching her?' I asked the woman again, partially to make sure and partially to remind her about my daughter. The women both seemed completely caught up in this unexpected reunion with the older man. She smiled and waved her hand at me, saying they weren't in a hurry and I should go on."

Circe took a deep breath as if going underwater. "I felt like I was diving into a pool as I started to run. Even when I wanted to breathe, the whole thing sort of took my breath away—the lightning and thunder, the ridiculously hard rain, the way it splashed up off everything. I was drenched in a second. My feet got heavy from the water soaking into my sneakers. I got to the car and frantically tried to work the key. I ripped open the door and fell into the driver's seat, banging my head on the door frame.

"What if I had run faster? What if I hadn't fumbled with the keys? What if I hadn't bumped my head? Would I have gotten there faster, in time to pick up my daughter and get her out of there?

"I sat there in the car, rubbing the sore spot on my head. The sound of the rain was like a waterfall. It ran down the windshield, blurring everything around me. I thought of my daughter and started the car. I backed out of my space, turning toward the store. And that's when I heard it."

Circe swallowed hard, as if she thought she might throw up or her body was trying to consume the words she meant to say. "The sound seemed both far away and right overhead. At first it was a dim kind of humming, like a mosquito getting closer. But I noticed that the humming was choked back at times, making it sound irregular, sputtering. It turned into a whooshing sound that came in over the parking lot, and I saw this thing drop from the sky and land right where my daughter had been sitting in the grocery cart."

Tears streamed down her cheeks, but Circe made none of the sounds I associated with crying. It was haunting seeing her like that, her eyes suddenly empty, staring out over the plains.

"It was a small airplane. It seemed so absurd, so out of my normal experience that I almost couldn't comprehend it. I sat in my car and screamed. It's kind of embarrassing, but that's what I did. I had my foot on the brake in the middle of that parking lot. I didn't get out and run to her. I didn't get out and call for help. I just stayed right there and screamed.

"The strangest part of it all is that I know Dan's brother had something to do with it, and that's why I'm here. That's why I'm waiting."

Her eyes were flat. It was as if she was talking about some other Dan, some other story that had nothing to do with me. I squeezed my eyes shut, pressed on my temples with my index fingers. I felt like more was coming back to me. Circe's memory stirred the dark bottom of my subconscious, and things were rising.

"I'm sorry, Dan," Circe said, and I didn't understand why she was apologizing. I glanced at her. She didn't look like she knew either.

"No one's at fault," Abe said. "These things are from long, long ago. If having these memories and talking about them will help you move on, then that's a good thing. If hearing someone's memories stirs up more recollections of your own, good! We're here to talk and, by doing so, move forward."

While my initial response to Circe's memory had been to recoil and not want to know any more, a kind of hunger remained. If these people were somehow connected with my brother, I wanted to know how. Maybe it would help me find him. Maybe it would help me bring him back.

"Would anyone like to go next?" Abe asked.

A few of them glanced at him, hesitation on their faces. A few kept staring at the ground. There was a long silence.

Po spoke, his normally whimsical accent terse and sharp, as if he was trying to hide his anger and doing a very poor job of it. He scared me. I finally understood why he had given me such a glare yesterday morning.

"I'll go," he said, running a hand through his red hair. His fingers trembled. "I'll tell you what happened. But I'm not rushing it."

13 PO'S STORY

I WATCHED ABE, hoping to get something from him, anything that might bolster my spirits. A smile, perhaps. A nod. But he looked intently at Po, and I felt very much alone. Po cleared his throat, and I felt a kind of helplessness, like I was being carried along on a river in rough water, not knowing how much longer it would be until I was sent careening over the falls.

"Jan and I had spent the previous week hiking in America," Po said, his words deliberate, rehearsed, "in some of the most remote areas we could find. All we had with us, we carried on our backs. She was a trooper too, and carried as much as me. She insisted on cooking, not because I thought she should but because she hated my food. 'You're always burning things,' she would tell me with a smile. 'You're always running too hot.' She giggled after she said that, and I would protest. 'What? My food is just fine, thank you very much.'"

Po stopped and smiled to himself, now fully immersed in his own story.

"'It's true,' she'd say, and she'd try to make up. She'd come over to me, hug me, and then pull away so she could look at my face. 'Maybe it's because of your red hair. Everything about you is burning.' That always made me laugh. At night by the fire, she'd run her fingers through my hair and talk about how much it looked like flames.

"Anyway, there we were, making our way on a trail, and she was hopping from one rock to another when she hurt her foot. I thought it was a pretty straightforward sprain—it didn't look like anything was broken—but it was bad, so I tried carrying her for a while. We weren't getting anywhere. She was trying to tough it out, but I could tell her pain was getting worse.

"We cut through the woods toward a spot on the map that indicated a road, and it was really slow going. The day was dying, and her foot was swelling, like a sausage ready to split. It definitely seemed worse than a sprain. I was afraid because I had no way to stop the pain. We'd rest every so often and elevate her foot to relieve the pressure. Eventually we got to the road where there was this narrow shoulder, so we set up camp there in the dusk and hoped a car would come. She was moaning and biting her lip and trying not to make a fuss, but she was hurt bad."

In the silence between sentences, when he stopped for a moment, all I could hear was the wind coming down over the mountain and sweeping past us. Sometimes when it picked up, the girl held her cloak so it wouldn't flap and Miss B held the corners of her shawl close to her chest. I could see the edges of the garden from where I sat. The corn tassels flailed wildly. I realized Po had stopped talking, and he was staring at me, not saying a word. It sent a hollow jolt through my stomach.

"It didn't take too long for a car to show up. It was this old woman," he said. "She drove past and went far enough that I was disappointed, like she had decided to leave us behind or hadn't seen us, but her brake lights came on and she eased to a stop. I saw her bright white reverse lights, so I walked toward her. I could tell she was afraid I might hurt her. She only put her window down an inch or so.

"I told her my wife hurt her foot pretty bad, and she asked if I was going to murder her. So I asked her if she planned on murdering me, and she chuckled, a nervous little sound. I thought she might drive away. I was sure I looked terrifying after being in the wilderness for as long as we had been. But I went back and told Jan this old lady was going to help us. I lifted her up, carried her to the car, and the old lady got out. I guess she had decided to trust us and let fate take its course. She opened the rear passenger door for me and I gently eased Jan in. I walked back to get our stuff, brought it to the car, and climbed into the rear seat with Jan. It was almost completely dark by this point.

"The old lady explained our options. The closest hospital was a five- or six-hour drive, and I couldn't tell if this was because it was that far away or because she drove slow. She was willing to take us there in the morning—she couldn't make the trip that night because she had already been away from home for too long and had to care for her husband. There was a small, private airstrip not too far off, and she thought they might be able to fly us to an airport close to the hospital. If she remembered right, the small plane flew back and forth twice a day, once at night and once in the morning.

"I honestly thought I was in some kind of a nightmare.

We were in America but couldn't get to a hospital? It was so frustrating. We decided to look into the plane option, so she drove there gingerly. Jan whimpered every time we hit a bump, and the old lady emitted a kind of sigh when she heard Jan, as if trying to apologize without words."

Po stopped, and the sudden silence made me look up, but this time he wasn't looking at me. He was staring up at the mountain. I followed his gaze and let my eyes roam the cliffs high above us, the snowy peaks, the fractured angles and jutting faces.

"I can't believe I'm remembering all of this," Po muttered. "Where did all of this stuff vanish off to? I feel like if I had remembered before now, I could have done something about it.

"Anyway, it was late when we got to the airstrip, which was nothing more than a large warehouse-type building flanked by a chain-link fence. I climbed out of the car and walked through the dark. There were trees all around. It was hard to imagine a clearing large enough for a plane to take off.

"A voice called out to me from inside the building, so I turned and walked toward it. As a man came toward me, I told him my wife needed to get to the hospital. He said the plane had already come back and wasn't leaving until early in the morning. I asked if he was the pilot and said we'd be willing to pay extra, but he said that wouldn't work. They didn't fly at night. When I pressed him, he gave me this sarcastic little grin and said his brother was the pilot and was drunk."

When Po said these words, a jolt went through me.

"I wondered how I could get Jan through an entire night. That's when he told me they only had one seat on the plane. I was so frustrated. This wasn't what I had in mind at all. I started pacing. Maybe one of the other passengers would sell me their seat in the morning. I asked him what time the plane left, and he told me six a.m. sharp."

Po ran his hands through his hair, looking frustrated, as if having the experience right there in front of us for the first time. "I asked him how I was supposed to get to the hospital.

"'We have a neighbor who sometimes rents out his car,' he said.

"'Why can't we just take it now?' I asked.

"He shrugged. 'You can, but it would probably take us just as long to drive there with the storms that came through.'

"'We'll take that last seat,' I said, and then I asked him if they had a place we could sleep. He said they did. I asked him if they had any Tylenol. He said they could do better than that."

I glanced around the circle. Everyone was caught up in the story. Misha's head was tilted to the side and her eyes squinted in a kind of wincing sympathy. Circe nodded.

"That night was like hell on earth for Jan. She was in so much pain, and I was really worried for her—a sprain shouldn't have been like that. Her foot was purple and green, and the painkillers weren't working. I didn't sleep all night.

"The plane was a Cessna 172. Don't ask me how I remember that when there are other things I can't remember and should be able to recall. That name and model number are stuck in my mind. Cessna 172. The runway was paved, kind of, with lots of loose stones. The pilot was barely sober, but we didn't have any other options. Jan was so out of it that she couldn't have had any concerns anyway. I watched them take off, and the wings dipped a little one way, then the other, and they were off. It killed me to send Jan off that way in her condition. He had promised me that his brother the pilot would make sure she got to the hospital. I had sent a wad of cash along to help him remember."

He looked over at me. "I guess by now you know you're the brother."

Po waited as if he needed my nod, my acknowledgment, before he could continue. I stared at the ground, closed my eyes, and nodded. Then he continued with his story.

"I was worried about the storm, and I told Dan that. He told me it would be fine, and he claimed storms moved in a certain direction there, pointing vaguely away from the spot where I had last seen the Cessna. I stood there for a long time watching the storm, noting how it wasn't moving the way he said it would. After that, he drove me to the other guy's house and I rented that car he had told me about."

Po stopped. He tried to speak again, but his voice had tiny fractures in it. He took a deep breath, raising his shoulders deliberately to take in more air. A sense of panic rested on me. I wanted to run. I didn't want to hear the end. I had a sense of what happened, and that was all I needed.

"I first heard what had happened on the radio. I was only a few hours into my drive, and the rain was coming down in sheets. I knew it when I heard it. I knew it was her plane. But I kept driving. I didn't cry. I didn't break down. Something in me thought that if I could keep driving, it wouldn't be true. I'd never have to face it as long as I didn't push the brake."

He nodded as if trying to convince us that every single word he said was true. He nodded over and over again.

"I drove around for a long time, just kept driving in circles."

14 WHEN THE PLANE FELL FROM THE SKY

WE SAT THERE for a long time, and no one said anything.

"Are you okay, Dan?" Abe asked, and I nodded, though it wasn't true. I wasn't all right. Their stories weighed on me. I tried to look out over the houses, stare into the plains, but there was no escape, not even there. I wished Miho would come over and comfort me in some way. I needed something. Anything. But their words were everywhere. They were inside of me. And a picture was revealing itself in my mind, an understanding of where these stories were going. I didn't know if it was because I was putting the clues together or because the memory was coming back to me.

"Let's take a break," Abe suggested, and there was a collective sigh.

Miss B stood up and stretched. Po slumped farther forward, his face in his hands. No one looked at me. No one knew what to do with my presence. I felt as if I had become superfluous to the proceeding, as if everything would move along better if I wasn't there.

"I'll get some food," Miho said, even though it was well after lunch. The sky had reached its brightest point a while ago. The afternoon was upon us, and at this rate dusk would settle with us still here, sitting around the fire pit. I glanced over at John and Misha and watched Miho walk away.

Even when Miho returned with the food, no one else said anything.

"We're getting somewhere, aren't we?" Abe asked quietly, but no one replied, so he took a bite of bread and passed the bowl of raspberries to his right.

Was Abe trying to work everyone through their issues so they would go east? But he knew I wasn't going anywhere without my brother. Did he want me to be here on my own? Did he think that if everyone else left, I would change my mind?

I watched the girl eat. She moved in tiny motions, like a mouse holding a small morsel, nibbling.

"Her name is Lucia," Abe said, and by the lack of reaction from everyone else, I could tell I was the last to learn this.

"Really?" I asked. "Did she tell you?"

"She wrote it down." Abe was clearly trying to be patient with me.

"Did she write anything else down?" I asked sarcastically. I couldn't help it. I felt cornered and defensive.

"She can't speak," Miho said in a flat voice, "but she can hear, Dan."

I sighed and closed my eyes. "I'm sorry." I couldn't remember Miho ever talking to me in that way, disappointment in her voice.

For a little while, the only thing I could hear was the sound of people eating, a fresh breeze coming in over the mountain, and eventually, when everyone was finished, John pacing in the grass behind us.

"John, your turn," Abe said, and his voice sounded hoarse.

John's massive bulk was striding back and forth with a nonsensical urgency. He was wringing his hands, muttering to himself. He nodded at Abe and came over. It didn't look like he was going to sit for this one.

"So . . ." He cleared his throat. He took up his pacing again, as if trying to decide exactly how to begin. His feet sounded like soft pads on the stone. His gaze roamed from one person to the next, finally landing on Abe. "I can't," he said.

"Take your time," Abe encouraged him.

But John had made up his mind already. He shook his head firmly. "I can't." He walked away, past Miho's house, past the tree, out onto the plains.

"John!" Abe called after him, but he didn't look back.

Abe seemed deflated. Why couldn't we all have hashed these things out privately?

"Well," Abe said, his voice a quiet breeze, his eyes vacant and far away. "Well."

"I can go," Misha said.

"Yes," Abe replied absently. "Yes, of course."

She looked at me the entire time she spoke, as if it was only us.

"The memory came back to me first in numbers," she said. Her voice was calm and deliberate, like a surgeon's. "The date, the hours of my shift, and the blood pressure of the woman we were helping in the back of the ambulance. I can't remember her name, but I remember another number—it was our third visit to her that week, and it was early in the week. She was always calling the ambulance. Sometimes we could placate her in the house, other times we put her on the stretcher, and occasionally we had to wheel her out and actually load her into the vehicle before she came around."

This was the most I had ever heard Misha speak at one time.

"I tightened the cuff and pumped it up and watched the dial drift down, stethoscope buds in my ears as I listened to the strong beating of her very old heart. I told her she was recovering, playing along with her as I had learned to do. My two colleagues had already returned to the front seat. They were less patient. She nodded, sighed, made some excuse, and I helped her back to the sidewalk, holding her arm as we climbed the three steps to her front stoop. She went in and closed the door without a word. I looked at the guys in the front seat and shrugged. They were laughing. I started laughing. But by the time I came around and climbed in through the passenger door, they had stopped laughing."

Misha's words came out calm, but her hands were busy: smoothing the fabric of her pants, tracing the veins in her wrist, squeezing into tiny fists.

"The driver pulled away quickly, and I told him to take it easy. My friend in the middle seat held up his cell phone and I stared at it. He had received a message from a friend at the grocery store before the call even came in. 'Small plane down in Kellerman's parking lot. Get here fast.'

"More numbers come back to me. The siren was on and the lights were flashing, and we flew past 4th Street, 5th Street, and 6th Street. I glanced at the speedometer—45, 50, 60. I was never afraid of blood, and my stomach never turned at injuries, no matter how gruesome. I could pull a stitch through someone's flesh without balking. I once held someone's scalp onto their head while we raced to the hospital. But there was one thing I could never get used to: speeding through red-light intersections, passing cars on the wrong side, slipping along the shoulder."

She paused. "The rain began to fall. Quite a storm." She exchanged looks with Miss B and Po. None of them smiled or cried or gave any kind of expression.

"Smoke already rose from the grocery store parking lot. We had to wind our way among the other vehicles blocking the way. Some people fled, afraid more planes would fall from the sky. Others sat in their parked cars, staring but not wanting to get close. Others did gather close and stood in the open as if the rain wasn't pouring down on them. There was no fire, but smoke rose from the plane's engine. Sadness rose in me as I saw multiple bodies lying motionless, but the mechanical, numbers side of me pushed the sadness down. I became a robot. We set up a small triage area, the three of us making our way from body to body. I prayed another ambulance would arrive, but none came, not right away. There were a few we moved on from. A baby. An elderly man. They were clearly gone."

I thought the man must have been Mary St. Clair's father. A small sound came from Miss B, like the homing signal on a piece of electrical equipment. Nothing more than a chirp or a hiccup. Circe was weeping hard without making a sound.

"I got to the plane first," Misha continued. "A pilot and three passengers. They all appeared deceased, but I tried to pry open the door to get closer, checking vitals with my hands, looking for signs of life. Through the shattered window of the plane I could see my colleagues working on two people. I cycled through the three passengers. They were gone. I reached for the pilot to confirm that he, too, was dead. You know those dolls made of cloth with sewn joints, full of cotton? You know how their legs fold and bend in any direction? That was the pilot's legs. They were folded and rolled up under him as if they had no bones."

She paused again. "Then he gasped. The pilot, I mean. He was alive. I shouted for the others to give me a hand. He screamed, the pain bringing him back to consciousness. We pulled him from the plane. I knew right away, when I grabbed under his arms and pulled, that he was intoxicated. I could smell it. We placed him gently on the pavement. The crowd had grown. Another ambulance arrived. And another. And another. We loaded up the bodies."

She shook her head. "I was soaked through, and my anger at the pilot rose up in me like a storm. He screamed the entire time he was being loaded into the ambulance. We covered three bodies, and I stumbled as I walked away from them. I heard a mother cry out for her little girl whose body was still under the sheet. 'But she's getting wet,' her broken voice said. Two officers held her back. I went over and held her close. It was Circe. 'But she's getting wet.' She kept saying that over and over again, and her voice turned into a whisper. But she didn't stop."

15 THE FIRE

CIRCE LET OUT a sound, a tiny sob, and Misha leaned over and put an arm around her. A tightness wrapped itself around my chest like a constricting band, and I found it difficult to breathe. My brother had done this. My brother had caused all of these people, my friends, tremendous pain. I wanted to run away, but I sat there like everyone else, not saying a word, not knowing what to do next.

That's when I felt something else—anger at these people who had called themselves my friends. These stories they were telling me, about how my brother the pilot had ruined their lives or stolen someone they loved seemed to invalidate my waiting. All this time! All these long days! I had been waiting for someone they now found despicable, unworthy. They had turned my brother into a monster.

Evening approached, with the dusk spilling in over the mountain. Shadows pooled around us, some filling up the alleyways and the hollows, some creeping in behind the rocks that lined the base of the mountain. I found my anger deepening into something close to hate. I couldn't look at them. I hoped Miho wouldn't tell her story, because I didn't think I could stay any longer if someone else spoke, if someone else piled their own bitterness onto my brother.

John returned wordlessly from the plains, a massive bulk of firewood in his arms. He knelt in silence before the fire pit, spread the wood, struck a match. I was suddenly glad he hadn't told his story. I didn't need to hear it all again from a different angle, over and over.

We all watched the fire grow as if it was the most interesting thing on earth, this concentration of heat, this speeding up of molecules, this splintering of wood, the way it turned into ghostly smoke. Our fire made the approaching shadows feint back and forth, this way and that. But out over the plains, a nameless darkness gathered, thick and new and frightening.

I thought of Mary, now one day's journey away. It seemed like ages since she had left. How many trees had she passed? How many long, empty stretches? Could she still see the mountain, or was it only a thin purple thread on the horizon?

I put my face in my hands. I felt spent, like I had run a long way, and I could tell the others all felt the same. Lucia sat hunched and almost disinterested, the way teenagers often do. She picked at the skin on her knee. She stared up into the sky.

Miho leaned toward me. Her hand moved, and I thought she was reaching for mine, something that would have given me a lot of comfort, considering everything that was taking place. But in the end, her hand dropped to her side.

"Miho?" Abe said. "Are you ready to tell your story?"

But I interrupted. I didn't even know what I was going to say. I would make something up. "I . . ." I began, but there was nothing. What words would make sense following all of that? What could I say that would make them stop? Miho of all people! I didn't need to hear her version of how my brother had ruined her life.

Then I started to worry. What if my brother showed up now, in the midst of all this? What would they do to him? Tear him to pieces? Only minutes ago I had been paranoid about being left here in town all alone, but now I wanted them to leave. I wanted them to go east without me, every single one of them, so I could wait for my brother in peace and welcome him. I could nurse him back to health. He would see what he had done and he would be sorry.

It's hard to remember the exact sequence of events after that. Everything seemed to happen simultaneously. Miho was staring into the fire, and its orange light spilled from her eyes. But it was too much light, and I realized she wasn't looking at our small fire—she was looking beyond it, out over the village roofs, and the fire reflected in her eyes wasn't the one in between all of us. No, there was a larger fire, growing like a monster.

"What's that?" she asked in a flat voice, dread leaking out.

Everyone stood, and sounds of surprise and alarm rose. A fire burned among the houses, the flames moving in a strange kind of synchronicity, darting up and down, flowing in and out of the shadows, peeking around corners and playing with each other.

While we had been speaking, a fire had started, spread out through many of the houses, and rose above the roof lines, seemingly everywhere. The flames farther up the hill rose higher, as if that was where the whole thing had started.

Farther up the hill. Toward my house.

"Grab your things!" Po shouted. "We have to get out of this place! It's time to go!"

"Wait a minute!" Abe replied, raising his hands, trying to calm everyone. But he was too late—the group had scattered. Even Miss B limped quickly down the hill toward the greenway, but she barely made it twenty yards down the greenway when the smoke clouded the sight of her and overcame her, and she collapsed. Her form came and went in the gray billowing, and I thought we might lose her.

"Miss B!" Circe screamed, running to her side and pulling her back.

The others, too, had scattered into the smoke and the flames. Abe followed one person, then another, trying to call them back to him. But it was total chaos. I could hear voices shouting, first for each other, then for help. Some of them came back to the patio after attempting to get to their homes, coughing and retching.

"We have to stay calm," Abe insisted, wiping sweat from his dark face.

Soon everyone had returned. No one had been able to get anything out of their houses. No one had even been able to get close. We gathered beside Miho's house, which by that time was also in flames, and the heat forced us farther away, back beside the oak tree. The crackling sound grew louder, the beams of her house split, and the roof caved in like a piece of rotten fruit.

"We have to leave. Now," Po said. "We need to head east. Something's going on. Maybe they're coming for us from inside the mountain. We have to go."

John echoed his agreement. The women nodded too. I

looked out into the darkness, in the direction of the first tree. Is this how it was all going to end?

Abe nodded, but he didn't look convinced. "Let me think. Just give me a minute."

"What's there to think about?" Po demanded. He paced and ran his hand through his blazing red hair. "How did this happen?" he practically screamed, waving his hand toward the flames.

Miho sat on the grass and wept, pulling her knees up to her chest and rocking back and forth. Lucia fell to the ground beside her, hugging her. I wanted to go to them, to comfort them, but a sudden suspicion entered my mind.

The fire had begun at the top of my hill.

Toward my house.

I sprinted away, following the greenway through the flames and the smoke.

"Dan!" I heard Miho shout, and the voices of the others joined her, calling out to me.

It was like another world in there, a foggy place full of nightmares and heat and flames. I pulled my shirt up over my nose and mouth and tried to run with my eyes closed, but they still teared up. The flames reached for me and my sleeve caught on fire. I slapped it until it went out, running the whole time, feeling the sting of hot embers glancing off my face.

The rain was the only thing that saved me. It came down in hard pellets, and while it didn't drown out the fire, it diminished it enough to clear the air. Soon I was on the other side of the scorched and burning village, running up the hill to my own house, the greenway slick beneath my feet. Everything smelled of smoke and heat and, somehow, also of spring rain and new life. It left me feeling incongruous, disconnected, and unsure of myself or of what to do next.

I ran to the front door and pushed it open. My house was not on fire. I saw her immediately, sitting in the chair that faced the glass doors, looking out over the plains. When she spoke, the pitch of her voice was willowy and light. I didn't recognize the sound of her at first, and I turned to see if someone else had walked in behind me, if someone else was speaking.

"You have to go get your brother," she said again, and this time I realized it was her.

"I can't," I whispered. "I can't go back in there."

"Not alone," she said, standing, and something of her old voice returned, soft and imploring. "Not alone, no, you can't go there alone. But you have friends. Good friends. They'll go with you."

I didn't think they would. No matter how sweet her voice, no matter how convincing, she didn't know them. I couldn't picture any of them coming with me back over the mountain, back into that hell. Nothing could get them there—not Po's anger or Circe's sadness or Miho's disappointment. We were all too afraid of that place. And besides, now they all hated my brother. Why would they save him?

No, wait. Abe would go with me. Abe would do it if I asked him. But I couldn't ask him. I couldn't.

And so it was just me. The thought of going over there alone sent such violent shudders through my body, I thought I might collapse.

"Did you do this?" I asked, trying to look into her eyes and failing. "Did you start the fire?" My voice was weak and tired, where hers was firm and unrelenting. But there was something there that seemed to be at its end. Was she losing patience? Did she feel something slipping through her grasp?

She gave a half laugh and shook her head. "No. Why would I have done that?"

"I don't know."

She looked at me with a smile that was almost sad, as if she felt bad about what she was going to say. "It was Abe."

"Abe?" I asked, shocked.

She nodded, and I thought I saw her smile turn a shade less sad.

"Why would Abe do this? And how? He was sitting with us the whole time."

She didn't say the question back to me, but it was in her gaze, as if the answer was inside of me somewhere if I would only look honestly. So I did. I don't know why I let her direct me in this way, but I followed the question as it looped around in my chest and my mind, and the answer came to me. When I spoke, my words came out in a whisper.

"Because he wants us all to go east?"

Again, she didn't confirm my answer with a nod or any sound. But the look on her face said, "And?"

"And Abe thought we'd stay here forever if he didn't do something drastic?"

She sighed. Anger swelled in my gut, pumped into my face, red and pulsing. I paced frantically, moving in a kind of frenetic pattern of distracted anxiety.

"He wouldn't do this!" But my words were shallow and had no bearing on what I had started to believe. "He wouldn't."

She didn't argue with me. She sighed again.

"But what about my brother?" I asked, again in hushed tones.

She shook her head. I thought of all the times Abe had reassured me there was no hurry. He would stay with me as long as I wanted to wait. Had even Abe reached his breaking point? Had he and Miho conspired without me, tried to figure out how they could motivate me to go? Were all the stories changing the way they felt about me? Maybe now that they knew what my brother had done, even they couldn't imagine staying with me.

Maybe Abe had instructed John to go around and start the fire, then come back with wood he had arranged beforehand. It was all coming together in my mind, and because lying came so naturally to me, it was easy to see it in others.

"Come," she said, holding out her hand. She led me to the front door of my house, out onto the greenway, and up the hill toward the canyon that led back into the mountain. I looked over my shoulder once, but all I saw was the village burning down, the flames already lower, the houses collapsing in on themselves. Smoke billowed up as the rain fell, but even the rain was slowing. I could hear the drops hissing in the charred ash.

Could Abe really have done that? Could he have destroyed everything that made up our lives?

We approached the gap in the mountain, the sliver of an opening that went back into the canyon. The woman's hand was soft and cool, and sometimes she reached over with her other hand so that she held on to me with both of them, leading me, beckoning me. The sign welcomed us to the opening.

> THROUGH ME THE WAY INTO THE SUFFERING CITY
> THROUGH ME THE WAY TO THE ETERNAL PAIN
> THROUGH ME THE WAY THAT RUNS AMONG THE LOST

The unreadable lines seemed to grow sharper, but the letters were still jumbled or too close together, or perhaps the words were written in another language. But the last line was still there, clear, breathtaking.

> ABANDON EVERY HOPE, WHO ENTER HERE

"I can't," I said.

She reached up and touched my cheek, the gentlest nudge, moving my face toward hers. "You have to."

"I can't," I repeated, shaking my head.

"If you don't, your brother will stay there forever. You are his only chance."

I stared into the canyon. For as far as I could see, it was nothing special, only a narrow path through the rock that seemed to widen out the farther along it went, gently going uphill. Maybe it wasn't as bad as I remembered?

"If you go in, if you go and look for him," she said, "I will convince the others to follow you. They'll be along soon to help you find your brother."

"How?" I asked, but I already knew.

"I convinced you, didn't I?" she said. Her words were like

those of a mother to a toddler, finally letting him in on her secret when it is too late for him to escape bedtime.

I sighed. She had convinced me. It was true. I was standing there picturing my brother, and there was no way I could turn and leave him. Not now. The village was gone—there was nothing there for me. Miho was gone. My brother had destroyed her life, and she wouldn't be coming back for me. Even Abe—surely the revelations about what my brother had done, the pain he had distributed to our friends, had turned him away from me. I had no one besides my brother, and if I didn't go find him now, I would have no one, forever.

I didn't even say anything. I took one step, then another step, then another, and before I knew it, I was inside the canyon. I was leaving the village behind, leaving Abe behind, leaving Miho behind. I was going to find my brother. I was returning to the suffering city.

The dread of it filled my stomach like a ball of lead. My hands were sweating. My tongue felt scorched from the fire, swollen and dry. I could still smell smoke on me, and I wondered, too late, if I should take things with me: food and water and supplies. But I kept going, one step after another. The sounds of the burning city vanished, and all that remained was a gray, filtered darkness, the pattering of heavy raindrops at the tail end of the storm, and a sense that everything had turned to bitter ash.

PART TWO

16 THE HOUSE

I EXPECTED MY first steps into the canyon to be difficult or heavy, as if the terror would be waiting for me as soon as I crossed over some imaginary threshold, but even though the light was dim and smoke followed me in from the burning town, I found the going strangely easy. And quiet. I knew the way in led uphill, into the mountain, but it felt like I was walking downhill. My senses were confused, so I turned around and looked back toward the opening. There was the split in the mountain, a dark line of nearly black sky between the shadows of the cliffs, the space that led down and out into the plains.

Was I actually doing this? Was I actually going back into the mountain?

The farther I went, the darker it became, until I couldn't see the difference between the cliffs on either side, the sliver of sky above me, or the boulders that lined the path. I kept tripping over dead stumps of trees. There was a short stretch of what felt like tall, brittle weeds that rustled and snapped off when I meandered through them.

I thought it might be best if I waited until morning to keep going, so I felt my way to the side of the canyon, waving my hands in front of me. It was narrow at that point, but the dark was so thick I couldn't see from one side of the canyon to the other. I found a series of breaks in the rock wall and cleared the ground of larger pebbles, sweeping them to the side with my bare hands. Even then the ground remained rocky and hard. But I was exhausted. Hearing everyone's stories, running through the fire, and my last conversation with the woman in my house weighed heavily on my mind. I fell into a fitful sleep, worried about Miho and Abe and everyone else. Worried that they had already left without me. Worried that they were following me.

When I woke up, an anemic light illuminated the narrow crag of sky at the top of the canyon, the color of blue-gray smoke. Everything was completely still. I realized that what I had been walking on was not dried-out weeds but rubble-strewn ground covered in old wasps' nests. A surge of panic filled me. There were hundreds of nests scattered along the canyon, so many that it was nearly impossible to walk without stepping on them. In a panic, I walked quicker, trying to avoid them.

But when I did hit them with my feet, their gray, honey-combed surfaces peeled apart like ash or tissue paper and floated around, lighter than air, so that I left behind me a wake of shimmering, sheer flakes hovering in that liminal space. I saw nothing alive among the remnants of the nests, nothing moving. As I walked farther into the canyon, they thinned out until there were only one or two here and there, hidden among the boulders or resting in the cliffs. I had a distant memory of walking through this same area when it was full of wasps, when they filled the air with their writhing, their buzzing, but it was too far away in my mind to grasp properly.

The tiniest of movements caught my attention, over along the edge of the cliff. One of the dead hives had twitched, but not in a way that was consistent with the movement in the wind or any other kind of natural trembling. I changed directions, drifted over toward the movement, but I lost track of where it had come from, so I stood perfectly still, close now to the right-hand canyon wall. I waited.

Again, the same twitching, and I saw where it came from. I moved closer. One of the gray wasps' nests sat precariously on a boulder that was about waist height. It shifted again, and a tiny black wasp crawled out from under the nest. I glanced around, a bit afraid that this was not the only one, that I might now find a million other lonely wasps crawling out from under those million dead wasps' nests. But no. Nothing. Only this one last wasp hovering above its dead nest, then landing again on the surface, spinning, exploring, and crawling back under.

It gave me a lonely feeling. It would die. I left it there, peering over my shoulder a few times with the strange sense that it might follow me, but it didn't. For as long as I could see the nest, it was dancing as if in the wind, but I knew better.

I remembered my dream again, the one in which I lied for my brother. Adam was clearer to me than he had ever been. I could see his face as if he was standing right in front of me. Wait. Was he standing right in front of me? Something seemed to be moving in the shadows, something with form, something human. I walked toward it, up the canyon. The place smelled of smoke and dust, and I could see a wind blowing up above the canyon walls, but the air down where I was remained still.

The shadows shifted, and what I had seen was gone. But I could still envision his face. I felt like I had found my way in among nameless things, as if all that I had forgotten would now come back to me. It was exhilarating and new, and again I had the sensation of walking downhill, even though I knew the path was heading up into the mountain.

The sky brightened as I continued, and the air cleared a bit, seemed more breathable, but my eyes were still watering from the dust and the lingering wisps of smoke. The canyon widened gradually, so that at first I didn't notice the extra space. But there were trees all around me, tall and thin, and they made it difficult to see both sides of the canyon. All of this transitioned into an even wider space that felt more like a forest than a narrow chasm.

That's when I saw the house in the woods.

I stopped for a moment, leaned behind a tree, and peered at the house only fifty yards or so in front of me. It was covered in weathered wood siding that was gray and split by the dry air. The windows were dark, and the front door looked like it might be partially open, but I couldn't tell from where I stood. From the chimney, a narrow, twisting thread of smoke rose up into the sky.

I stayed there for a long time. I sat down, waiting to see if anyone would show themselves. I peeked around the tree and pulled back again. But there was also a huge sense of relief building in me, even in the midst of the fear—after waiting for my brother for such an incredibly long time, I was finally doing something about it. I was no longer sitting in my own never-changing house at the edge of the plains, wondering if he would be the next one to come out.

There was no way to pass the house without going within view of the windows. If someone was in there, they would see me. I could sneak from tree to tree, but then the house would be behind me, and I still wouldn't know if anyone was in it or if they had seen me. Or if they were following me. Going farther without knowing what was inside that house unsettled me more than the thought of walking up and knocking on the door. I had to search the house before I could pass it by.

I stood up and went out into an open space between the trees, where I had a clear view of the front porch. "Hello!" I called out.

The resulting sound was alarming. I should say the lack of resulting sound was alarming. The canyon swallowed up my shout in an instant. It was the polar opposite of an echo, as if I had not even said anything. The sound of my voice died the moment I stopped shouting, the "o" of "hello" cut short. It sent a shiver down my spine.

I took a few steps closer to the lonely house, walking under some low-hanging branches. The trees, while being alive and having leaves, drooped in the heat and the stillness. I reached up, pulled down a leaf, and realized it was brittle, even on the branch. It crumbled in my hands.

"Hello!" I shouted, and again my voice died in the air. I was closer to the house now. The light reached its peak in the sky above me, and I nearly forgot I was in a canyon.

The door of the house creaked open a bit, an abrupt sound that set my heart racing. I felt my muscles tense instinctively to run. I steadied myself by reaching over and holding on to one of the trees. The bark disintegrated under my fingers, and the fragments fell to the ground without a sound.

If it wasn't for the house, I felt like I could have lost track of which way I was going. I looked out from behind the tree again. I was still thirty or forty yards from the house, but I saw a woman come out to the porch. She wore a black dress, and her long, dark hair was up in a tight bun. She peered out into the woods as if looking for something specific.

I opened my mouth to shout again, but I wondered if she would even be able to hear me. I gathered my courage and walked toward the house and the woman. She watched as I approached, but she didn't say anything. I got closer, so close that I could see a thin layer of dust covering everything—the rails, the wooden porch floor, the front door handle. Her narrow feet had left a path through the dust from the door to where she stood. The inside of the house was dark.

Above us, the light was fading. I needed to get moving. I needed to travel farther before the darkness fell again.

"Hello," I said, and when the word was swept away, I said it louder, trying to lodge it in the air. "Hello."

She nodded. Her face was plain, and once I was close I could see she had dark rings around her eyes. Wrinkles radiated out from their corners. She gave a weary sigh, closed her eyes as if she had already had enough, and crossed her arms, not in a defiant way but in the way small children sometimes cross their arms when they are cold.

"Hello," she said in a wispy voice. "Who are you?" Even though it was a question, it came out more as an exasperated statement. *Who are you, and why are you bothering us?*

I swallowed hard. I hadn't expected to see anyone on this

side, at least no one besides Adam, and certainly no one living here, this close to the entrance. Why would anyone stop here? Why would anyone live here?

"I'm Dan," I said. It gave me a breathless feeling, talking in that quiet place where any words spoken were caught up in an unseen river and swept away.

"Dan," she said quietly, as if she could decide everything she needed to know about me simply by saying my name. "Dan."

"What happened to the wasps?" I asked, and immediately I wondered why that particular question had escaped.

Her eyebrows raised, and I thought I could almost see a smile gathering at the corners of her mouth, an amused expression. It felt mocking. Or something else, something I couldn't put a finger on.

"The wasps?" she asked, tilting her head back and appraising me. "The wasps are gone. We are nearly at the end. Yes, nearly."

"The end?" I asked, but she ignored that question.

"In the next strong wind, more and more of their fragile nests will be swept away. Dan." I had the feeling she was trying to decide what to do with me. "They crumble and are blown away like dust. From dust they have been made . . ." Her voice trailed off.

A creaking came from inside the house, along with the slow knocking of labored footsteps and a rhythmic *thud, thud, thud*. If anything of the grin remained on her face, the tiny hint of a smile that my questions had nearly brought out of her, it vanished at the sound of those footsteps, and a deep sense of dread was pounded into me, deeper with each wooden knock. I considered running back the way I had come, back through the trees and the dust and the lifeless wasps' nests, back through the narrow part of the canyon and down into the plains. Could we begin again? Could we rebuild our town and return to what we had?

A man came through the door. He wore a red flannel shirt faded to almost pink under denim overalls covered with rips and snags and holes. Neither the man nor the woman wore shoes, and their feet were cracked, calloused, and cinnamon colored from the coating of dust. He had a white beard, a bulbous nose, and gray eyes. Red varicose veins crisscrossed under the translucent skin of his cheeks and seemed to continue into the whites of his eyes, which were bloodshot and irritated and had large bags under them.

He clenched his jaw—I saw it in the way his beard bulged around his cheekbones and his lips bunched up each time, the way lips will scowl on the face of someone who has no teeth. He leaned on a weathered gray cane. When he saw me, he breathed hard, taking in great gulps of air and blowing them out through his nose like a winded horse.

"Hello," I said, but he didn't move from his spot just outside the door. He didn't stop that labored breathing. He hated me. I knew it as clearly as I had ever known anything, but I had no idea why.

The woman looked at the man and waited. When she seemed to accept the fact that he was not going to stop all that blustering and blowing, she turned back to me. She might have been beautiful once, a long time ago, but her hair had been pulled so tight, and apparently for such a long period of time over and over again, that she had bald spots above her ears and a bald line down her part. She had a strand of a scar that ran from the corner of her left eye almost to the edge of her left ear, a shallow scar not easily spotted at first, but when the light hit it in a particular way it flashed like a vein of silver in rock.

"I'm Sarah," she said, looking at me with a question in her eyes and then glancing away quickly. Was that a bashful look? Had she expected me to recognize her?

"Does your friend have a name?" I asked, surprised at the forwardness of my question. I was getting used to the fleeting nature of my own voice in that stifling air, and somehow it made it less intimidating to speak. The words were gone almost before anyone heard them.

He seemed to be calming down, not because of any kind of acceptance of me but because he appeared to be growing tired. "His name is Karon," Sarah answered.

We stood there for an awkward time.

"Karon?" I asked.

She nodded.

"Why are you here?" I asked. "I thought everyone had left."

When Sarah spoke, it was with great reluctance. "Come." She turned and walked through the door.

The man didn't look back as he followed her into the house, his cane louder against the wooden floor. It seemed his anger at me had been transferred from his heavy breathing and blowing to the force with which he thrust his cane against the floor. *Thud. Thud. Thud.*

They left the door open to me, but I hesitated. I could still see the rock wall of the canyon hidden among the trees. I took a few steps away from the door to the edge of the porch and glanced toward the back of the house. There, farther into the woods, I could see the other side of the canyon wall. I couldn't see the top of either side of the canyon, because the canopy of the forest was high and thick.

"What should I do?"

A whisper of a breeze moved through the canyon, only a few seconds' worth, but enough to lift the fine dust and swirl it around. The brittle leaves seemed to whisper, "Shhhh." The dust settled all around me, on my shoes, my arms, even my face. I closed my eyes, reached up with both hands, and wiped my skin, finding a thin layer of the finest powder.

When I opened my eyes, the woman was standing in front of me. I jumped.

She almost smiled again. "Come," she said, but this time she didn't turn around until I moved to follow her.

17 THE RIVER

A GREAT SADNESS filled the house. There was an emptiness, not only in the corners but even in the areas where we stood or sat. Even when the rooms were full of us, they felt vacant. The sadness coated everything, like the dust or the shadows that deepened as darkness fell.

I followed Sarah through the front door into an old kitchen, the counters warped and yellowing around the edges, the cabinets misaligned with doors that didn't close quite right. Beyond that was a kind of dining area, as sparse as you can imagine, with a small round table and four chairs. The walls were yellow, whether by choice or due to age, I couldn't tell.

Karon had already sat down, his mouth scrunched together, his old, watery eyes looking past me through the door that Sarah had left open. She walked in a kind of glide, never in a hurry, and pointed toward a chair, indicating I should take a seat. But I didn't sit down right away—I put my hands on the back of the chair and stood there. I watched her sit down, quietly, calmly.

The two of them were quite a sight.

"Why are you here?" I asked again. I realized in that moment that they had given me the seat that would leave my back facing the still-open door, and something else followed me into the house along with the dust and the sadness and the emptiness—a pinprick of fear that started in my gut and moved outward, threatening to make my hands tremble. It was the same fear I had felt ever since the woman had come into my house. Was she out there somewhere?

Sarah took a deep breath, looked at me and then over at Karon, glanced past me almost imperceptibly, and rested her hands on the table, one on top of the other. She had wonderful posture. She sat there like an etiquette teacher.

"That's not important," she said.

"Well," I began, but she interrupted me.

"We have been here for a long time. A very long time. From the beginning, in fact, and now time has nearly run its course. The important question is, why are you here? You do know you are walking the wrong way?"

Again, the hint of cynicism—or was it sarcasm or genuine amusement?—crept in around the corners of her mouth, the edges of her eyes. I decided to be completely truthful with her, and it was a strange sensation, this letting go of all the lies I had clung to for so long.

"I don't remember seeing you here when I left the mountain the first time," I said.

"You wouldn't," she said. "The condition people found themselves in when they were leaving was . . . overwhelming. It would have been difficult to pay attention to anything but your pain and your guilt."

I nodded slowly, accepting her explanation. "I'm here for my brother. He's the last one, the only one left."

She looked at Karon as if he might want to weigh in on the subject, something that surprised me, considering his inability to speak. She turned back to me and stared hard into my eyes, looking for something. Maybe trying to detect truth from lies? I couldn't tell.

"Have you considered that it might be important for people to leave this place under their own volition? Under their own motivation?" she asked.

I shrugged. "I can motivate him."

This time she smiled for real, a smile full of pity. "Oh my."

"What?" I asked.

"This is not a place you can be rescued from." She hesitated. "That's not exactly the right way of saying it. Maybe this is closer to the truth—this is not a place where someone can come and whisk you away."

"What kind of a place is it?" I asked, not sure what she was getting at.

"It's the kind of place you have to leave on your own. Everyone who has ever left has battled their own way out. In this place, our guilt consumes us."

"Do you mean guilt as in that sense of feeling guilty, like shame, or as in being found guilty? A guilty verdict?"

The old man practically roared at this one, and I jumped at his outburst. Sarah reached over and held his shoulder in a gentle grasp, but she did not look away from me.

"Yes. Both. It is through the maze of guilt that someone must find their way out."

"So, it's some kind of motivation? Determination?"

"Do you really remember nothing about this place?" she asked. Something about it felt like an insult, but I didn't feel offended as much as embarrassed.

"No. Nothing," I mumbled.

She clenched her jaw and shook her head in a barely perceptible way. "The only thing that can rescue anyone from this deep darkness is grace."

"Grace?" I asked. That didn't sound like anything nearly strong enough to bring my brother out safely. But I didn't say that. I stared down at the table. If I somehow managed to find my brother in this hellhole, was I sure I could persuade him to come with me? Doubt made its way inside of me and settled, a seed.

The three of us sat there in the silence. Karon worked his mouth from side to side and up and down, his lips twisting in on themselves something fierce, so heavy was his hatred toward me. Or so I imagined. Sarah sat completely still for long periods, her unflinching nature interrupted occasionally by deep sighs, during which she closed her eyes and tilted her head back.

A strong breeze blew through the canyon, coming from the direction of the plains, the direction I had come from. It rustled the leaves of the trees, at first gently, then sending them into a chattering panic. It was a loud, roaring sound, one that the stillness could not sweep away. I looked at Karon once again, and for the first time he seemed calm. Perhaps by the sound. His shoulders slumped and his eyes crept toward closing.

A grayness came with the wind, a tangible dimming of the light, and a weightless substance like flakes drifted around and through the house. It was like ash or a very fine dust. I reached up and caught an especially large piece, and it disintegrated in my hand.

"What's that?" I asked.

"The old wasps' nests," Sarah said.

When the wind subsided, the gray flakes were every-where—on the table, the countertops, the floor, even our shoulders and the tops of our heads. Sarah stood and brushed herself off, but most of it clung to her clothing until she ground it in with all the brushing. I did the same. But old Karon just sat there, the lighter-than-air wisps resting on him, fluttering slightly even after the breeze had passed.

"How do you expect to get to your brother?" Sarah asked.

I didn't know what to say. I didn't have much of a plan except to go back in, all the way, and then go all the way down.

"There's only one way in, isn't there?" I asked.

"Yes. But there are . . . obstacles."

"Like what?"

She picked up a larger piece of nest, a shred resting on the table, and it disintegrated. "Only one that we might be able to help you navigate," she said, glancing at Karon.

Again he began huffing and puffing through his nose and toothless mouth. His indignation only minutes ago had terrified me, but now I realized there was something endearing about it.

"What is it?" I asked.

"You don't remember?"

I tried to think back, but there were still so few distinct memories of my time here in the mountain. I shook my head.

Karon rested his knobby, weathered fists on the table. His knuckles were like knots in thin branches, and all the ash-like wasp paper that he hadn't brushed off drifted backward as he leaned forward suddenly.

"The river," he said in short gusts of breath.

He barely moved his mouth, so at first I wasn't sure what he had said. I glanced at Sarah, but she was still looking at Karon.

He erupted again, this time incorporating a kind of groan that added body to his words, if not clarity. "The . . . river . . ."

A sense of drowning overcame me, and the smell of blood, and the warmth of muddy water, and a desperation to rise, rise, rise. I stood up in response to this overwhelming sense of claustrophobia, and my chair fell over backward. Had his words awakened a memory? Or a kind of nightmare?

A premonition?

I turned to pick up my chair, and the open door caught my eye. All of the light had fled, and I realized that complete darkness had descended, the kind I had only ever seen and felt in the canyon during the previous night. Or was it two nights ago? Or more than that? I exhaled with disappointment. I had wanted to make more progress before the light left. I had so far to go.

"You will spend the night here," Sarah said. "Tomorrow, at first light, Karon will take you to the river and help you cross."

What could I say? The darkness was so thick outside that the opened door looked like a portal into an ocean of black mercury. There was a small lantern lit on the kitchen counter, and I didn't know if she had only just lit it or if it had been burning when I first walked in. Its light was tepid.

"What has happened to you?" I asked. I stood behind my chair, and the dark doorway behind me felt like another person, someone else I needed to be mindful of. "Why are you here?"

She stared hard at me again, as she had been doing almost the entire time. I was becoming used to her gaze—something about it grounded me in reality, kept me from becoming lost in the dizziness and the dark. If she saw me, then I was.

"Sit down," she said. "I can tell you a little."

I eased into the chair, and at the same time, Karon stood. He stared at me, his mouth wrenched into that same old scowl. His breathing had dimmed along with the light, so that each exhale seemed to illustrate his weariness, deflating him slowly. He turned and thumped his way into another part of the house, and all went silent.

"He doesn't like to talk about this," Sarah said, her voice suddenly kind. "Where did you go when you left the canyon?"

"Not far," I answered, shaking my head. "I stayed in the same town, the one barely outside. I wanted to wait for my brother." My weak words vanished quickly in that dark soundlessness.

"I know the town. If you stayed there, you understand how many people traveled through. Karon and I have waited here for a long, long time. He has helped more people cross the river than either of us could ever count. This was what we chose."

"Why didn't you ever come all the way out?" I asked.

"We took a few steps out, once. I saw your town. But we have been waiting for a long time too, and this is where we decided to do it. You understand how this feels. Some time ago, a woman came along, worse off than many, perhaps not as bad as some. But she bore a great resemblance to the one we were waiting for, and Karon immediately went to her and brought her into the house. Once I saw she was not who we had hoped, I thought we should send her on her way. It didn't make sense for someone to stop here. There is nothing here, in this house or in this canyon, for anyone."

I began to ask if there was anything there for her and Karon, but I stopped. I felt like I was asking too many questions.

"We nursed this woman to health, against my better judgment. This is no place to grow healthy. It's much too close. But we did it, we took her in and helped her, and the past is the past."

I heard Karon's knocking again. At first I thought he was protesting our conversation, but I realized it was the thudding of him walking the floor above us from one end of the house to the other.

"Her name was Kathy, and she soon became like a daughter to Karon." Sarah said this with great loneliness in her voice, and deep regret. "For a long time she stayed here with us, a very long time, and when she was well she took care of us. I began to doubt my doubt, so to speak. I wondered if I had misjudged her. She was very pleasant, and Karon was happier than I had ever seen him."

I found it difficult to breathe. I knew what was going to happen.

I knew who she was talking about.

"She began going out whenever someone was passing by, someone making their way out of the canyon. She would walk up to them and have long conversations, even though they were barely rational. It seemed to me that she was asking a lot of questions, and again, I thought it inappropriate. Karon and I had always let these passersby go along their way. Of course, Karon helped them along the river, but after that, they were free to go. But Kathy would sit with them. Some of them became disoriented after talking with her, wandering the woods here around the house, calling out the names of people they were looking for. Sometimes I can still hear them."

Her voice had not changed, but her face was pale.

"I spoke to Kathy about this. I told her she shouldn't distract the people walking by, that they were on the right road and would find their way. Once across the river, they did not require our aid or intervention. Do you know what she said to me?"

I shook my head.

"She smiled a nice smile and whispered, 'Through me you pass into eternal pain.'"

A chill spread from my neck all the way down my arms. I swallowed hard.

"Soon after that, people stopped coming. I assumed no one was left. Or very few. Once the flow of people stopped completely, only recently, she left us alone." Sarah stared vacantly past me, over my shoulder. "Karon fell into a bottomless sadness, not because he missed her but because he was convinced she had passed beyond the canyon in order to bring people back into this place. He thought we should have stopped her. And so we remain, no longer helping people leave but guarding the way back."

"Why do we let our guilt consume us," I whispered. It was not a question but a kind of statement.

I felt a numbness moving throughout my body. The woman didn't seem to notice my distress. She kept talking.

"This is why Karon was so upset by your appearance. You are the only person to ever come back through the canyon. He assumed she had sent you back this way. His hatred for her is difficult for him to contain."

Finally, she looked at me, and her gaze was piercing. I could tell she wanted to ask if I had returned because of Kathy. I felt frozen in place. I was thinking of all my friends outside the canyon, our destroyed village. I suddenly wondered if Kathy was trying to convince any of them to come back in as well. Perhaps to save me?

As we sat there, I felt a kinship with her and Karon. If I had not been on a search for my brother, I would have stayed with them for a long time, perhaps forever. It was lonely there, and dark, but there was a peace to be found among the shadows of the trees, and the confines of the canyon seemed a welcome enclosure. The feeling I had identified as a deep sadness was something else, something I couldn't put a name on, but it wasn't entirely negative.

"You can stay here, but you can't live here," Sarah said, as if she could read my mind. "There is no life here. Only dim light and ash."

"But you're living here," I said.

"Not much longer," she whispered. "Come." She stood up from the table and walked into one of the side rooms. I followed her, and miniature clouds of dust swirled up under each step, as if the world was decaying and its remains were rising in slow motion, trying to re-form it into something new.

It was a tiny room, more like a closet. There was a dingy window, the glass so dirty I doubted I'd be able to see through it even during the day. On the floor was an unrolled, navy-blue sleeping mat an inch thick. I did not think of myself as being tired, but as soon as I saw the mat, a weariness split my marrow and my eyelids sank. Again I tried to remember if I had slept for one or two nights in the canyon on the pebble-strewn ground. I was fairly certain it had only been one. But I couldn't be sure.

I turned to look at Sarah, and I realized she had moved closer to me. I saw for the first time what it was that made her beautiful—those flat gray eyes, in the dim light, were like horizons. I felt myself leaning toward her, falling in, so tired I needed someone to lean on. But she lifted her hands in the space between us, held me away from her, held me up.

"Lie down," she whispered. "Sleep."

And from there I descended, yes, down onto the mat, but I went deeper than that. Deeper than the floor of the house, deeper than the foundations of the canyon, deeper than dreams or nightmares or memories. I stayed there in that depth, and I slept like I never have before and will probably never sleep again, there on the edge of the river Acheron.

WHEN I WOKE up, I rose up through all of those layers of darkness, back up to the floor of the house, back up to where I slept on the mat, back up to the canyon. I realized something hard was jabbing me. First it prodded my leg, so I pulled my leg away, and then it was in the middle of my back, a straight rod grating against my spine. I rolled over, and the thing rammed my eye. I howled, reached up, and grabbed it.

Karon was scowling down at me. We both held tight to the cane, and I could feel his anger trembling through it.

"The river," he said. Whether it was because I had heard him say it before, or because a good night's sleep had cleared up his speech, or because he wasn't as angry as he had been, I could understand him. The words even sounded like actual words people use in real sentences.

I released his cane. He looked me over as if trying to decide where next to deliver additional pokes, then let out a burst of air, disgusted at my laziness or some other shortcoming, and turned, limping out.

I sat up. A dusty light came through the window. I stood, walked to it, and peered through the dirt, but all I could see were smudges of dark trees and the empty spaces in between them.

The room where we had sat the night before felt new, completely different. Because of the light, it was almost cheery. Someone had spent a good amount of time mopping and cleaning the countertops and dusting the high spaces, evidenced not only by the shining room but also by the four wooden pails of dirty water sitting beside the open door. There was a loaf of bread on the table, but the house didn't smell like someone had done any baking. I tore off a piece. It was stale but I was hungry, so it tasted delicious. I gulped down a cloudy glass of water.

The air outside was somehow new. Sarah and Karon sat on the chairs on the front porch, staring out into the dim day and the rustling trees, now clean.

"What happened to all the dust? And the wasps' nests?" I asked.

"Didn't you hear the wind last night?" Sarah asked.

I shook my head.

"You must have slept well," she replied, that small smile finding the corners of her eyes and mouth. "A strong wind blew for most of the night."

"Does that happen often?"

It was her turn to shake her head. "No. Very rarely, in fact. And it's a beautiful thing when it does. Karon thinks it's a good omen for you."

The trees seemed not so dead in that early morning. The forest was actually quite beautiful now that everything had been cleared away—the brittle leaves were gone from the forest floor, the dust had been removed from the leaves, the remains of the nests no longer clung to the roots and the trunks.

I sighed. I needed to leave. I didn't want to, but Sarah's story about Kathy concerned me. I didn't know how much longer it might be until she convinced the others to follow me, and I needed to find Adam before they did.

"I have to go," I said. "I want to stay, but I have to go."

"Yes, of course," she said. "We're ready."

They walked off the porch and I followed. I kept looking behind us, down the canyon path that cut through the mountain to the town and the plains. I kept waiting to see someone walking out from among the rocks or emerging from behind a tree. I listened. But I knew I wouldn't hear them until they were right up next to me, not with the way sound died so soon in that heavy air.

I turned to see where Sarah and Karon were going, and they had already stopped, the house still visible through the trees. In front of us was a river more wild and alive than any I had ever seen.

"We never expected to take anyone this way, back over the river," Sarah said quietly. She paused, and it seemed to me she still wasn't sure about helping me go back, farther into the mountain.

"Have you always done this?" I asked. "Have you always helped?"

"One day we were standing here, the two of us, and we saw someone approaching from the other side."

I peered across the raging water. It was hard to see the far bank.

"I turned to Karon to see what he thought we should do, but he was already in the boat, pulling himself across. When he returned, he had a young man in the boat with him. The boy was badly beaten. We didn't ask him what his name was or what he was doing. He simply climbed out, crawled a short distance on the ground, rose up on shaky legs, and continued along the path."

Sarah smiled. Even Karon seemed to have a pleasant look hidden among the deep wrinkles on his old face. "The river," he said.

"Yes," she said in a whimsical voice. "The river. After that, we came down every day, and if someone was at the far bank, Karon went over and brought them across." Tears were in her eyes, but she didn't move to wipe them away. They sat there like diamonds. "Soon we were bringing them over in boatloads, every day, twice a day, three times a day. Sometimes all through the night. Yes, even in this inky darkness. We could hear their cries."

The sound of the river was loud and alive. I thought the cries must have been very loud, to hear them all the way from the other side.

"If you want to know why Karon looks so old, it's because he worked so hard for so very long."

I looked over at him, his white hair, the wrinkles etched in curving lines around the movement of his face. He stared back at me, and this time he didn't growl. He seemed content to let me stare at him, to let me explore, but I couldn't hold his gaze for long.

"Even after Kathy arrived, we kept bringing more people over, although by then the flow had slowed to a trickle. She was here, as I already told you. And after she left, there were no more from the far bank. Now, you."

Karon's mouth curled up in anger and he snorted, but it wasn't so scary now that I knew his anger was not aimed at me.

"I'm ready," I said.

Their faces held a subtle pity that said, *You can't possibly be.* Karon looked embarrassed by my ignorance. He turned away and bent over, and I realized he was reaching for something. I had not noticed the boat, shallow and gray, bobbing against the bank. Mist from the raging water had partially hidden it. When Karon moved toward it, I nearly laughed, thinking he must be joking. There was no way that boat would make it across. I might as well hurl myself into the water and hope for the best.

If Sarah noticed my doubt, she ignored it. "Over there, that's where it truly begins," she said. "This is nothing. This darkness, this ash, this dust: it's only the wild edge of what's waiting for you. Once you cross, you will see things you can never unsee. You will hear sounds and silence that will split you in two. It is a horror." She paused. "I will ask you this only once."

I saw again the beauty in her gray eyes. Again I wanted to stay. "What?" I asked.

"Will you please reconsider? Stay with us. Wait here for your brother. When he is ready, he will come out."

In that moment, it wasn't her gray eyes that struck me, and it wasn't the fact that she reached out and put her hand on my arm. It wasn't even that, when I glanced over at Karon, he had tears in his eyes. What struck me was the sound of the word "please," the way it sank into me, the way it latched on to my better nature, my best self. It was the "please" that was so convincing. I couldn't say no, but she could see it in me, I guess, because she turned away.

I helped Karon drag the boat to the bank. The ground was slick with mud, and as we struggled with the boat, Sarah put something around my neck. It was a knapsack made of burlap, and heavy. We situated the boat so that it pointed down into the water.

"Food and water," she said. "For your journey. It won't last long."

I nodded my thanks. I didn't know what else to do, what else to say. Karon grunted, motioning for me to sit at the front of the boat, and I climbed clumsily aboard. The inside was wet. There was a small bench that ran across, up toward the front. I sat down and realized I was terrified. I gripped the sides and closed my eyes, trying to breathe slowly. I looked over my shoulder to see if Karon was going to push us off, and I caught him leaning toward Sarah, kissing her cheek. They were both crying.

The boat shifted backward as Karon crawled in, bearing a long oar. "The river," he growled, and we slid down the short bank and into the rapids.

The water immediately lashed our boat to the right, downstream, and I nearly went overboard in those first moments. The front of the boat rose and fell once, smacking the water. I shouted my alarm, holding even tighter to the sides, leaning forward so as not to get tossed into the muddy, churning rapids. We moved from side to side, mostly facing downstream but also making our way to the far bank. I heard a loud sound from Karon.

He was laughing. His white beard was wet and blown to the side by the strong wind that now swept over us. His wide eyes burned with a strange fire, and he was smiling a fierce, almost delirious grin. Every time a large wave hit us and I thought we would turn over or take on too much water, he would laugh uproariously, his eyes flashing. He was no longer the bent old man from the dusty house in the canyon—he was Karon, some kind of seafaring master. Something not human. Something beyond human.

I turned back around, and the boat slammed into another huge wave. I pitched forward, striking my head on the bow. Everything went black.

18 INTO THE ABYSS

IN THE DARKNESS of my mind I heard a gritty scraping, and I realized only once it stopped that the sound had been that of my heels sliding along a sandy beach. Someone's hands were under my arms, dragging me along, and then they dropped me to the ground. I groaned. I could hear them walking away, their feet scratching along the sand, then the long, slow sliding of something into the water.

I opened my eyes, reached up tenderly to touch the side of my head, and groaned again. My head felt split in two, and as if to mirror the feeling, a long grumble of thunder crackled around me. But there was no rain, no lightning. Only the pealing of thunder, one long, low sound after another. It was a persistent, faraway call, and it filled me with loneliness.

The satchel Sarah had given me weighed heavily on my neck, an anchor. I sat up, looked out over the river, and was surprised to find that the water had calmed. Karon stood in the prow of the boat, steady and strong, his white beard billowing out to the side. I wanted him to look back, wanted him to wave, but his stoic silhouette never turned toward me. Soon he was a tiny speck at the far side, and I saw him pull his boat up onto the bank. Sarah must have already gone back to the house.

There, on the far banks of the Acheron, I sat for what felt

like a long time, thinking about all that had happened. And all of it in such a short time. I wondered about Miho and Abe, where they had gone after the fire in the village. I thought about the woman whose name I now knew, Kathy, living in my house, her dark hair soft and shining. I thought about sitting beside her when she was in my bed, kissing her, and shame smothered me. I dwelt on the story Sarah had told me about how Kathy had deceived them. Or had she? I still had trouble placing any blame on her. Maybe she had been trying to help.

A sound moved around me, and at first it moved so subtly I was unaware of it, focused on my own thoughts, my own problems. But gradually I became conscious of it—a deep sighing, a long, heavy moaning. Was it the river? The wind was strong, drying me off, parching my lips. Another gust of wind, another long, low sigh, so heavy it ached in my bones.

I turned away from the river, my head still throbbing. I thought of my brother. I had to keep going. I couldn't turn back now.

The thunder continued to rumble, though the sound of it seemed to come farther and farther apart. My clothes still clung to me, and a mist moved in, a fog that made me feel even more alone.

What was I doing? Why did I think I could go back inside and even find my brother, much less bring him out with me?

I thought again of Sarah's words. *It's the kind of place you have to leave on your own. Everyone who has ever left has battled their own way out. In this place, our guilt consumes us.*

Our guilt consumes us.

I was guilty. I had lied to my friends, kept secrets from

everyone. I loved my brother, the same brother who had hurt so many people. Was that a guilt? Was that a transgression? And now I was there, on the other side of the Acheron—even that seemed some kind of sin I would have to atone for. Having barely entered this foreign land, I could already feel my guilt rising up around me, an acid eating away at me.

The mist settled on my skin, and the satchel swayed against my side, bumping me with each step. The day was cool even as it rose toward midday. Distant thunder moved around me like the sounds of a faraway battle. I waved my hand gently through the mist, and a kind of dew gathered on my fingers. I licked a finger, but it tasted almost stale. Not quite salty, but there was a sharpness about it, and it sat on my parched tongue. I shook the satchel and could feel the slosh of water, but I knew I needed to save it for as long as I could.

The mist became so heavy that when I arrived at the edge of the abyss, I nearly fell in. It was an immense hole, wider than the river, so deep I couldn't see down into it. This was the place from which we all had fled. I would have to be quiet now. I would have to be careful.

Were they still down there?

Our tormentors?

The wind picked up, the mist melted into strands, and the strands sifted up and away. For a moment I could see all the way across the hole. It was like a caldera, except there was no visible bottom, and it was not the black color of hardened lava but granite gray. Was it a mile across? Two? I couldn't tell, but as I took it in, I saw the path that wound its way down into the great hole, clinging to the edge of the rock like a thread.

I stared at the path and found where it spilled out of the hole, not far from where I stood. I walked to that ledge and started down, then stopped. I looked back toward the river one last time. I couldn't hear it. I couldn't see it. I almost couldn't imagine it anymore, that river I had been sitting alongside minutes before. Or had I been walking through the mist for hours? My mind was weighed down with the unknowing. The place had a way of making me forget.

The mist descended around me again, cool and heavy. I stayed there at the edge an extra moment, remembering Sarah's words and wondering if perhaps Kathy had persuaded someone else to come back to this side of the canyon. Maybe she had persuaded all of them. I stared into the mist, looking for someone, anyone. Part of me wished someone had come so that I wouldn't be alone. But another part was frightened for my friends, frightened about what would happen if they did come with me or what they would do to Adam if we found him.

Then another thought.

What if Kathy had followed me in?

Another rumble of thunder. Another gust of wind.

And down I went.

EVERY SO OFTEN, as I followed the path down into thicker mist, it widened out. I hadn't circled the great pit even once before I came to the first one: a small glade of trees up against the face of the cliff with four seats made up of wide, cut logs. I stared at them for a minute. I thought I should know why they were there or who they were for. Everything about this place felt familiar, which made sense to me because I knew I had passed that way once before, but nearly all of it was so deep in my mind I couldn't quite remember it.

I sat in one of the seats and stared out over the narrow space, out over the abyss. The mist seemed lighter there in that place, but it hung heavy higher up. The bare wooden seat was worn smooth, as if it had been used over and over and over again, so often that it had been buffed into something that felt like silk. I touched the rough bark of the sides. I felt like I could sit there for a long, long time, going even deeper into my thoughts.

I heard a sound up the path, the direction I had come from, but I couldn't see anything through the mist. What had I heard? Footsteps? Or perhaps the dew had gathered on a crumbled ledge and the ledge had fallen? Maybe it was only another rumble of distant thunder? The thunder never seemed to stop.

The remarkable thing about loneliness is how the mind begins to turn further and further inward. I found myself latching on to memories, following them to their source. I remembered getting the news about the plane crash, and the long way into darkness I followed after that.

I went deeper and deeper inside of myself. I could stay here forever. I could sit here for a long time until I remembered everything, until the mist cleared. Perhaps my friends would come and find me, and this suddenly seemed like a good thing. I imagined four of us sitting there on the wooden seats, perhaps me and Kathy and Miho and Abe. We could tell stories, talk about the old days in the village. The hint of a dazed smile lifted the corners of my mouth, I took a deep breath, and I sighed.

There was no better place to be than right here.

A loud crack of thunder seemed to come from right above me, and I ducked my head, nearly falling off the wooden seat. I was bent over so low that I felt the ground under my hand, rocky and solid, and the movement also caused Sarah's knapsack to move on my shoulder.

What was I doing?

Why had I stopped?

I shook my head, trying to clear some space for the present moment. I stood up and was surprised at the effort it took. I felt like I was waking up from a dream.

I remembered again the morning of the crash, the morning my brother had wrecked the plane. I thought about helping the injured woman into the plane. Po's wife. I remembered the two businessmen climbing in, long-limbed and cramped in the small seats, made even more uncomfortable by the woman moaning in pain. The black man leaned forward, put his hand on her shoulder, and whispered a few questions. Miss B's husband. She answered without opening her clenched-tight eyes, nodded, bit her lip.

I waited impatiently for my brother. Where was Adam? What was taking him so long? I looked over the plane once, twice, even though I had already checked it twice that morning, and stared down the runway. This was what sat at the heart of our brotherhood: his constant return to failure like a dog to its vomit, and me waiting, waiting, waiting, the responsible one, clearing his path of all obstructions. Lying to keep him free.

The truth was, we were staring down the end. This last business venture, this tiny warehouse and adjoining airstrip in the middle of nowhere, was one that I had sunk every last penny into. And we were walking the edge. I hadn't slept well the night before and ended up roaming restlessly around the building, listening to the woman's quiet pain, Po's insistent caring. I tried to think our way out of our debt. But there was no way. We had to keep going and hope our luck broke through.

And the morning found me waiting beside the plane, waiting for Adam to come and fly it, to keep this dream going. One more lost flight and we were finished.

I WAS CONFUSED. I had thought I was back at the airstrip with my brother, waiting for him beside the plane. But the lashing wind and the drenching rain reminded me that I was walking down into the abyss along the narrow path. But no, I wasn't walking, I was sitting, huddled up against the rock face. The darkness I thought existed only in the pit itself had crept up to the path. A storm shook the rock. Water rushed down over the edges in small waterfalls, formed small rivers that ran along the path or plunged over the dark edge.

I didn't care. The memories swallowed me.

I WALKED AROUND the plane one last time. It was sunny there, in my memory. It was warm.

One of the businessmen poked his head out the door. "Are we leaving soon?" he asked, concern in his voice. "I don't think this woman is doing well."

I stared at him, wanting to shout at him in frustration. I slapped the tail of the plane twice, not hard, but it still made a sound. He leaned back into the plane. But I knew he was right, so I walked to the warehouse, back toward my brother's room.

The early morning sky was cool blue on that day when I found my brother passed out drunk on the floor in his room. I went out and retrieved a bucket of water. I didn't care anymore. I threw the bucket of water on him, and he barely made a sound. It was the lightest of groans, as if he was lost so deeply inside of his body that not even a bucket of cold water could find him. I got another one. And another.

By the fourth bucket, he was sputtering, sitting up. He wiped water from his eyes, shook it from his hands, and stood unsteadily in the small lake I had created. He looked at me with tired eyes, eyes pleading to let him sleep, let him go, let him be. Let him live his own way. He had chosen his lot in life—that's what his eyes seemed to say. And I almost did. I almost gave him what he wanted. But there was still that thing inside of me that had to keep going, had to keep pushing, had to make sure this little flight got out, had to keep my brother on the right path.

"Adam," I said quietly, "if you don't go fly that plane, we're done. We can't take another loss like this. We'll lose these customers, and that will be the end of it."

And after much pleading—and a change of clothes, a hat,

sunglasses on his bloodshot eyes, and help to the plane—he agreed. He crawled in, he taxied, and they took off.

I SAT THERE on the path, in the storm, and the realization of it all took my breath away.

It had been my fault.

Everything that had happened, all of that death, had been because of me. Everyone waiting in the village to exact revenge on my brother should have been waiting for me. When I forced him to take that flight, I had sent them all to their deaths.

I was the guilty one.

I leaned against the rock. The rain came down so hard that I didn't even hear the person approaching. I didn't hear their feet on the wet ground. The only reason I knew they were there was because they reached down and touched my shoulder.

19 VOICES

MY INITIAL RESPONSE to the light touch was terror. I flailed my arms and legs and pushed myself farther down the path. The wall left deep scrapes along my spine, but I didn't slow down until I was far enough away to stand up. I ran, and all that time the rain was coming down harder and the wind sounded like voices shouting up from the bottom of the abyss.

I got about twenty feet down the path, moving as fast as I could while keeping one hand on the cliff wall so I didn't plunge over the edge, before my feet slipped out from under me, my head hit the ground, and a black curtain drifted down, covering me along with the rain. The thunder seemed to be very far away—perhaps I was dreaming it? The sound of it echoed inside my head, a comfort. I moaned and rolled onto my side.

Again the soft touch of a hand on my shoulder. But this time I was too exhausted, too hurt, to move. The hand was small, but it was filled with strength, and it seemed to be trying to lift me to my feet.

"I'm not going back without my brother," I mumbled.

Again the strong, gentle tug on my arm. I tried to look up, tried to find the face that was behind this soft encouragement, but the rain was blinding. I could barely open my eyes. I was confused. Had Sarah followed me across the river? Was it Kathy?

"I'm not going back," I said again, my voice fading. "Not without Adam."

I stood and the hand moved down to mine, and the person led me along. The rain stung my face, and as we made our way down, the wind seemed to always be at our back, pushing us farther into the depths. We stayed as close to the rock face as we could. I closed my eyes and let myself be moved along. The farther down we went, the lighter the rain, the calmer the wind.

Suddenly, all went still. I looked over at the person who had helped me travel down the path.

It was Lucia.

THE INSIDES OF my eyelids burned and scratched like sand whenever I blinked. The muscles in my neck ached, and my head felt heavy on my shoulders. Every so often I tried to stretch, arching my back and straining my neck from one side to the other, but nothing loosened up. Every other breath seemed to emerge as a sigh. My legs were heavy and on the verge of cramping. But we kept walking.

I took off the knapsack and rummaged through it. I pulled out the water, took a swig, and offered it to Lucia. She barely took a drink.

"Go ahead," I encouraged her. "Keep drinking."

She shook her head, her quiet eyes staring into mine. I couldn't hold her gaze. It felt like she might see inside of me.

Ahead of us the path narrowed, became more of a ledge than anything else, and I peered over the edge. There was a gray sort of undulation running toward the other side of the abyss as far as I could see.

"Is that the bottom?" I asked her. I didn't know why I kept talking to her. She obviously wasn't going to speak to me. But there was comfort there, even in the sound of my own voice, even in my own unanswered questions. We both looked over the edge, and Lucia's mouth drew tight. She shook her head. She didn't think it was the bottom.

"What is it?" I asked. "Wait. Are those . . . clouds?"

A sadness filled her eyes and she nodded. She took a deep breath and let it out, then another.

"So, you mean that even once we get all the way down there . . . we'll still only be in the clouds?" I asked, as if it was her fault.

We stared down into the depths. Lucia didn't move. She didn't look at me. She just stood there at the edge of the abyss.

I sat down. "I can't," I said, although I couldn't even vocalize exactly what I couldn't do. I couldn't go on? I couldn't keep hoping? I couldn't bring myself to slink along that narrow ledge with the entire abyss waiting for us to fall in? I couldn't bring back my brother?

Lucia sat down beside me, put her head back against the cliff that rose at our backs, and quickly fell asleep. The air was clear around us, although up above, high above, the mist we had descended through stretched out like a flat white covering. A breeze came down the path, and wisps of Lucia's hair trembled around her face, her fair skin, her small ears.

"What are we going to do, Lucia?" I whispered. The words had barely escaped my lips, hadn't even risen up in the cool air, before I, too, fell asleep. It was a sweet feeling, giving in to that weariness, resting my head back against the rock, feeling the dust of the path under my palms.

Sitting there with Lucia, I felt something I hadn't felt in a long time: hope. Her unexpected appearance in the abyss, her kind face, her gentle disposition, awakened something lovely in me, something peaceful and patient. I wasn't sure what to do with it. I wasn't sure how to be. I wondered if this was how it felt to have a daughter. While I sat there, her head against my shoulder, I felt like I could breathe again.

It was a heavy, dreamless sleep, more like a fog than a darkness. My eyes shot open. I thought I had heard something, and it seemed strange, this idea that a sound had woken me, because everything was so still. The air was clearer than it had been when we were higher up, but there was still a humidity to it, a kind of mistiness, and the cliff walls were damp, shining in the dim light.

I sat there staring out over the abyss. Lucia was still asleep. My legs were stretched out in front of me, and my feet nearly reached the edge. I looked down the path, and my heart raced again as I saw how narrow the ledge became. If it continued to narrow, we'd never make it down. Even if it stayed the same, I wasn't sure I could trust myself to walk along it, when one wrong step, one tipping of the balance, would send me into the abyss itself. How long would it take me to fall to the bottom? Could I count to five? Ten? Twenty? One hundred?

Was there a bottom?

I heard the sound again, the sound that had woken me up.

I sat up straighter, and Lucia slowly lifted her head off my shoulder. She cleared her throat, coming up out of sleep, and it was a tiny sound, pebbles tumbling. I held up my index finger.

"Quiet," I whispered. I heard it again. "Voices. Did you hear that, Lucia? Voices. Or at least one voice."

She nodded, propping her hands underneath her as if she might spring to her feet at any moment and run. She trembled like a deer aware of a predator, trying to remain still, struggling not to spring away. I could feel the energy of it course through her body, a jolt.

"Slowly," I whispered. "Slowly."

We stood like children playacting, moving in exaggerated slow motion. I bumped the cliff and a small rock fell out, striking the ground at our feet with a miniscule thud. It terrified me, the thought that I might have given us away. But the faraway sounds I heard didn't change, didn't come more quickly.

We looked up along the cliff, but the way the rocks jutted out and the mist hovering above us meant it was impossible to tell how high above us the path had last circled by that spot. I couldn't tell if the voices were straight up, which meant they still had a long way to go to catch up to us—one entire revolution of the abyss—or if they were up the path from us, which meant they would see us at any moment.

"We should go," I said, adjusting the knapsack on my shoulder and moving toward the place where the path narrowed. It was too thin to walk forward on—with only a foot or two to work with, we had to turn sideways and shuffle, our backs to the cliff, our faces looking out over the abyss. I told myself again and again not to look down, but the gaping space in front of us almost had a personality of its own, one I could not look away from indefinitely, so after we had made our way twenty or thirty yards along the ledge, I looked down.

The curved cliff walls were wet and shimmering. A fair distance below us, those clouds sat thick as a blanket. Would they hold us if we fell? Maybe Lucia was wrong. Maybe they weren't clouds but snowdrifts or rolling plains covered in white ash. Or frost. I wanted to jump, and the desire scared me. I wanted to fly through the air and feel the breeze on my skin, the weightlessness of falling, the plunging into those clouds. The disappearing—that was it. I wanted to disappear. I wanted to feel the end.

But Lucia was beside me, and again I felt that calm surge of hope. She shook her head, but whether she had read my mind and was telling me not to jump or had heard the same call and was saying no to it, I couldn't tell. She swatted her hand about her head as if trying to clear off a stinging fly.

The whole oppressive place, with its shimmering granite rock and its narrow ledge and its mist and its hopelessness, was like a voice in the back of my mind. *Jump. You can do it. It would be so easy. Not even a jump—a fall. A slow leaning forward. Go on. Let go.*

"No!" I shouted. I couldn't help it. I had to do something to scatter the voices, and for a moment I felt that presence, whatever it was, withdraw as if cut. The air cleared, and even the mist seemed to dissipate. A brighter light came down to us from above, through the haze. But only for a moment.

"Dan, is that you?" a voice called out, muffled and far away.

I thought it was a woman, but I couldn't tell for sure who it was. Miho? Kathy?

"Hurry," I said to Lucia. "Hurry, we have to get going."

We descended faster, our feet shuffling, almost reckless. My breathing was labored, and not only from exertion—the air itself became harder to breathe.

A long time passed—hours? days? weeks?—and we were down among the clouds, disappearing into the fog. Yet always above me, fainter and farther away than the first time, I kept hearing the voice.

"Dan! Dan! Is that you?"

20 DAD

A MEMORY CAME to me there on the ledge, my back to the cliff, my hands sliding along the damp rock. In the memory, a woman came out of my father's bedroom.

"You can go in now. He doesn't have long," she said. She was a nurse or a caretaker. I nodded, and after she passed by, I took a deep breath and went into the room.

The lights were dim. It was the house I had grown up in, and the walls were the same dark paneling, the ceiling fan still swaying back and forth as it turned. Mom was long gone by then. I knew that as the memory came back to me. My mother had died. Did she pass before or after the airplane crash? I thought it was before, but I couldn't be sure. I hoped it was before.

My father didn't move when I entered the room. His eyes didn't open. His hands were still on top of the beige sheet. The place hadn't changed much. Mother's old figurines were still on top of the dressers, the old lamps she had chosen still sitting on small bedside tables on either side of the bed. Neither of them were turned on.

"Dad," I whispered. It was strange speaking to him like that, calling him "Dad." We hadn't spoken in the weeks leading up to that moment—maybe it had been months—and I couldn't remember the last time I had called him "Dad," but I didn't know how else to address him. "Man"? "Mother's husband"? His name was Virgil, but I never called him that either.

He stirred, and his lips parted, seemed to mumble some words, but no sound escaped. I moved closer, leaned in over him, and for the first time felt genuinely sad at his passing. We had never understood each other. Had we ever loved each other? I wasn't sure. I didn't think I could remember ever loving him.

"Dad," I whispered again.

There was a chair positioned beside the bed, and I pulled it over, sat in it, and put my hands on the bed, close to his right arm. He had always been a very hairy person, his arms practically furry in his old age. Hair sprang out of his ears, and his eyebrows were wiry with strands standing up here and there. Tufts of chest hair came up out of his shirt collar. His hands were still the hands of a trucker, cracked and etched with deep lines of dirt, the kinds of stains that would never come out no matter how much soap was applied. His fingers were thick and his hands were powerful. His nails were a mess, chipped and raw around the edges.

Even as he slept, his hand sought mine out, drifting toward my arm. "My son," he said, and tears rose to my eyes. He had never, ever called me that. He had always spat my name out like profanity: "Dan!"

But there, he called me "son." I leaned closer. His eyes wouldn't open, although his forehead seemed to be trying to lift his eyelids by sheer force.

"I'm here, Dad," I said, and the word "Dad" came easier that time. "Are you okay? Are you in a lot of pain?"

His head shook, lulled around, and it took some effort for

him to steady it. When he spoke, his words were slow and slurred. "No, fine. I'm fine, son."

Again, I melted at the title of "son."

"Can I get you a drink? Anything?"

He held tight to my arm and didn't answer. He took in a breath and moaned the exhale, not a painful sound but a tired one. "Just wait," he said, trying again to open his eyes, to no avail. "Just wait."

I sat there for quite some time, so long that I thought he might have fallen asleep. Or died. Had he died? I put my ear next to his mouth and nose and thought I sensed some stirring, like the air outside a cave that has another entrance miles away.

"Son," he said again, the word a balm. "Adam."

Wait. What? I wasn't sure. "What did you say, Dad?"

"Adam." The word escaped from him like a breath.

He thought I was Adam. That's why he had called me "son."

"That's not me," I whispered. "That's not who I am. Dad, Adam's in prison. He killed a lot of people in a plane crash that was his fault."

"Adam," he continued, his voice otherworldly, breathless. "You are the one. I have left everything to you."

I tried to speak, but I could no longer use the word "Dad." It wouldn't come out. I couldn't say it. I hated him. In that moment, when he thought I was my brother, when he called me "son" only because he thought I was Adam, I hated him with everything inside of me.

"You have had a hard time of it," he mumbled.

"Yes," I whispered, even though I knew he wasn't speaking to me.

"Oh, Adam."

And then he died. I didn't have to check his pulse or lean in close to know it. There was an incredible stillness that settled in his flesh, a kind of anti-animation where every one of his cells appeared to harden. Lifeless doesn't even begin to describe it. He seemed to immediately turn gray, a darkening that blended into the wood paneling and wooden furniture. The room dimmed, perhaps because a cloud passed over the sun, or perhaps because the ghost of him shrouded the window on its way out. I didn't know. To be honest, I didn't care. He was dead. I thought that might rid me of the voices, the ones that had told me throughout my entire life that I wasn't quite enough, that my father didn't love me, that I had no one.

But the voices never left.

21 CROSSING OVER

THE MIST GREW more and more dense as we made our way down, and the ledge became narrower. My toes reached over its edge at some points, with only my heels finding space to stand. Lucia and I leaned back into the cliff face. I didn't know how much farther we could go. I kept peering into the fog, hoping to see a place where the ledge opened up again to something the size of a normal path, but I could see nothing beyond the next ten feet.

"Are you okay?" I asked Lucia over and over again, looking back at her, hoping she had enough bravery for the both of us. She nodded, nothing more than a twitch of her head. Sometimes she looked at me, her soft eyes almost smiling.

Smiling. And there it was again: hope.

I could still hear the voice calling my name, but it was much more distant now, faint, and I wondered if it was a real person or some trick of the mountain.

"Dan!"

It called to me like something from the past.

"Dan!"

When we reached the bottom, at first I thought the ledge had vanished. I thought we had gone all that way for nothing and would now have to shuffle our way back up to the path or jump. But the ledge hadn't left us stranded. It had led us to the bottom. There it was. Flat ground.

The fog still hung about us, but now it held a sickening smell like rotting mud. It was the smell of composting vegetation and dead fish and lingering water. We stumbled off the ledge and I fell to the ground, my legs trembling. Looking up, I could see nothing but mist. The walls of the abyss, the sheer cliffs, spread out and away from us on either side.

How long had it taken us to get to the bottom? A day? Two days? A month? Without any change in the light, it was impossible to say. We stood there for a moment, both of us completely still. I tried to peer into the fog to see if our tormenters would show up, come racing out of some cave and tie us up, carry us away. But after all the time we had spent in the pit so far, I hadn't seen signs of anyone. It was so strange.

"Now where?" I mumbled, but Lucia was already off and running, plowing through the fog. I hoped she wouldn't run into anything or over any other cliffs, but I could hear her feet in the distance, and they were a continual patter. Searching. Wandering.

"Come back!" I shouted, and immediately covered my mouth, not wanting the voice that was following us to know we were there, that we had reached the bottom. I had hoped that the narrow cliff would prove to be too much for the person to navigate. But there was no response to my shout. The bottom of the abyss seemed to have the same sound qualities as the area around Sarah's house—the sound of my voice was immediately swallowed up.

Lucia emerged from the fog and grabbed my hand, pulling me after her.

"What?" I asked. "What did you find?"

I followed her into the haze, and when the ledge disappeared behind us, and then even the walls of the cliffs, I felt
disoriented. There was nothing around us but the swirling
mist. No sound. Even the light seemed too dim, so that we
were cloaked in a grayness. The ground went from rock to
packed clay to pebbles on a kind of wet dirt, but we hadn't
walked far before the mist cleared a bit and I saw the water.

I couldn't tell if it was a river or a lake or an ocean, although I would have guessed lake because the water wasn't
moving. Reeds grew along the bank, oozing up out of the
muddy mess. Beyond them, the water seemed a bit deeper,
but still very brown and full of silt, a gray kind of mud. In
front of us, as if placed for our purposes, was a small row-
boat.

Lucia bent over and lifted an object out of the mud. It
came up like something peeling and hung from her hand. It
appeared to be a shirt coated in the gray muck. She threw it
out into the reeds and it spun end over end, making a wet
slapping sound where it landed. I realized the whole bank
was coated in mud-covered clothing. I had thought they
were only strange shapes in the mud. I bent over, grabbed a
wrinkled ridge of mud at my feet, and lifted a pair of jeans up.

We moved closer to the boat grounded among the reeds.

"Can we get to it?" I asked.

The boat was only ten or fifteen feet out from us, but the
mud was oozing and liquid, nothing that could support us.
I shuddered. It seemed a particularly horrible way to go.

I took in our surroundings, paying closer attention. There were tiny white flowers growing up around the reeds, barely out of the mud, concentrated in circles. The sheen of their spiky white petals, even in those dire surroundings, was not beautiful. The bright red stamens rising from their throats looked hazardous. I glanced down at my feet to make sure I wasn't getting close to any of them.

The reeds were brown and jagged, the same color as the mud, or perhaps a bit more yellow. I touched one to see if we could perhaps lay them down as a kind of bridge to the boat, but their edges were sharp and slicing, like upright blades. The air was almost unbreathable, and I coughed, trying to hide the sound in the crook of my arm. I listened again for the one coming behind us.

A strange coldness pooled at our feet, moving in like a breeze, and the slow pace of it made it seem sentient, as if it was picking its way along, choosing where to go, where not to go. The cold unsettled me, but it did seem to clear the air, the mist rising above our heads so we could see farther in both directions.

Lucia gave a quiet coughing sound as if the air was catching in her throat after her run, but soon she was off again, this time along the edge of the undefined bank between land and mud. She bent down and seemed to be pulling article after article of clothing from the mud, throwing them over her shoulder. Was she digging a hole?

"Lucia," I said, trying not to be too loud. "What did you find?"

I walked carefully in her direction. This place had that effect, with the ascending and descending mist, the creeping cold, the knowledge that all around us, the cliff face rose hundreds of feet, thousands of feet, with the only way out being that narrow path. The voice behind us. The always-present question about what had happened to those who had tortured us. And the bog. Even the bog seemed to hate us, to hold a seething animosity. I wondered if anything living swam in its dark depths, out in the middle.

A long-lost phrase came to mind like a memory. *I will put you in the cleft of the rock and cover you with my hand until I have passed by.* I could not remember where those words had come from.

Lucia was down on her hands and knees, tugging at something, wrestling a shape from the mud and the clothes and the smell of the bog. I arrived where she was and reached out to touch it, my fingers sliding along the muck. It looked like an oar, the long kind a gondolier might use to direct a flatboat along a shallow canal.

"How did you see that in the mud?" I marveled.

She didn't quite smile, but it was there in her eyes.

I followed her back along the soft bank to where we had stood staring out at the irretrievable boat. She dropped the oar to the ground and worked over it, wiping as much of the muck from it as she could, leaving small piles of mud that sank back into the earth without a sound. The wood, partially cleaned off, was quite light colored. It reminded me of pine.

Lucia placed the oar between us and the boat and walked on it, balancing herself above the mud. Moving along it like a water bug, she got to the end and hopped into the front of the boat. When she turned to look at me, her eyes were wide with exhilaration, almost joy.

The cold came in deeper, approaching from the far side of the water, and it was rising, no longer swirling around my ankles but rising to my waist, my shoulders. With it, the bog smell lessened. But it was cold. Very cold. I clutched my arms to my sides.

Lucia's smiling face flattened out in a way that said, *Come! Hurry!* She reached over the side, lifted the oar, and laid it back down in a new spot so it wouldn't be implanted in the mud. All around us, the little white flowers seemed to bloom in the cold, opening their petals, turning toward the swamp like rotating red eyes. The reeds made a whistling sound, or seemed to, even though there wasn't a discernible wind. I could see no far bank.

The cold was deeper, up to my chin. I could feel it the same way someone who cannot swim would feel the rising tide gather over their shoulders, their neck, their mouth. I could still breathe, but my exhale clouded out of my mouth. I glanced at Lucia perched at the very front of the boat, looking as though she was prepared to jump out and retrieve me if I fell off the oar and sank. She made me brave, though I doubted she would be strong enough to pull me from the muck.

I took a few steps out onto the oar. It was slick, and one of my feet slipped off, went into the mud. I pulled it out, back on the oar, another step.

Lucia looked at me anxiously.

Another step, another. The oar was sinking in the mud. I walked faster, arms out at my sides for balance, feet sliding here and there, one step off the oar, quick back on before it sank, another step.

"Dan!"

The shout came from behind me.

"Dan!"

It was Miho. I knew it. I looked back. I had to see her. And because the cold had driven away the mist, I could see all the way across the flat space, all the way from the edge of the boggy lake to the cliff wall and the thread of the tiny ledge.

Miho edged her way down quite quickly, twenty feet from the bottom. Fifteen feet. Ten. She jumped from there, hit the ground hard, fell, stood, and came running.

I turned back toward Lucia. I slipped but then reached the boat. Her skinny arms pulled me in and I fell into the bottom, hitting my shoulder on one of the crosspieces. She leaned out over the edge and I clung to her legs to keep her from falling in. She hauled in the oar, and it was longer than I remembered—it didn't even fit in the boat.

I sat up on the seat and watched Miho come running. Closer, closer. Lucia's eyes filled with questions, and she thrust the oar into my hands. I nodded without really knowing what to do, but I wedged the oar into the mud and pushed, leaning against it with all of my might.

"Stop!" Miho shouted, standing on the bank only fifteen feet away, close enough that I could see the tattoo that edged her hairline. I missed her. An ache filled me, and I wished I could go back and do it all differently. I wished I would have told Abe the second I saw Kathy coming down the greenway. I wished I would have shared my memory with Miho.

She didn't look well. She was so thin I could see her collarbones clearly, and her arms were sticks. Her eyes were weary, and she kept giving her head a little shake as if trying to wake up. But even with her in that condition, even with the affection I felt rising in me, I knew we couldn't bring her along. I had no idea how Adam's actions had hurt her or what she would do to him given the chance.

"Don't stop," I whispered to Lucia, though she wasn't doing anything. "Keep going. We have to keep going."

She stood and grabbed the oar below my hands, and we both pushed. The boat edged backward, away from the bank.

"Dan, I'm coming to you," Miho said in a determined voice, as if she couldn't believe I would leave her there. She took a few steps toward us into the mud. Her feet sank immediately, down to her shins.

I didn't say anything. I couldn't. Again I leaned against the oar with Lucia, we both pushed, and the boat moved. The farther we went, the less muddy the water and the easier we moved.

Miho took another step. She sank up to her knees. "I'm not stopping, Dan," she said, and her voice was calm. "You can't do this. You have to come back. You can't bring Adam out. He has to do it himself. You know it's true!"

"Why don't you want him to come out!" I screamed, and emotion split my voice. I was crying and I didn't even know why. "Why do you want to keep him here?"

I had so many more things I wanted to say, but I knew if I kept speaking, I would lose the argument. I shook my head, a poor defense against the sadness and doubt gathering inside of me. The reeds made a rasping sound against the wooden sides of the boat. We went through a pool of white flowers, and their stamens burst in a cloud of red pollen.

"Dan!" Miho shouted. "Dan!"

"I can't!" I finally said. "I'm sorry!"

I watched as she wrestled her way backward and fell onto her back, her arms sinking in the mud. For a moment I thought she might be going under, and I grabbed Lucia's arm, holding the oar still.

"Dan!" Miho screamed, and there was an edge of terror in her voice. One arm vanished into the mud all the way up to her shoulder, but she wrestled backward, rolling, plunging, like a wild animal struggling to stay up out of a swamp. Eventually she dragged herself back onto the bank. She was covered in the brown-gray muck, and she stayed there on her hands and knees. I could tell she was sobbing, though I couldn't hear it.

"How could you leave me in that?" she shouted, but the mist around us swallowed up her words.

"I'm sorry!" I shouted again, my voice cutting short, and there were so many things I was sorry about that I didn't even know which one I was apologizing for. But the bog swallowed up my words too, and I didn't think she heard my apology.

The boat drifted slowly away through water almost completely clear of any reeds. Above us, the mist descended again. The cold grew sharper.

I let go of the oar. Lucia pushed us out, one hand over the other, the oar reaching deep. Then she sat, and the oar trailed in the water as some current tugged us away. I put my forehead against her back and wept.

22 ADAM'S ROCK

"I CAN PUSH for a little bit," I said, moving toward the back where Lucia had settled after turning the boat around and setting out across the muddy water. She slid forward to the bench where I had sat and handed me the oar. I thought for a moment how disastrous it would be to drop it.

My legs wobbled underneath me as I stood, and I grabbed the oar with two hands, stabbed it into the water. The shallowness surprised me. I had expected to have to reach far into the depths to find the bottom, but it was only three or four feet beneath us. I got into a slow rhythm of plunging the oar, pushing the boat forward, lifting, bringing the dripping oar back beside the boat, and dropping it in again. The movement helped keep me warm.

Lucia sat completely still, staring forward. All around us the water moved, creating small crests. I looked back, but the bank was far off. I couldn't see Miho.

In front of us, far in the distance, a dark rise became visible, a thin line along the gently swelling surface. I had nearly forgotten about the knapsack. It had become a part of my body, an extra appendage, and the way it bounced against my side as I walked had become a kind of comfort. We reached in and took what we wanted, and soon the small bits of food were gone. A small amount of water remained. How would we ever hike back up with so little water, with no food? But this was not a question my mind attached itself to. The only remaining desire was to get to the bottom and see if my brother was there. After that, who knew?

The far bank came up on us quicker than I expected, and our boat ground up against rocky beach. Lucia and I crawled out, dragging the boat farther in until it was lodged firmly between two boulders. I pulled the oar up onto the flat slab that made up the rest of the bank. I wished Lucia would say something—I thought I would feel less lonely if she did.

"Here we go," I said, hoping for some kind of an answer.

She nodded, her eyes bright again, eager. She took off in a slow jog, her feet padding ahead, away from the water and into another narrow canyon. It was maybe twenty feet wide, flanked by the same kind of cliff walls that made up the rest of the abyss. I wondered how she could run—gravity felt heavier there. My feet were a burden to lift with each step.

I had lost track of the shape of our surroundings and the direction we were walking. Our wanderings had gone down, that I knew, but once at the bottom of the ledge, once we crossed the bog and left Miho behind, any sense of direction disintegrated.

Beneath our feet was hard rock, and the path twisted and turned even deeper into the mountain. I had a sense that if I could see high enough up, there would be a sliver of blue sky, but the cliffs rose up all around us. The light was dim.

"Lucia," I said.

She slowed, turned to look at me. But I had no other words. I had only wanted to hear my own voice, to make sure I wasn't disappearing.

We came to an iron gate. It was tall, too tall to climb over, and its imposing doors swung on hinges somehow attached to the stone. They were tall and narrow, formed with metal fastened to itself with rivets. There were no signs of rust.

I walked up to the gate and stared at it. I swung the knapsack around in front of me and reached deep inside, my hand sliding along the seams. There it was. The key I had found, the key Kathy had always been asking me about. I pulled it out. It was cold in my fingers, and something about it made me afraid. I handed Lucia the knapsack, and she slung it over her shoulder and watched me with expectation in her eyes.

I put the key into the lock. It didn't go in smoothly, but as I struggled to turn it, the entire gate groaned, and there was a loud splintering sound as the latch was freed. The gate moved toward me almost imperceptibly, and I reached my fingers along the inside edge and pulled. It was heavy but swung soundlessly, as if it had recently been oiled. Lucia didn't run ahead of me. She nodded, and I couldn't tell if it was a movement of agreement or a lifting of the chin indicating, "You first." I reached back and slipped the key into the knapsack now dangling over her shoulder.

We walked through the gate, and I noticed there was no lock on the inside. This gate was not for keeping people out of the area we had just entered—it was for keeping people in. I stared at it. Would it stay open? If it closed, would it lock us in automatically? I searched for anything to wedge in the gate and hold it open until we returned, but there was nothing.

I turned away from the gate, and Lucia sidled up beside me. We put our arms around each other to stay warm, and I felt such a fatherly affection toward her. Her presence was a gift. I wondered again where she had come from, why she was here.

The cliff walls pressing in on us widened into an open space of what appeared to be deep, rich soil, and the light increased, if only a little. I could feel my spirits rise. There were large, beautiful trees everywhere, their heavy limbs swaying in a breeze. The cold that had felt nebulous or intangible solidified there in that glade, made itself present in a way it had not been anywhere else.

A light snow fell as we walked among the trees. They were shaped almost like people. The wide bases of their trunks split into several exposed roots before plunging into the frozen earth. Could there be a warm undercurrent of water? But what of the lack of light? It was a strange and nonsensical place, the lime-green leaves coated lightly in white snow, the rich earth carpeted with grass and filled with glassy puddles, the trees whose branches moved and shifted like arms.

Lucia ran off, vanished among the trees, and her absence left a lonely, frightened space inside of me. The shadows in that place were strange. They seemed to move of their own accord, somehow separate from the object that made them. A tree's shadow might appear to be billowing in a storm while the tree itself was standing nearly still. Or the dim shadow cast by the walls where we had entered shimmered and moved like a liquid, but the walls were fixed.

From some of the deeper shadows I thought I could hear something. Voices? Or maybe it was only the wind? I was so cold. So cold. Could I even trust my senses anymore? How much longer until my body gave in to hypothermia?

"Lucia!" I shouted, a sense of frustration rising toward the girl. I did not like being left alone in that place. Why was she always running off?

The snow fell heavier, and I moved farther in among the confusing trees with their incongruent shadows. It was like a swirling of my vision. I realized the ground had gradually gone from grass to icy puddles and then to a solid block of ice—the trees somehow grew up and out of that shallow, frozen lake. The trees looked more and more like terrified people waving me off, motioning for me to go and never return. Warning me.

"Lucia!" I shouted again. The wind blew harder, and the snow stung my eyes, blinding me until I stumbled out into a clearing, all of the trees shrinking back from this open space. Here the ice was clear all the way down to the depths, and the snow stopped suddenly. I wondered if I was dead or alive. The stillness was vast.

"Lucia!" My voice was weak and hoarse, scratchy in the cold, and puffs of steam escaped every time I shouted. But she did not reply, and I grew more frustrated, nearing anger. Where was that girl?

Across the vast pool of black ice I saw movement. Lucia? But no, it wasn't movement so much as something that didn't blend in with the complete stillness, something that didn't move so much as shift. I looked closer, peering through the darkness.

Adam?

I walked forward carefully, skeptically. Could my greatest hope be right there? But I hadn't taken more than five or six steps forward when a sound made me stop suddenly. I was awakened by fear. It was the sound of creaking and a grinding split. The ice under my feet was not as thick as I had thought, and a gentle thread of water oozed up through the crack. I stopped. I peered into the darkness again.

Could it be him?

A man Adam's size, with long black hair, down on hands and knees, was isolated on a tiny rock island in the middle of the frozen lake. I took another step toward him, and this time the ice cracked in the shape of a spiderweb. I took a step backward.

"Adam?" My voice came out tenuous like the ice, cracking in the cold.

Somehow in that great stillness, he heard me, and he looked over. It was too far away to see his eyes. He didn't have a shirt on. His pants were torn and frayed and sliced so that they hung around his legs like rags. He seemed to be looking for the source of the voice, then turned his face upward, toward the nothing sky, and gave a maniacal laugh.

"You fooled me again!" he screamed, and in his voice I could hear every torment known to man. "Well done! Yes! Well done!" He slammed his hands against the ice and his shoulders shook. I thought he must be weeping. I wanted to shout for him again, but I didn't want to cause the same reaction. He was obviously hurting himself.

But I couldn't help it.

It was him.

"Adam!" I shouted, looking frantically around for another way across the ice. I took a few steps back, slid to my right ten or fifteen yards, and walked forward again tenderly, leading with my toes. The ice was turning to fire under my feet. But when I had walked the same distance forward, the ice groaned and split.

"No," I groaned. "Adam!"

Immediately I wished I hadn't called for him again—my voice seemed to be making him crazy with agony. He struck his forehead on the ground in front of him. He screamed. He grated his fingers along the rock.

I felt it before I saw it, a blur of movement to my left, coming out of the trees. Lucia ran across the ice, and as she did, a word erupted from her. It seemed to have the force of all the gathered words she had held in.

"Daddy!"

I caught my breath. I stopped blinking. The world spun.

Lucia, running toward Adam, was shouting "Daddy!" over and over again.

My throat swelled and I knew it was true. Maybe I had known the first time I saw her, recognized something in her eyes or the way she looked at me or how she pushed her hair away in some familiar gesture of Adam's.

"Lucia!" I shouted, trying to warn her. "The ice!"

But she didn't stop. She only glanced at me and sprang from side to side, here and there. In some places I could tell the ice had split under her while in others it remained flat and firm. She didn't run straight but seemed to follow some pattern. Maybe she could see where the ice was thicker. Maybe a shallow place ran from where she had emerged out to the small island where Adam knelt. Or maybe she was simply lucky.

I watched the knapsack sway and bounce on her back, the precious knapsack holding the last of our water. And the key.

She arrived at Adam's rock, clambered up, and sat quietly beside him. He did not look up. I wondered if he could see her. Maybe he thought she was simply another in a long line of hallucinations. She studied him, her head tilting to the side, then she reached out a hand and, with the gentlest touch of her index finger, lifted his chin so that his eyes rose to hers. They were like a precious statue, the father on his knees, the daughter lifting his face so that he could see her.

Even from where I was, I could see him begin to tremble, first in the weakness of his arms, and after that his hips, and eventually his whole body. Lucia lifted her other hand and held his face, her tenderness propping him up. She leaned forward and kissed his forehead.

The ice under my feet cracked further, and I shifted back and away from Adam's rock, alarmed at the distance growing between us. I stared down at the ice to see if things were stabilizing, but hairline fractures were still forming, so I took a few more steps back. When I looked back up, Lucia was taking off the knapsack and placing it on the rock. She took out the water and funneled some into Adam's mouth. I worried about how much she was giving him and if we'd have enough to get us back out.

Adam drank, sat back on his haunches, and stared at her as if she was a vision come to life. He said a few words I couldn't hear, and she leaned forward and hugged him, even in his wretchedness, his filth. This time his shoulders trembled, but in sobs. He kept leaning his head back and looking at her in amazement, then embracing her again.

The water under me churned, which was strange because I hadn't moved. I looked out over the black expanse of ice, and it all seemed to vibrate as if in an earthquake. The ice trembled. Some distance off, at the edge of what I could see, a large piece of ice broke from the rest and stood up on end. The whole earth seemed to groan.

"Lucia!" I shouted. "The ice!"

We must have realized it at the same time: this was not a lake we were on but a river, one so massive I couldn't see the far bank. The water beneath us was moving, and the ice was beginning to break up. The sound of it was like the splitting of the mountain. I became more and more frantic as the seconds passed, as the river moaned, as the ice fractured.

"Hurry!" I screamed, my voice as broken as the river, and yet still they remained on the rock. I could tell she was pleading with him, and he was shaking his head, his long black hair swaying in pendulum movements. She wept, she pleaded, she hugged him, and still he remained, sitting back on his heels, refusing to move.

She pointed across the ice. He looked at me. Our gazes locked, there at the bottom of the abyss, with the world collapsing around us. I wanted to shout to him to get moving. I wanted to raise my hands and gesture wildly for him to hurry, the ice was breaking, this was his chance. I wanted to get on my knees and plead. But all I did was stand there, my shoulders slumped.

I had caused this. He was here because of me, because I had forced him to fly that day, because I was more concerned with my own reputation and possessions than anything else. I wondered if he had somehow discovered that it was my fault, that the accident never would have happened without my insistence that he get out of bed that morning and fly the plane.

He stood. Lucia was tiny next to him, but strong. He leaned on her and they climbed gingerly down the shallow side of the rock and began making their way across the ice. She ran ahead, I guess because their weight together would have been too much, and beckoned to him. As they grew closer, I could hear her voice encouraging him, pleading with him to keep coming, telling him he could do it. He followed her, barely able to walk, sometimes falling to his knees. At one point his legs went through the ice, and he sprawled forward, spreading out his weight, inching himself forward.

It started snowing again. Lucia arrived to me before he did, and we backed up, hoping to find thicker ice or shallower water farther back toward the trees. Still he kept coming. Now he could walk, his bare feet white on the ice. I was shaking with cold but also warm from the exertion, the stress, the emotion.

There he was, standing in front of me. Could it be true? I waited for him to evaporate, a mirage. I had waited so long for this moment.

He wouldn't look directly at me. His eyes flitted here and there, nervous and unstable, and I understood why Lucia had reached out and taken his chin in her hands, directing his uncontrolled glances. But I waited, and eventually our eyes met.

"Adam," I said, my voice shattered, miniscule, lost.

"Dan," he said.

For a moment I thought I was truly looking at myself, another version of me, one that had never made it out of this place but had withered away here at the bottom for endless years, endless decades, tortured by all the wrong I had done. It should have been me. All along, it should have been me.

"I'm sorry," I said, and his gaze sharpened, but he said nothing. "I'm sorry," I said again, and I put my hands on his shoulders as if I was going to shake him. He seemed so lost.

"The knapsack," Lucia whispered, her voice barely registering in the midst of the river's chaos and my overflowing emotions.

"What?"

She didn't answer. She sprinted back onto the ice that continued to break up, clashing against itself, upending in sharp angles and shards.

"Lucia!" I shouted.

Adam, too weak to continue in the midst of everything, fell to his knees and broke through the ice. The ice around my own feet followed, and I plunged through. For a moment we clawed at each other, trying desperately to rise. The water was dark underneath the ice, and in a panic I lost my sense of up and down. But it was shallow there where we stood close to the trees, and my hands soon found the muddy bottom. I pushed off, up, and burst through the surface.

My brother had already pulled himself to safety and crawled the rest of the way to the trees. He sat there, his back against a trunk that resembled a forlorn mother with branches reaching down like arms. The trees' shadows were darker then, like bottomless ditches. I pulled myself aching and frozen from the water. How long could we survive, wet as we were, hungry as we were, cold as we were? I gathered myself on all fours and the ice creaked. I didn't think I had the strength for another submersion.

I crawled along a line where I thought I would be safe, looking toward Adam's rock for Lucia, wishing she would show herself. I choked back tears at the thought of losing her there, in that lowest of places. Just when I gave up, she appeared, coming up out of the icy water, gripping the rock, pulling herself up. She lifted the knapsack and started to put it over her shoulder but stopped. She stared at it. She peered through the darkness and spotted me.

Freed from its icy bonds, the river flowed faster than before, and the flat spaces of ice had become bobbing, miniature glaciers sliding away. Lucia seemed to gather her courage. She jumped from one floating ice island to the next. She vanished into the water, then pulled herself up again, crawling onto a slowly spinning slab. She was swept toward me briefly, jostled by other moving pieces of ice. She prepared herself to make another running leap, had second thoughts. Her face was sad. Her lips were a straight line. All around us was the sound of ice colliding, cracking, creaking.

She threw the knapsack hard in my direction, her arm a slingshot, and I crawled toward the spot where it landed, on ice in shallow water. I grabbed it, and a wave of relief washed over me so that I almost felt warm again. I looked at her, a smile on my face. She gave me a thumbs-up. Throwing the knapsack had knocked her to her knees, and she paused there for a moment on all fours. She tried to smile, but I could tell she was afraid.

Then the ice she was on tipped up at one end. She slid toward the other edge, bracing herself, clawing for something to hold on to.

"Lucia!"

She went under, and I lost sight of her.

23 HOW FAR
WE HAVE FALLEN

I DON'T KNOW how long I waited in that spot, holding my breath. The water was a mess of ice collapsing in on itself, mounding up in some areas, spreading out in others. It was like a flat field full of debris left behind after a village is leveled in war. I gasped for breath. I held the knapsack in one hand. I wanted to scream.

But the cold, the cold was breaking my bones. I turned and crawled, and my body creaked with the weariness of it. Once I was closer to what I thought was solid ground, I stood gingerly and walked toward where Adam still sat against a tree. They were haunting, those trees. Their roots, where they showed through the black ice, seemed to pulse like veins. I knew it was some trick of the light, perhaps the shimmering of the ice, but it still repulsed me.

I stopped beside Adam and sat down. The snow had been coming and going ever since Lucia and I had arrived in that place, but in that moment, it was so light that I thought it had stopped. Except every so often a lone flake would fall, lost. The sky was only low, gray clouds, like a hovering fog. I thought about the rim of the abyss beside the river Acheron and the immeasurable distance between us and that place. I wondered how far we had fallen.

Adam mumbled something that sounded like a question. I looked at him again, trying to find the brother I remembered hidden there among the gaunt flesh, the long hair, the broken skin. His knees bled from kneeling on the rock for who knows how long. He flinched every few seconds as if being prodded.

"What?" I asked him quietly. I wanted to hug him. I wanted to hold him. After so much time with Lucia and her silence, the sound of another human being's voice, even indecipherable, was like balm. But there was something between us, something I couldn't identify. There was a kind of strangeness there, and years, and misunderstandings that might be too far gone to clear up.

"The girl," he muttered, his voice still hoarse. Saliva pooled in the corners of his mouth. He was crazed. Would the hike out help him heal, or had he left whatever shred of sanity that remained on that rock in the middle of the frozen river?

"Where is she?"

I took in the shifting ice. When I didn't see her, a sob came out of me, a wave of grief, but I cleared my throat to hide it. I knew in that moment I could never tell him about her, or he wouldn't leave. I was the only one who knew she was his daughter. Had been his daughter. There was no reason to tell him now.

"What girl?" I whispered.

"The girl," he said, his voice stronger, his eyes searching mine. "The girl who came over to me."

I shook my head slowly. "I don't know, Adam." I paused, swallowed. "I didn't see anyone."

He stared hard into the deep blackness of the ice beneath us. There was another blistering crack from the river, a moaning creak, and Adam shivered convulsively. The ice was on the move. I wondered what had set it off.

"I've seen a lot here," he said. "I've imagined a lot."

I nodded.

"Are you sure?"

"I didn't see a girl," I insisted. "I saw you look up at me across the ice, drag your way through the river. That's all I saw."

He clenched his jaw. Shook his head. "I could've sworn . . ."

"We should go." I stood up, moving gingerly away from the tree on the ice, but my caution was unnecessary. The water there remained solidly frozen.

"No use," he said.

What?

"No use," he said again. "There's no way out. The gate is locked."

"Have you been to the gate?" I asked.

He nodded. "Once. Long after everyone left. Long after she left. I managed to crawl all the way there. When I found the locked gate, I gave up hope. So I crawled back out to the rock."

"She?" I asked.

"What do you mean?"

"You said, 'Long after everyone left. Long after she left.' Who's 'she'?"

He shuddered. "The one in charge. The one who ran this whole place, every circle of it, every tree, every corner."

"It was a she?" A sense of dread slunk through me. "Did she have a name?" I asked in a hushed voice.

He nodded again.

I raised my eyebrows in a question. *What was her name?*

"Kathy," he whispered.

Kathy. I had left everyone with her, and they didn't even know who she was. A thought dropped into my mind— what if I was here because of her? I was, wasn't I? Hadn't she been the one to convince me to come back in, to get my brother? But he couldn't have gotten out without me, could he?

What if she was now convincing the others to come in and retrieve me? What if she walked east and found others to convince?

She would fill this place again.

"We should go," I said. I was filled with fresh urgency to get him out, get us out, and find the others.

"Who are you?" he asked with none of the urgency I was looking for.

"Me?" I asked. "I'm Dan." I decided to leave it at that. For now.

"Dan," he whispered, and he was lost again, searching through hidden realms in his mind, perhaps searching for me. He emerged moments later. "The gate." He sighed.

I reached into the knapsack, searched the bottom corners of the cloth, and pulled out the key. I held it up in front of him, and he looked at it in awe, as if it was the strangest of all the strange things he had seen, the least believable.

He reached up, not to take it but to touch it. "Is it real?"

"Yes," I said, again seeing the movement of Lucia's arm as

she threw the knapsack. I saw her clinging to the ice, sliding toward the edge. I saw her going under.

Adam tried to stand, and when he couldn't do it on his own, I reached down and took hold of his arm. He felt like a bundle of twigs. We both continued to shiver, so I put my arm around him and we tried to live off each other's warmth. I didn't know how we would walk, how we would leave this place. I thought of the bog we had to get through, the ledge we'd have to maneuver. The river. Maybe Karon and Sarah could help us. If we made it that far.

The ledge. I had left Miho by the ledge, assuming she wasn't a figment of my imagination. And now we had to get past her too, make sure she didn't exact some sort of revenge on Adam. I had never heard her story, but I could guess. The crash had affected her in some way. She hated my brother. She was waiting for him like all the others.

"Do you see people a lot down here? Imaginary people?" I asked.

He nodded as we walked stiffly through the trees and over all those strange shadows. The ice felt solid under our feet, but I was still expecting it to break at any point. The water that was on me felt like it was freezing, turning me into a block.

"Do you think I'm real?" I asked.

"No," he said, and as we shuffled along, this was the closest he'd come to giving me a smile.

"Fair enough."

We found the entrance to the narrow canyon and left the trees and frozen river behind. And Lucia. We left Lucia behind. The guilt was crushing me, even though I knew there was nothing I could have done. I could not have walked across the ice. I could not have jumped in and pulled her out. I could not wait here long enough—she was gone. Not telling Adam about her felt like both a gift and a terrible betrayal. I told myself I would tell him someday. Far in the future. Far from here, when everything else was better.

The gate was still there, open, just as I had left it. Adam seemed so intrigued by it that I slowed and let him lead the way. He stopped directly in front of its opening, walked from side to side, and caressed its cold metal. He examined the lock, the doors.

"I stood at this gate, beating on it with my fists." He rubbed his hands together. "I screamed until my throat bled. How did you get the key from her? How did you come here?" He seemed to finally be accepting the fact that I was real and that I was with him.

"Do you know who I am?"

He nodded, his face blank, his hand still on the gate.

"You do?"

He nodded again, but he still didn't say anything.

"We have a lot to talk about once we get out of here," I whispered. I glanced away from him, feeling my face form a kind of wince, before walking over and gently taking hold of his elbow to guide him farther along. He kept looking over his shoulder at the gate, as if it might transform into a monster and chase us down, devour us in that rocky canyon.

"You should lock it," he said, his voice suddenly lifeless.

"What?"

"The gate. You should lock it. We can't leave it open. What if she comes back down? What if she brings someone else here to keep them prisoner, like she did to me and all the others?"

"I don't think we have to worry about that," I said. I would have locked it had it not been for Lucia in the frozen river. Somewhere among the ice. Locking the gate suddenly felt crucial. Every evil I knew would come through if I didn't.

"There are horrors there," he said, stopping. "There are things in there, in the water, in the woods, you cannot even imagine. They will follow us. They will get out."

His voice was quiet, but it was impossible for me to ignore the terror he clearly felt in that moment. Have you been with someone who is in the midst of a panic attack? There is no rationalizing, no explaining. Nothing I said would convince him that all the things he had seen had been illusions, the constructs of a broken mind. But I could not lock Lucia into that place. It was the very bottom. If she had somehow survived, the way needed to remain open for her.

To appease Adam, I walked over to the gate and pushed the doors against each other so that they appeared to be closed. I held up the key so he could see it, then inserted it into the gate. I turned it so that it locked, but I also turned it back so that it unlocked again. When I took out the key, the unlocked gate budged only a fraction.

When I turned to look at him, relief left him sagging, like someone who has finally relaxed. He had not seen the slight movement of the gate shifting open. In his mind it was locked and all the horrors of this place would be contained. Seeing the gate from that side, he raised his hands and covered his face, and the sound of his weeping echoed off the rock. I did not go over to him, not that time. I only watched and waited. His crying went on for a long time.

We finally continued through the canyon and had nearly reached the bog when I noticed that the cold was not so cold. My feet and fingertips were no longer numb. I put my hands up to my mouth and blew into them, and I could feel the warmth spreading. I looked over at Adam and could tell he was feeling it too. His joints didn't seem so locked. His face had regained some color, although his black hair did still emphasize the paleness of his skin. He reached up with a swollen finger and pushed a thread of hair out of his face.

"I can't believe this is all here," he said. "A way out."

We walked slowly, and the scuffing sound of our feet on the hard earth was lonely and peaceful. Every so often, one of us would need to stop to rest, and the other would stop as well, leaning against the canyon wall or sitting on the ground. We had reached the limits of our exhaustion. I could not let myself think about how far we still had to go.

I pulled out the water and we each took a sip. I put it back in the knapsack and thought about the price of it.

"How long?" he asked, staring at the ground between his feet.

"How long?" I repeated.

"How long was I in there?"

That was a good question. I had no idea. The passing of time in the small town on the edge of the plains had felt immeasurable. It could have been ten years. I thought of all the harvests we had seen, all the times we had pulled vegetables and fruits from the garden and the orchard. It must have been longer. Twenty years? Could it have been longer than that?

"I don't know," I said. "Time doesn't pass the same way anymore."

"Why'd you decide to come and find me? Why now?"

"Things were ending. Our village was destroyed. Kathy was there."

"Kathy?" He didn't actually say her whole name out loud. He said it the way a child might whisper a curse, knowing they'd be in trouble if anyone heard.

I nodded. "She burned down our village. At least I think it was her. She was trying to cause chaos, trying to break us up. I don't know. I don't understand completely. I think she wants everyone back in here again."

"But you're here because . . . of her?"

"No. I'm here because of you. I waited a long time, Adam. For you. I couldn't come back here. I couldn't. But then, when everything fell apart . . . I don't know. I had to do something."

We walked on, and I could tell he was thinking hard about something, thinking through all I had told him.

"You shouldn't be here," he said. "Nothing she wants to happen is good."

I didn't know what to say, so I didn't say anything.

He spoke again. "If she wanted you to be here, you shouldn't be here."

24 BROKEN THINGS

THE ROCKS ROSE up in front of us, a kind of jetty that held back the bog waters. We made our way up, exhaustion stiffening my fingers, but after the cold of the forest and the canyon, the rocks felt almost warm. We got to the top and spotted the boat and the extra-long oar, and we wound our way down among the boulders. It took both of us to lift the boat and slide it into the water, and I'd imagine we both looked pitiful in our pain and weariness.

Adam climbed in gingerly, and I followed, dragging the oar with me. It took one easy push and we were back in the water. Again I searched behind us for Lucia. I willed her to appear. How could she ever cross this water without a boat? How could she ever leave this place on her own? I took heart in knowing that anyone who had ever escaped from this part of the abyss before had done so on their own, perhaps even without a boat. But it all felt so unlikely.

We drifted silently across the still water, and after a while the bank we had come from disappeared behind us. It wasn't until this moment that I realized there was no fog, no haze. The clouds were so high that they looked like a flat sheet, stretched, without any breaks in them.

Adam sat in the front, his back to me, leaning forward

with his arms out and his hands gripping the bow. He could have been in prayer. He could have been asleep. He could have been plotting some escape. I wondered how his clothes still clung to him after all that time, torn and shredded as they were. His hair had dried in coarse clumps like wet straw, and between the strands I could see long, deep scratches on the back of his neck. Were they the marks his abusers had left, or were they gouges of guilt, self-inflicted? This place was even stranger than I had imagined, and what had happened to all of us seemed less and less clear.

He whispered something in his hoarse voice.

"What?" I asked, not even sure if he was talking to me or to himself.

"The water." He pushed the words out. "The water. Do you remember? The lake. Do you remember the lake?"

I was about to say no, but an image came into my mind. Adam and I in a lake house that one of my father's trucker friends had said we could stay in. It was a rough hunting cabin, and there was no running water inside, although there was a pump out front and an outhouse. Thirty yards down the hill from the house, the lake lapped up against a stony beach, and a long, narrow pier jutted out into the cold blue water.

Adam and I were roughhousing one afternoon, and in a series of events that happened too fast to replay in my mind, our wrestling caused a large pair of elk antlers to fall off the wall, strike the floor, and break. The two of us sat suspended in time, me on the bottom, nearly pinned. We craned our necks to find the source of the loud snapping sound.

We could fix it, I told myself. We could glue it, or hang it back up and pretend nothing happened, or throw the entire thing into the lake. But neither of us could move, because we heard the creaking of the bedroom door, and our father emerged without saying a word. He didn't even look at us—we still hadn't moved from the floor. He stared long at that broken set of antlers, his friend's fractured trophy.

"Come on," he mumbled in a voice that terrified me more than any shout could have.

We disentangled ourselves from each other, and I felt alone, afraid, and somehow naked. With Adam, even when he was pinning me to the ground, I felt part of something, something strong. But standing and following my father, walking wordlessly behind Adam, I felt even less than what I was, which at the time was a frightened twelve-year-old boy.

Still not looking at us, our father walked outside and down to the pier. It swayed under our weight, and I nearly fell in a couple of times. I considered turning around and running, once even looking over my shoulder into those wooded hills. I imagined the feeling of safety I would have, running through the shadows of the trees, building a shelter in the wilderness where I could stay. Escape.

But I didn't run. And neither did Adam. We trailed behind our father, all the way to the end of the pier, by which point my legs were trembling. He climbed into the motorboat, also owned by his friend, and motioned for us to get in with him.

"The rope," he said, and I knew he meant for me to untie the boat from the dock.

I tentatively untied the rope, and the boat bobbed for a moment in the water, independent of the pier, independent of me. Again I considered running. I could be halfway back to the dock by the time he climbed out of the boat. I could be in the woods before he could catch me. Would he even chase me? Probably not. Maybe that's the real reason I didn't run—I couldn't face such a tangible sign of his indifference.

I jumped in and the boat shook. Adam and I moved to the front, gripping the sides, and the motor roared to life, easing the three of us out into that flat, beautiful lake. Soon we skimmed the water, and there were no waves to slap the bottom, no waves to skip us up into the air. It was a droning, constant propulsion to the deepest section, where the far banks were barely visible in all directions. A cold mist blew into our faces. I looked at Adam. He couldn't help but grin.

Our father cut off the engine unexpectedly, and the boat limped to a stop, pitching this way and that ever so subtly. There was no wind. The sky was huge, a beautiful blue dome that held everything, the entire universe. There was even happiness in that moment of quiet, that moment of peace, and I could nearly forget that Adam and I had broken something important.

"Get in the water," our father murmured. Had he been drinking? I couldn't tell. Adam reached for one of the life jackets, but our father stuck out his foot and stamped it down in the bottom of the boat, where an inch or so of water had gathered. "You won't need that."

We looked at each other. We had on normal clothes—khaki shorts and T-shirts. We had planned on going out for dinner. I reached into my pockets to make sure they were empty, taking out only a few small pieces of lint, a penny I had found on the dirt road that led to the cabin, and a movie stub. I moved to take off my shirt, but a hand ripped it back down.

"Get. In. The. Water," he said again, each word existing entirely on its own. When Adam and I paused at the side of the boat, he shouted so that his voice broke the dome and brought the universe caving in around us. "Get in the water!"

We jumped in, our splashes nearly synchronized. The water was clear and cool but not cold, a perfect day for swimming. I could feel the colder currents moving around my legs like fingers reaching up for me. We both hovered there, treading water, waiting to see what we were supposed to do next. But our father sat in the boat, staring off at the distant horizon.

Adam and I drifted closer, but as soon as one of us came within arm's reach, our father cleared his throat and said in a light voice, as if he was wishing us a good afternoon, "Don't touch the boat."

"It was an accident," Adam said, sputtering as a small swell rose up over his mouth.

"You two. You just go through life thinking you can have or take or break whatever you want. You're like two little animals. It's pathetic."

"We didn't try to do it," I chimed in. "We're sorry."

"You're right, you're sorry," he said, staring down at me.

My arms and legs ached, and the water was cooling. I hadn't noticed when we first set out, but the end of the afternoon was near. I wondered if he was going to make us swim home. The shore was nearly invisible from where I was, down in the water. I put my head back and floated, eyes closed. The water drowned out all other sounds, and I was gone, far from there, in a bathtub or a swimming pool or hunched under an umbrella after the rain has stopped. It was quiet there. Peaceful.

I stayed that way for a few minutes, and when I looked up, I found it hard to believe how far I had drifted away from the boat. Adam was still there, still treading, although the look on his face was strained. His skin had gone pale. He floundered, coughed, righted himself.

"Adam!" I shouted. "Float on your back. Get some rest."

But he wouldn't. His dark hair was wet. His breathing was hoarse. His arms splashed. Then he was under.

"Dad!" I screamed. "Adam!"

Our father eased his way over to the edge of the boat and stared into the depths. He plunged his hand in and grabbed Adam first by the hair, then by the scruff of his T-shirt, pulling up on it so that it came up under his chin, a noose. He dragged Adam into the boat and dumped him like a marlin. I heard Adam coughing over and over again until he threw up. Our father sat at the front of the boat as if nothing had happened. He wasn't smiling or frowning. He was sitting. Waiting.

I floated on my back, trying to preserve my strength. I knew in that moment what he wanted—he wanted me to feel that gentle slipping under, the panic of no air, the sense of him saving me from death, literally pulling me up into life. And I would not give him that satisfaction. I floated on my back, the water plugging and unplugging my ears, the sky cool and far above me. I treaded water for a few minutes. Then I floated again.

The boat coughed to life. I straightened up, kicked in the

water, moved my arms around. I felt instantly suspicious because my father never gave up, never at anything and especially not when it came to waiting. He showed Adam the motor, how to steer, and sat in the front of the boat again.

He had never let either of us drive the boat, no matter how many times we begged.

As they trolled past me, he spoke one last time, and again he did not look at me but sent his words out to some other place. "You little cheat. Floating isn't allowed."

The boat powered past me, leaving me in the middle of the lake. I caught Adam's glance and could tell he was worried for me. He looked nervously over his shoulder to see if our father was watching, then he pushed a life vest over the side. It bobbed in the water, pushed aside by the wake. Our father turned toward Adam again, and at first I thought he had seen the life preserver, but he only instructed Adam on how to give the boat more throttle. It stood up out of the water, a higher pitch, before sitting and speeding away.

I swam, exhausted, to the life vest and tangled myself up in it. It held me, and I could finally catch my breath. I started kicking slowly, asking myself if it was even possible for me to swim all the way back to the shore in front of the cabin.

There is a particular feeling that comes in the night as you float on your back, when the deep water is still and the sky is reflected back to you. I moved slowly, sometimes using my arms to paddle, sometimes my legs, and I made it through the dark, all the way back.

The boat thumped against the pier in a gentle rhythm. There were waves, tiny ones, enough to lift and lower the craft. A hand reached down and helped me up, and once on the pier, sitting on that solid thing, I felt like jelly, like my entire body might melt. I was so tired.

"You okay?" Adam asked.

I nodded. We sat there for a long time, saying nothing. Then we stood and walked back inside. Our father never said a word about it. He used glue to reattach the antler. No one ever noticed the difference.

"I SHOULD HAVE come back for you," Adam said as we approached the muddy banks of the bog. "I should have brought the boat back out and found you."

"It was dark," I said. "It was a big lake. You wouldn't have found me, not at night."

"That's not the point. You came back here for me."

Back here. For a moment, in that memory, my mind had escaped to a place where the sky was bright blue and the water clear, where the trees that lined the distant banks were green and full and the cabin's red metal roof was like a siren's call. Back here, though, the muddy water was thick. The only bank that was visible was the one coming into view, loaded with those sharp reeds growing up out of the mud. The sky was dull, a kind of brown-gray, and while the cold had dimmed, the warmer air smelled of rotten mud.

"If you are real," Adam said, staring straight ahead, leaning into the bow of the boat, "if you are real . . . where did you come from?"

"Outside of the mountain."

"And what is it like there? Outside?"

"It's very green," I said. "It's quiet, and the air smells of living things. From there, the mountain looks like something beautiful. I live in a small stone house at the edge of a village." I paused and decided not to tell him about going east, not yet. "There are a few others there."

I wondered if they were still there, if all of the houses had burned or if any had been saved. Was Abe still waiting for me, as he always said he would?

"You can choose a house. There are some empty ones. But we still have a long way to go to get there. You were at the very bottom."

Adam turned around and faced me, leaned back, and wedged himself into the bow. I could tell he was on the edge of passing out.

"You know what I miss the most?" he said, his voice weak and see-through.

"What?"

"The birds," he whispered. "The swallows swooping down over our heads like bats, the pigeons in the barn, the doves in the eaves, the robins hopping along, eating worms."

"I never knew you liked birds."

He nodded. "I stared into the sky for years here, or decades, I don't know, just looking for the birds."

"Mother loved birds," I said quietly.

He nodded. He leaned his head back on the point of the bow and spoke toward the flat clouds above us. "You know, I remember how Mom used to stand beside the window and watch the birds."

"Yeah," I said. "Me too."

"One day I saw her standing there, and there was such love

in her eyes. She held a cup of coffee close to her face, and the steam moved around her mouth, cheeks, and ears. I had never seen such love before. I wondered if she was looking out the window at Dad, but we both know that wasn't what it was." He gave a wry chuckle. "I walked over to stand beside her and see what she could possibly be looking at with such love, such fondness." He laughed as he said "fondness," as if he knew it wasn't a word he usually used. "Do you know what she was looking at?"

I shook my head.

"She was looking at you, Dan."

The oar stopped in the water, and our forward motion slowed. For a moment we were adrift, and the boat, because of the distribution of weight, an underwater current, or something else, slowly spun, pointing us back toward the far bank, the path through the gate, the frozen river, and Adam's rock.

She had loved me. And yet, I had only ever been concerned about my father's love.

I gripped the oar and braced my weight against it, sending us in the correct direction, back toward the muddy side of the shallow brown lake. When we weren't speaking, there was nothing but the sound of the boat in the heavy water, the oar dipping in and drops falling from it when I lifted it out.

I did not want to tell him that there were no birds in the plains.

"Have you seen Father in any of your travels?" Adam asked me.

I shook my head. "No."

"So, he found his way out."

This was something I could not contemplate. If he had left the mountain, if he had been in this place and fled, it must have happened before I had found my way to the village, because I had seen many hundreds or perhaps even thousands of people come through, but never him.

"I guess."

"I thought I saw him here, once," Adam said. "But it was from a distance, and it was when there were still a lot of us. I don't know. Probably my imagination."

Now Adam was looking right into my eyes. He scared me, because I couldn't tell if he was sane or not, if all this time in the abyss had unhinged his mind or if this was the brother from my childhood. If it was him, I didn't recognize him.

"I hated him," Adam said, his words reluctant to come out. "I don't remember much about this place. I've been here for so very, very long. But I do remember that I wasn't always so deep inside the mountain. It was my hatred for him that drove me down here, looking, searching. I wanted to find him. I planned on killing him. But this place . . ." He motioned all around us. "This place was so full of people moaning, screaming, pulling on me, needing, needing, needing."

He ran his hand through his long, tangled hair and winced, gritting his teeth. He was getting himself worked up. I wanted to say something that would calm him.

"I wish you would have come out. I wish you would have joined me."

He shook his head, put his face in his hands, and sat there like that for so long I thought he might have fallen asleep. But then he spoke.

"I do too. When I heard your voice, and the voice of that imaginary girl, it was like all of that hate broke up inside of me. The fog lifted. I don't hate him anymore." He paused. "Do you, brother? Do you hate our father?"

I didn't know what to say. I had barely thought of him, except perhaps when my memories came back to me. I was so focused on Adam that my history with our father slid easily through my fingers, but here, deep in the abyss, I could feel that hatred rising. It threatened to pull me down.

I shook my head uneasily. "No," I said, frowning. "I don't know."

I didn't want to talk about our father anymore.

"What else do you remember? What else do you miss?" I asked.

He looked at me, squinted, and I knew I had been found out, that he could tell this was me grasping for a change of subject. But he went along with it.

"I miss the sunrise. Remember when we had that airplane business and I'd go on an early morning run? The plane lifted easily off the runway, barely clearing the trees, and there it was—the sunrise. I can't tell you how many times I wanted to keep flying, all the way into it."

I was amazed at how many memories he had. I was amazed at how quickly he seemed to be recovering, transforming from that torn man kneeling on the rock, and I didn't have the heart to tell him. This place we were going to had no sunrises—only the soft dimming of light in the evening, which was beautiful and peaceful but was no sunset, and the dark of night, and the early morning brightening, which was gentle and quiet, but it was no sunrise.

Would we ever get out of this place? Would I ever see the green grass of the plains stretching out in front of me?

I felt a nagging sense of fear that something was coming for us, that I should have locked the gate no matter what that might have meant for Lucia. The desire became so strong that I nearly turned the boat around. Again I scanned the horizon for any sign of our tormentors. I dug in the oar, and now it was a struggle to pull it out, because it sank into the muddy bottom. Bubbles rose in the water every time I lifted it. I scanned the bank for Miho. Nothing.

We got the boat as close as we could. I told Adam to avoid the reeds and the flowers. After we had struggled to push the boat farther through the mud, we lay in the bottom, exhausted, panting. I arranged the oar the same way Lucia had placed it, on top of the mud, stretching out to the bank.

"You have to walk along it or you'll sink," I said. I took off my shirt and threw it to the bank. "In case you need an extra step."

Adam scurried along the wooden oar, his feet slipping, and he did not have to step on the shirt. I followed him, and the oar sank in. My last few steps were in knee-deep mud, so tight, resisting each step with such powerful suction, I thought I might lose the skin on my legs. But soon we were resting on the bank, the bog and the gate and the icy hollow behind us. Now there was only the long, steep ledge, the climb to the top, and the river Acheron.

But . . . Miho. Where was Miho?

Maybe we didn't see her coming because we were exhausted. Maybe we didn't sense her approach because she was still covered in mud, blending in with that whole place.

Maybe I didn't want to see her, frightened of what her presence might mean. But she was there, and she came out of nowhere. Before I knew what was happening, she had leaped onto Adam, pulled him backward onto the ground, and had her arms tight around his neck, choking him. Adam's eyes bulged out of their sunken sockets. He held tight to her forearm, the one that was choking him, but he didn't have the strength to pull it away.

25 LEAVING

WE BECAME A blur of bodies, of arms pulling and scratching, of lungs gasping for breath. Someone bit me. I grabbed hair and pulled. A rake of fingernails tore lines in the side of my face, and I yelped, turned away, kicked with both legs. Three of us, on the ground, and Adam barely fought back. Miho wasn't going to let go—she was like a python, squeezing, squeezing, even after death. The only thing I could think to do was to put her in a choke hold as well, and soon she released Adam's neck and started hitting me.

This was what I remembered about this place. This was the abyss—not the quiet passing over water or the insistence of cracking ice. But this. This fight to stay alive. This confusion. This self-preservation. This pain.

I fell away and rolled over again and again, trying to create distance between us. She heaved three loud sobs, let out a scream muffled by her own hands, and ran to the cliff wall, wedging herself into a narrow space in the rock beneath the ledge. Her body shook with cries and tears and sobs.

I glanced over at Adam. He was curled up on his stomach, twitching as if he had the hiccups. Moaning. I took a deep breath and sank onto my back, relieved that it seemed to be over if only for a few moments, staring up into the gray sky. The cold air swirled around us, but there were touches of something warmer.

What was happening to us?

I reached up and held my face, touched the cuts, then looked at my fingers and saw thin clouds of blood. I could taste it in my mouth too, perhaps from the shot I had taken to the lip. I spit it out. I searched for the knapsack, picked it up, and crawled over to Adam.

"Are you okay?" I asked.

He nodded without looking up, without moving.

Miho was ten yards away, still crying, still pulling on her short hair. This place would destroy us. I didn't know how I knew that, but I did. We had to get out.

"Miho," I called out.

Adam looked up slowly, not in fear but in resignation. He had bright red marks on his cheeks from where someone had struck him—it very well could have been me in the confusion. I didn't know. One eye was swelling. His neck was raw, and he kept rubbing it, gently clearing his throat.

"Miho," I said again.

She stilled herself and sat down, her knees pulled up to her chest, her face down. The three of us sat in that silence for a long, long time. I focused on my breathing. Adam lay back down on the ground. I stared out across the water, thinking of when my father had left me in the lake. Thinking of Adam waiting for me on the pier. Thinking of Lucia going under.

Miho's silence turned again into sobs, and her voice choked

out words in a strange rhythm. I stood on shaky feet, held the knapsack over my shoulder, and shuffled toward her.

"I can't," she said. "I can't. I can't. I can't."

I sat down wearily beside her. I didn't care anymore if she hurt me. I was too tired to care.

"Miho," I whispered, "we have to leave. We have to get out of this place."

Adam made his way over to us and sat beside me, so that all three of us were resting in the shadow of that cliff. Again I thought of the long, narrow way out. My muscles were so weary they trembled and cramped every time I tried to move. I couldn't imagine how we would ever make it up.

"I hated you for so long," Miho said.

"Me?" I asked.

She shook her head. "Him. I hated him for what he did. He killed her. My mother. She was at the store the morning the plane crashed. She was killed along with all the others you heard about. She was the sweetest, kindest woman." Miho paused. "I tortured myself for years over that, blaming myself for not taking her inside the store faster. I wished I hadn't agreed to watch the child—if we only would have gone in, she wouldn't have been there when it happened. I couldn't get the sound of it out of my head for years. Any loud sound would send a panic through me."

She took a deep breath. "I always had a hunch that I was staying in the village because I was waiting for someone. It was this idea hovering at the edge of my mind. But after the memories came back that night, I realized I was waiting for your brother. And once I realized that, once I remembered his name and all that he had done, all that he had taken from me, I hated him."

"What changed, Miho?" I asked. I was so tired.

She looked at me without any expression. "I hated him until I saw him here on the bank, and I saw you."

"If you didn't—" Adam began.

"I attacked you because I couldn't hate you anymore. That made me so angry. The thought of revenge had sustained me, but when I saw you, I knew I couldn't hate you anymore."

"Why not?" Adam asked.

"Because of love." She said this simply. Matter-of-factly. "In the village, I came to love Dan. Even though my love wasn't for you, love changed me."

I felt many things in that moment. I felt a rush of love for Miho, the old feeling that had grown between us. But I also had a sense that it was leaving, that everything that had happened was putting a small crack in the glass, and anything special we'd had between us was slowly fading away.

"What happened in the village?" I asked her. "What happened after the fire?"

"The rain came. A woman walked toward us through the embers and the ash." She looked at me as if she knew I would never believe something so ludicrous. "She said she had just come through the canyon, but I knew she was lying because she seemed fine. She didn't look tortured at all. She looked rested and, well, good, like she had been out for at least a few days. Maybe a week. She told us we should all go after you, because she saw you going into the canyon. She said you told her you were going to look for your brother, but that we should go in after you and stop you. She asked if any of us had a key."

Miho spoke in short bursts. She sounded confused by her own story, even though she had been there.

"I don't know, Dan. It was all so strange. But she was adamant. We needed to go in after you. All of us."

"I think I know her. This lady," Adam said.

We both looked at him.

"There was a woman, when the place really started to empty out. She was actually trapped in the ice all the way up to her chest. She never made a sound, but I saw her digging at the ice until her hands were bloody. Clawing at it like some kind of animal, or like a machine that couldn't feel any pain. I shouted at her a few times and told her to stop, she was hurting herself, but she didn't listen." He nodded softly to himself. "That's her. That's who you're talking about. She broke free somehow. I don't know. She found a rock or a shard of ice and picked her way out with it. She was the last person I saw down there."

I looked over at Miho. I didn't want to dwell too long on Kathy. I didn't want them to know that I had kept her in my house, sheltered her, helped her.

"And only you came?" I asked Miho, my voice timid.

"We all went up to the entrance. You know, beside the signpost. We had a long conversation about what we should do. Abe was saying that it wasn't smart for all of us to go in. Po said he wouldn't go in anyway, whether it was smart or not. Most of the others didn't seem to think they could make the trip. They were too afraid. John wanted to come with me. Lucia, the girl? She ran in before any of us could stop her. We all ended up having a terrible fight about it. I wanted to follow her in. Abe said to wait. John wasn't sure."

She paused, and I looked up. The clouds were coming down.

"That woman was there the whole time," she said, "not saying a word."

"But you came," I said.

She nodded, shrugged, as if her trek here was nothing worth mentioning. But then her eyes lit up. "Lucia was with you in the boat."

"What?" I asked.

"When you left me on the bank. Lucia was in the boat with you."

A surge of panic raced through me. Somehow I had completely forgotten that.

"I don't know what you're talking about," I said quietly, firmly.

"This place will mess with your mind," Adam whispered.

Miho looked at me, glanced away. "I could have sworn I saw her."

"It's strange you both would have seen the same thing," I admitted, trying to sound confused by their visions of a young girl. What would they do if they found out I had left her behind?

"What about everyone else?" I asked, trying to steer the conversation back. "Where did they go?"

"Everyone else went east. They said they had waited long enough. They thought Adam was probably dead, and even if he wasn't, they were ready to move on. Kathy kept saying these things that tugged at all of us, things that made it hard to walk away. But eventually they did. Then it was only her and Abe and me. As I walked into the canyon, I could see the two of them there, standing side by side."

Adam's voice sounded groggy. "What do you mean, they went east?"

"I'll explain later," I said. I couldn't imagine trying to explain one more thing to him. I closed my eyes, rubbed my temples. The scratches on my cheek were stinging, and I rubbed them gently with the very tips of my fingers.

"Are you sure you didn't see her?" Miho asked Adam.

"See who?" Adam asked.

"A girl. Lucia. She's only a teenager."

"The person you were just talking about is a girl?" Adam was suddenly alert, leaning forward so he could see Miho on the other side of me.

She nodded. "She showed up a few days before all of this happened."

Adam's voice was full of confusion. "I saw a girl when Dan came for me. She crossed the icy water and helped me to the bank. When she ran back out to the rock, I lost sight of her."

I shook my head. "I told you, Adam, it was your imagination. You were seeing all kinds of things down here. Kathy in the ice up to her chest?"

"What did she look like?" Miho interrupted me, throwing the question at Adam.

"Thin. Light brown hair. A pretty face. A soothing voice. When we were out on the rock, she told me I could do it—I had to do it. It was time for me to leave. And for some reason,

I believed her." Adam gave out a half laugh, disbelieving. "So I did."

"What's going on, Dan?" Miho asked, turning to me.

"I have no idea," I said emphatically before sighing. "Anyway, Lucia couldn't speak, remember?"

This seemed to turn the tide of Miho's belief. "True," she said.

"We have to get out of here," I continued. "We shouldn't be waiting here. When you stop moving in this place, it's so hard to get started again."

"Dan," she asked, doubt in her voice, "did you see Lucia?"

"No." My jaw clenched. My heart raced.

Silence. They both stared at me.

"We have to go," I said. "Can't you feel this place? It's coming for us. Something here is coming for us."

That part I was not making up. They could sense it too. I stood up, walked over to the ledge, and started inching my way up, pressed along the wall. Enough. I would leave, even if that meant leaving alone.

"C'mon, Adam," I said. "You next. Stay close."

When he started up the ledge behind me, he was so shaky I couldn't imagine him ever making it all the way to the top. But with one sliding step in front of the other, up we went.

I looked at Miho now fifteen feet below me. "C'mon, Miho," I said, trying to speak in a steady voice. "We have to go."

She sighed, stared back over the bog. The clouds were so low now that my head was nearly in them. I thought that was probably helpful—none of us would have to worry about a fear of heights if we could barely see down past our feet.

Miho walked over to the ledge and started up behind Adam. Our backs were to the cliff wall. She took a few sliding steps up, stopped, and held her face in her hands. She cried again, softly, and I thought I knew why: she knew I was lying. She knew we were leaving Lucia behind. But she didn't have the strength to go back and find her.

26 UP

WE INCHED OUR way up the ledge, small pebbles falling in front of us and disappearing into the fog. Soon we were so high up we couldn't hear them hit the ground. Every so often I stopped and waited for Adam and Miho to catch up—Miho always looked calm, sometimes closing her eyes, taking centering breaths. But Adam grew less steady the higher we went. His legs trembled from exhaustion and fear.

I thought about the view we would have if it wasn't for this impenetrable cloud we were climbing through. The short, dusty space between the cliff and the bog. The long brown water that Lucia and I had crossed together, and the thread of a canyon that led to the final, frozen river and the island of rock where Adam had knelt. Could we see it all from here if the clouds cleared?

I doubted it. There was something about this place that seemed to operate outside of reality, as if the journey into the abyss was actually taking place inside of me, in a place you couldn't see from far away. I thought that if the clouds cleared, we would probably see a long emptiness, a dreary landscape, and maybe a small brown puddle.

But the clouds never cleared. Adam constantly wiped his hands on his torn pants. He licked his dry lips quickly, like a reptile. I could count the ribs in his side. He looked up the ledge at me, his eyes wild, before looking at Miho. Sometimes the mist was so thick I couldn't even see her.

There was a particularly narrow section of the ledge, and after I shuffled my way through it, I waited to make sure Adam would be okay. He came sliding along, his feet scraping the stone, and small bits of dust and tiny pebbles bounded off the edge. At the space where the ledge was less than the length of his feet, he balked. Trembled. Swayed out but somehow caught his balance by bracing himself against the cliff face.

He froze.

"Adam!" I moved back down toward him, but the change in direction threw me off for a moment, and I nearly fell. "Miho!"

She came up, a calm look on her face. "You're fine, Adam." Her voice sounded like a gentle breeze moving through the mist.

"I can't," Adam said, the words coming in short bursts, his lips pursed. "I can't."

She reached up and took his hand. He looked so shocked by her touch that it nearly sent him over. "We can do this together."

If she wanted to kill him, I thought, this was when it would happen.

But she didn't. She spoke quiet words to him, so smooth and low I couldn't hear them, the way a trainer speaks to a spooked racehorse. He nodded, seemed to find himself, and shuffled one side step, another side step.

"Take his other hand," she told me.

I hesitated, because if he fell, I didn't want him dragging me over the edge with him. But I thought of all those years, all that time I spent waiting for him in that stone house. This was my brother, my long-lost brother, and if I returned without him, what was the point?

I took his hand, and his fingers felt the same as mine. I had the strangest feeling, almost like vertigo, that he was me, that it wasn't him we were leading out of the abyss, but me. I took my eyes off the ledge and looked over at him as we moved along, and I wondered why I wasn't happier in that moment. I had waited so long for him. And now we were leaving, escaping the abyss, both of us alive. But I couldn't shake this deep sadness, so heavy it nearly pulled me off the ledge. It turned every breath into a sigh, every thought into a spiral.

Miho held his other hand. Our eyes met, and it felt like the first time we had really seen each other in that place. She was sad, I could see that, and disappointed. I couldn't help but feel that it was there on the narrow ledge that all of my lies finally ended whatever it was we had been so close to having.

That was how we made our way along the narrow ledge, sliding up until we reached the place where the path widened. We fell to the ground with exhaustion and relief, sitting side by side once again, our backs to the cliff. I reached into the knapsack and took out the water container. It was nearly empty. I handed it first to Miho, and she took a small sip, the tiniest of draws. She licked her lips, trying to spread the moisture around, and handed it to Adam. He took a large gulp, and I could see his throat lurching. I closed my eyes and imagined the coolness of the water, the smoothness of it running over my tongue, silk on the sides of my throat.

Adam handed it to me, but I knew before raising it to my mouth that it was gone. I sighed and pretended to drink, because I didn't want Miho feeling sorry for me. But nothing came out, not even a trickle. I held it up for an extra moment, then put it slowly back into the knapsack. I glanced over at Adam. The smallest drop rolled down from the corner of his mouth, but I could not tell if it was water, sweat, or the buildup of moisture in the air. It was now on his skin, drifting down. It was like a globe, like a small world to me. He reached up and wiped it away.

Without saying a word, we stood and trudged upward, the abyss now to our right, the clouds thinning as we climbed, until all at once we were in clear air again. Clearer air than I had seen at any point inside the mountain. I could nearly see to the far side of the round abyss. Once again, the clouds filled the abyss like drifts of snow.

A realization snapped into my mind like lightning. "Miho," I asked, "are they waiting for us?"

"Who?" she said, her voice cracking. I didn't think it was from lack of water.

"The rest of the group. Abe. Kathy."

"Why would they wait?"

"You said the rest of them went east, but do you believe that? Or are they waiting for Adam?"

"Why would they wait for Adam?"

I stopped walking and turned on her. "Can't you answer a simple question?" I demanded. "Why do you keep asking me questions in return? Are they waiting for Adam? For revenge?"

She shook her head, but her words were less assuring. "Maybe, Dan. I don't know. They said they were leaving."

"But they wouldn't have gone far unless they forgave him. They wouldn't have left the town behind unless they were free of that."

Adam glanced back and forth between us. We were talking about him as if he wasn't there. "It's okay," he said in something like a whisper. "It's okay. I'm getting out—that's all that matters. I remember now. Remember it all. What can they do to me that's worse than this place?"

Miho and I stared at each other for quite some time, as if we were feeling each other out again, trying to decipher where each of us stood, whose side we were on, and who we should be concerned about. But Adam seemed genuinely unaffected by the conversation.

Up we went, up and up and up, and finally there was the top, way ahead of us on the curving path, up above us like the lid of an eye. The roaring of the river became audible in the still air, a kind of fearful rumbling. I had tried not to think about how we would cross.

Once we scaled the path and stood at the top of the great abyss, we all looked down over the ledge, the clouds far below us, nearly invisible in the shadows. Lucia came to mind, little Lucia with her soft face and quiet eyes. I had to turn away.

We followed Miho toward the Acheron. She walked straight to the river, made a sharp right at the bank, and kept moving. Up ahead, I saw Karon's boat.

"How?" I began, not knowing what else to say.

"I found this boat on the far side when I came in after you," she said, shrugging.

"Did you see Karon?" I asked.

"Who?"

"The man who belongs to the boat. Or the woman who was with him?"

"I didn't see anyone," she said. "Help me turn it around."

The three of us grabbed the smooth wooden sides, and in our weakness it took a great effort to drag it, turn it, hold it. There was Karon's one small oar, the bench where I had sat at the front, the bottom of the boat where I had passed out. Across the river, above the foaming white rapids, I could see the far bank, the trees.

"Didn't you go to the house?" I asked Miho.

She shook her head. "There was no way I was going in there. Are you kidding?"

"Sarah lived there," I said quietly.

"What?"

"Nothing," I said. "Nothing."

As usual, Adam watched us, his eyes taking us in, his long black hair swaying like a pendulum.

I felt a sort of numbness as we climbed into the boat. I imagined it was the same feeling someone might have before they take their own life, knowing the end of all things is only moments away. I couldn't see us surviving this river.

We all shifted our weight together as best we could, and the boat lurched once, twice, three times, four times. Finally we were in deep enough to drift, and already the current yanked us downstream. Adam and I sat in the front and Miho perched in the back, small yet strong with the oar, thrusting it in and pulling, pulling, pulling against the current.

The white water was rough and choppy. I noticed then— and it seemed a strange time to see such small things—that the wood of the boat was smooth, and the metal sheath that held the bow together was burnished from so many cross-ings, bearing dents and scrapes from collisions with rock. The bottom of the boat was slick with a kind of black-green algae, like moss, and slippery as ice.

On the far side, in the direction Miho fought to take us, I thought I saw Kathy waiting.

I stood to get a better look. I slipped, striking my head again, and darkness took me under.

27 FORGIVENESS

MY EYES OPENED, and everything was silent. I was in an uncomfortable bed in a drab room, staring up at a yellowing ceiling. The only light came in from a window along the wall behind me and a bit to the left, and through it fell tan, dusty rays. My vision went blurry and I blinked to correct it, and with that blink a searing pain radiated from the side of my head, down and out my arm. A few realizations settled on me like birds returning to a wire after being frightened off.

I was in Sarah and Karon's house.

I was in Sarah and Karon's house alone.

Miho and Adam had left me.

I deserved it.

I was hot, so hot, and I pushed the blankets down off my fevered body, but as soon as I did, I realized how cold it was in the room. How had I not noticed this before, not seen my breath rising like the clouds in the abyss? My body trembled, and I pulled the covers back up. The cold had followed us all the way from the icy lake, the stone island, and had caught up to me here.

I felt an absurd relief at my pain, my loneliness, my confusion, because finally this place inside the mountain had become what I always remembered it to be: a place of horror, of ongoing dread and sickness and lack. I was somehow relieved to know I hadn't made up that part in my mind. This was a horrible place, and I was back in it, and I would never be able to leave.

Lucia walked into the room, her skin a whitish blue. "It's your fault," she said. "It always has been. Your brother. The accident. Me falling in. It's your fault."

I knew it wasn't her. I knew it was a vision handed to me by the mountain, but I still wept and trembled. I pulled the covers up over my face before plunging into a feverish sleep.

I WOKE AGAIN, and this time it was dark except for a weak, trembling light that came in through the doorway. A candle? A fire? I no longer cared. The pain in my head was a constant companion, a worm working its way deeper into my mind. I scratched at my scalp to try to find it, dig it out. I scratched until I bled.

I heard the sound of footsteps on the creaking floor, and I went from a state of fevered numbness to sharp fear. Who was coming for me? Was it Lucia again, to torment me? A shadow stretched across the dim light, a firm shadow of utter blackness, and fear eclipsed the pain.

Kathy.

I knew it. She would pick me up and carry me to the boat, throw me into the abyss, drag me through the gate, and lock it with the key I had in the knapsack.

The key! What had happened to the key! I groaned in despair. She came across the room, lifted her hand, and again everything went black.

I STOOD FROM the bed and walked outside, walked through the cold, and there among the trees was the large building my brother and I had used for our airplane hangar. *Where is the runway?* I kept thinking. *Where did all of these trees come from?*

I walked through the oversized garage door into the barn where we parked the plane, and there was a bright light in the back corner over the door that led to the room where my brother used to sleep. I stopped outside the room, my hand on the knob, frightened of what I might find.

The door eased open silently, and I looked inside. He was there, passed out. His eyes opened. He tried to talk, but his tongue slurred all the words. He stopped, shook his head, and tried again.

"I cannnn't do it todaaaaaay. Not nowwwww. Leave meeeeee alonnnne."

But I picked him up, surprising myself. Wasn't I sick? Wasn't I weak? I carried him to the plane and stuffed him in, not finding the sudden appearance of the plane remarkable in the least. His arms and legs were limp and refused to comply.

"You have to!" I screamed. "You don't have a choice!"

Then the plane was taking off, and I realized what I had done. I chased it through the trees, but he was gone, flying away, disappearing into the sky.

I OPENED MY eyes, wincing at the light that came through the window. It wasn't exactly bright, but my eyes weren't used to it. I blinked again and again.

I heard someone pushing a chair in under the table in the dining room, and the sound had a particular quality of realness to it, the untidy feel of concrete reality. This was not a dream. I was still in Sarah and Karon's house, but I was not alone.

I sat up slowly, trying to remain silent, but the bed creaked slightly. I froze. I didn't think the sound was loud enough to alert whoever was in the kitchen, but I waited to see. As I came up from under the blanket, I realized just how cold the air was. I looked over at the window to see if I could open it, if it was low enough for me to crawl through. I would make my getaway, escape before my captor knew what had happened.

I became convinced that Miho and Adam had left me behind, which was no surprise after my never-ending lies and refusal to own up to what I had done. Kathy had come back. I was sure of it. In a strange reversal of roles, she was in the kitchen and I was in the bed; she would tend to me while I recovered, as I had tended to her. But I didn't want to see her again.

The cold air would have been refreshing if it wasn't so dusty, and when I pushed the blanket down off my legs, it was the cold that woke me completely. The pain in my head still throbbed. My fingers explored sensitive, deep cuts from where I had scratched too hard in my dreams, trying to get to the pain in the middle of my head. The gashes down my cheek from when we had fought with Miho were dried out, but they burned when I touched them.

I moved my legs around and gingerly put my feet on the floor beside the bed. I waited again. The person in the kitchen took a few more steps, the floor giving them away, but the sound moved to the front door. I heard it open. I heard them go out onto the front porch. I tried to stand, but my legs turned to jelly and gave out under me. A rush of blood to the head and I fell to my knees. I felt disoriented and dizzy. I hoped I hadn't made too much noise, but I heard footsteps coming quickly through the house.

Tears filled my eyes, but I didn't know why—desperation? regret? sadness?—and I tried to claw my way up, pulling on the windowsill. But my arms were hopelessly weak, and I fell to the dusty floor again. Sobs wracked my body. The footsteps stopped inside the bedroom door. I didn't even want to look. But I did.

Miho stood there with Adam. They stared at me, and I didn't know what to think or what they were thinking or why they had stayed behind.

"Why are you here?" I asked quietly.

"You're hurt," Adam said.

"We couldn't leave you behind, but we're too weak to carry you," Miho explained. "We tried."

"You wouldn't be here if you knew me, if you knew what I did," I said, not daring to look at them any longer.

"We know," Miho whispered.

"No, you don't," I said.

"We do," Adam said. "You practically told us your life

history while you were sleeping. Your dreams, your night-mares, you talked about it all."

Shame dropped me farther to the floor, if that was even possible. They knew it had all been my fault from the beginning.

"Lucia?" I asked, staring hard at the floor.

"We know," Miho whispered again.

"So why didn't you leave?" I asked, my voice barely strong enough to muster the words. "You should have left me."

"We love you," Miho said.

"We forgive you," Adam said.

A harsh wind kicked up and blew the front door open, and a bitter cold raced in around us.

We forgive you. Those words soaked into me like sunshine. *We forgive you.* Had those words ever been uttered in this place, in this mountain? I didn't know how to respond. I didn't want to believe it could be true, but I was too weak to run away from it. I wondered if that was the only gift this place could offer—a weakness so intense that you simply could not do anything on your own. You could not flee when penance was paid on your behalf.

"Did you see Sarah or Karon?"

"Who?" Adam asked.

"They lived here before. This is their house."

Miho shook her head. "We haven't seen anyone."

WE WAITED IN that house for a long time, trying to recover enough strength to go on. Days. Maybe weeks, I don't know.

We used Sarah and Karon's meager stores of food and water. Inside the mountain, it was often hard to tell if night had come or if clouds had simply shadowed the canyon, choking out the light. At other times, night seemed to stretch on endlessly, and the three of us would sit at the kitchen table, quiet, staring intently at the dark windows, feeling a nameless fear.

Sometimes, when the light came around, we sat on the front porch. I always stared in the direction of the Acheron, silently pleading for Lucia to come across. I hadn't gone down to the riverbank, so I assumed the boat was still on the near side, which meant she had little chance of coming across. Still, I wished I would see her small form coming through the trees.

While we sat on the porch one afternoon and the light faded and the ominous shadows of the trees gave way to a broader darkness, Miho looked over at me. She was sitting on the other chair. Adam stood at the corner of the house, leaning against the wood siding. I thought I could sense something between them, something new and growing, a green sprout pushing up from under a small stone. It made me feel unsettled, and happy, and jealous, and sad.

"I think we're ready to leave," she said, and she did pretty well at keeping any semblance of a question from her voice. But it was still there. I knew it. They wondered if I felt ready.

I nodded slowly, cleared my throat, decided not to say anything.

"So, in the morning?" Adam asked, and there was a childlike eagerness under the surface of his voice. I could understand that. He had been here in the mountain for a long, long time. I couldn't wait for him to see the land opening up in front of us, the plains stretching out as far as he could see, the green space alive and warm and calm.

"It's colder," I said, hugging my arms to my chest.

"That's another reason we should go," Miho said.

"And Lucia?" I asked, barely able to say her name.

"We'll talk to Abe," Miho said in a determined voice, as if she had already argued this point many times with Adam. "Abe will know what to do."

I sighed, a kind of quiet acquiescence. I was ready. Truth is, I had been ready for some time, but I found it hard to leave Lucia behind. I thought for a second of going back, of boarding the boat and crossing the Acheron again, making my way down the path, down the narrow ledge through the clouds, to the bog, across, through the canyon, through the gate, to the frozen lake. But I didn't even know if she'd be there, if she had somehow managed to survive. The thought of the journey, or perhaps the memory of her—I couldn't tell which—brought tears to my eyes. And I couldn't have done it anyway. I was too weak.

I stood and limped back into the house, into the bedroom, and crawled under the covers. They had seemed much too thin recently, the cold reaching under them. The cold was growing. It felt like it was spilling up and out of the abyss.

When I woke up and walked into the kitchen, the small bucket of water we had kept in the corner was frozen. Miho and Adam stood on the front porch, clapping their hands together and blowing into them for warmth. We were clothed in leftover garments we had found in the house, Karon and

Sarah's final gifts to us. We looked at each other and no one said a word, but Miho led the way off the porch, into the trees, and toward the narrow canyon that led to the village and the plains.

As we walked, it started to snow.

28 THE CROSSING

I WISH I could tell you about the look on Adam's face when we walked through that canyon and came out into the great wide open, how awestruck and happy he was, how he fell to the ground weeping and smelling the grass, feeling the sunshine. I wish I could tell you how he hugged Miho and me, how he started healing immediately, and how we sat out back just like the old days and looked out over the plains.

I wish.

Truth is, when we got to the opening that led into the plains, right beside the wooden signpost, I wasn't even looking at Adam. I was looking out into that wide-open space, and I felt nothing apart from shock, confusion, and sadness.

Because there was nothing to see except snow.

But it was beautiful. Yes. The landscape was pristine, the snowflakes fell heavy and thick, and before we knew it, our hair and shoulders had a fine layer of white gracing them. Glaring white for as far as we could see, completely covering the tall green grass.

"Is this it?" Adam asked.

Miho and I didn't say a word. The village itself didn't look any more welcoming. Most of it was blackened, charred from the fire, and the snow only served as a greater contrast against that burned wreckage.

"What happened?" Miho whispered as I walked out in front of them. Somehow the snow had been light in the canyon, but once I stepped out into the greenway, it was ankle deep at its most shallow points. Some of the drifts reached my knees. I pushed through it, the cold wetness soaking into my pants, leaking down inside the shoes I had taken from Karon's room. It had drifted up against my door, and when I opened it, some fell inside the house and began melting on the wooden floor.

That reminded me of when Kathy had first arrived, how she had let in the rain, collapsed inside the door, and lay there in the puddle.

Miho and Adam came in behind me, and after I pushed the door closed, everything went silent. The three of us stood there without moving, looking around. The white snow glared its light in through the back doors, but the rest of the house was dim and gray. I held my breath, waiting for Kathy to emerge from the bedroom, but after waiting a few moments and realizing everything was deathly still, it was clear no one had been in the house for a long time.

"Is this it?" Adam asked again. "Is this the village where you live?"

"It's not usually like this," I said.

"It's never snowed before," Miho said, as if explaining away some small defect.

"It's never been this cold before," I added.

We searched the house for anything we could burn, and soon a blaze glowed in the fireplace, crackling legs of wooden chairs and smoldering pieces of the oak bed frame and hissing smoke from the spines and pages of books. That hurt me the most, nearly caused a physical pain—when Miho pulled the books from the shelves and tossed them into the fire, splayed open, pages moving. But we were cold and tired, and long after the other two had fallen asleep on blankets on the floor in front of the fire, I watched the paper blacken and curl. I stabbed at the books, pried them open with the metal poker, so that the pages would burn completely. Even then, I could see that some of the words would survive.

Long after dark, I heard a knock on the door. At first I wondered if Adam or Miho had gone outside. But they were sleeping, and neither moved at the knock. Was it Abe? Or one of the others, come back to have their revenge on Adam? I walked to the door and stood there for a full ten seconds before reaching down and taking the knob, turning it, opening the door.

Kathy.

We stared at each other as she stood in the snowdrift, light from the dying fire flickering on her face, her back to the mountain and the nighttime shadows. I felt gaunt and stretched, filthy, worn down. I felt like she must have felt when I had first seen her.

"Hi," I said in a tired voice. My knees were suddenly weak.

"Dan," she said, compassion in her voice. She looked like she might cry. "You're back."

She filled me with competing desires. I wanted to slam the door in her face. I wanted to embrace her. I wanted to care for her. I wanted her to care for me.

"What happened?" I asked. I couldn't help it—accusation slipped into my voice.

Her dark eyes hardened like water freezing in fast motion. "Whatever do you mean?" she asked, her voice barely louder than the wind that swept the snow into the house. I could hear it, the icy rasping of the snow scraping along the floor. The cold breeze rustled the fire, fanning it.

"All of this happened after you arrived," I said, but the accusation had taken a backseat to genuine confusion. "The fire. Me going into the mountain. The chaos." I paused. "The snow. Everything fell apart."

She gave a mocking grin. "You think I caused the snow?" Her voice was the one used to speak to older children about nighttime monsters and fantastical creatures.

I stared at her. Yes, actually, I did. I did think she had brought the snow. "You started the fire. I know that."

Her mouth hardened. She blinked once. Twice. Her piercing eyes took me in, devoured me. "I know what you did," she said. "I know who you left behind."

My face flushed with shame.

"You should rest here, recover your strength, and go back in. Find her." Her voice was very convincing.

"I can't," I said.

"You left a small girl in the abyss. Think about it. What chance does she have?" She turned and walked through the snow as if it was warm water, as if her body was nothing more than a mechanical shell made to transport her mind through any condition. I walked out into the snow and watched as she vanished into the darkness, down the hill, in among the burned buildings.

A voice called to me from the house. I turned in a daze. "Dan!" the voice shouted again. "What are you doing?"

I walked slowly back through the snow, feeling as helpless as I ever had. At the end of me. We could not stay here, that was clear. I did not have the strength to go back and retrieve Lucia. But without her, I didn't think I could go east.

I came to the door of my house and walked past Miho, her confused, beautiful face. She leaned aside to make room for me to go through. "Dan, what were you doing out there?"

I sat down in front of the dying fire. I threw in another book. And another. And another. "I thought I heard someone," I said.

IN THE MORNING, we stood by the back doors and took in the plains. Because the sky was a glaring white, it was almost impossible to distinguish the horizon. The entire world was a white space, empty and never-ending. The first tree outside of town, off in the distance, was black against the white backdrop.

"We have to go east," Miho said, and neither of us replied. We stared out at the snow.

In the stillness, I heard the sounds of someone approaching the front door through the snow, pounding their hands together, kicking through the drifts. I didn't think I had the mental fortitude to argue with Kathy one more time. If she insisted I go back, I would. I would take a flask of water and whatever food I could find in the burned houses, and I would return. I knew I would die there, either drowning in the river or falling from the ledge or starving. But if it was her, I knew I would go back.

Adam and Miho looked at me as the sound of knocking echoed in the quiet house. I wondered why one of them didn't go answer the door, but I was also afraid of what Kathy might do to them, what she might say to them, so I took on the mantle of their expectations and crossed the room. It was my house, after all.

I opened the door.

It was Abe. His arms opened wide, and I fell into them, weeping.

ABE SAT IN the armchair. Miho sat on the floor beside him, closer to the fireplace. Every so often, she leaned over and plucked a book from the shelf and threw it in. It hurt a little, how easily she did this.

Adam sat across from them, his back to the fire, facing the back doors, staring out over the plains as if it was the most beautiful thing he had ever seen. Even when he spoke, he barely shifted his body.

And I sat wrapped in a blanket, my back against the wall across from the fireplace. My gaze went from Abe to Miho to Adam to the fire and back again to Abe. He was the only one who made eye contact with me. When Miho's gaze met mine, it flitted away like a doe into the undergrowth. Adam refused to look at me. They had forgiven me in the canyon, but here, where our trip east became real, where we would turn our backs on the mountain and Lucia for the final time, the reality of what I had done was hard to forget.

When Abe first arrived, we'd greeted him and said a few pleasantries. We'd settled into our current spots. And then we'd said nothing. Where were we supposed to begin?

"How did we end up here, Abe?" I asked quietly.

"Here?" he asked.

"This place. The mountain. This village. What is this? How is it connected to the memories of these lives we lived so long ago?"

His face was almost expressionless. "I think you already know."

"Maybe, but I want to hear it from you."

He seemed to be considering his options, and he started nodding before he even spoke. "Yes, you know. I think you all do, if you're honest with yourselves."

Miho held her hand up over her face, tears rising to her eyes.

"The memories you have," Abe said in a kind, hesitant voice, "are from a life you lived before you died."

"So this . . ." Adam began, his voice trailing off.

"This is all in a time and place after life," Abe said.

"We're dead?" Miho's words came out with a kind of dread. But Abe's smile warmed us.

"Do you feel dead?" he asked.

Miho shook her head.

"That's because you died, but you're not dead. You're here. You came through the mountain. You lived in this town for a long, long time. And now you have to decide what to do next."

I knew that Abe was talking to all of us. I had died. This was not a surprise to me. In some ways, him saying that out loud felt like the final piece in a puzzle that I had been able to see for quite some time. But even though Abe wasn't delivering a revelation, we still sat there in silence for a long time, trying to connect everything.

Finally, Miho broke the silence. "What now, Abe?" She sounded like a lost child.

"There's not much food," Abe cautioned. "The others took most of what they could find with them for the journey. I hope they made it out in front of this snow." His voice faded, and I imagined our friends forging through knee-high drifts, collapsing in the cold. How could Miss B ever make it through this?

"So, we can't stay," Miho said in a matter-of-fact voice.

"Why would anyone stay here?" Adam asked.

"You should have seen it." My voice erupted almost without my permission. "You should have seen this place when times were good." I stared into the fire. "I could hear the laughter from up here. Everyone down in the village on a cool night, the fire roaring. Sometimes there was singing." I looked over at Adam. "Sometimes there was singing," I said, as if that alone would be enough. My voice sank down into a whisper. "You might as well know it all now. There's no reason to keep it from you. You already know I left Lucia behind, not that I could have done anything, but I lied to you about it and I accept responsibility. But there are other things too."

I felt Miho stare at me in that moment, and it felt like everyone was holding their breath.

"I knew Kathy was here. I welcomed her into my house when she came from the other side." I waited for admonishment, yet there was nothing but kindness in Abe's eyes. "I don't know why I didn't tell you all about her. I thought I was doing something good. At least in the beginning."

This time Miho didn't look away.

"She kissed me." I shook my head. There were so many things I wanted to say, and all the words were getting clogged up in a drain too narrow to accommodate the flow. "But that's not even the worst of it." I laughed, as if the extent of my false life was ludicrous. And it was. It suddenly seemed almost comical to me. "The worst is that the plane crash wasn't even Adam's fault."

Now they all looked surprised. Even Abe.

"It's true!" My voice started sounding maniacal, even to me. "It's true. Adam wasn't fit to fly that plane. He was drunk. Do you remember that, Adam? You were a raging alcoholic."

He nodded. "Yeah," he said, but he didn't seem ashamed. That made me even more jealous, and I felt like I was losing myself, like my sanity was tethered to me by a thin string and the tension was building, and if the string snapped, all would be lost. "I do remember that," he said.

"Well, I found you that morning, and I forced you to fly. I laid it on thick—we'd go under, we'd be broke, you had to do it. And so you did. If I hadn't walked you to that plane, you never would have flown, and no one would have died."

I looked between the three of them, my heart racing, my eyes bulging. I stared at everyone again. "So. That's it. Everything—Lucia, Kathy, the crash. It's all my fault."

We sat there in the silence that rushed in after my out-

SHAWN SMUCKER

burst. The fire died down, and I willed Miho not to throw any more books in it, and for some reason she didn't. She was staring into the glowing embers, somewhere far away. Adam had stood and walked over to the doors, standing so close to them I thought he was going to pull them open and go blundering into the snow. Only Abe returned my gaze. He said something under his breath, to me or to himself, I couldn't tell. But the shape of his words seemed to say, "Well done."

He sighed. "All of this is in the past. I'm glad you've said what you've said, Dan. There is nowhere to go now but forward. In this moment." He waited to see if Miho or Adam would say anything. When they didn't, he continued. "It seems to me," he said in a humble voice, as if he was completely open to disagreement, "that the most important question is the one Miho asked a moment ago. Namely, what now?"

Miho shook her head, still staring into the fire.

"I'm just along for the ride," Adam said.

"Our options have not changed much." Abe smiled. "They are, in many ways, what they have always been. We can stay. We can go back into the mountain, this time to find Lucia. Or we can go east."

"We?" Adam asked.

Abe shrugged. "I think, at this point, the best thing we can do is stick together."

I weighed the options. I could try to go back and get Lucia, but that seemed impossible. I had used up everything I had to get Adam. I had nothing left. Going east felt equally as difficult, and I didn't know the path or what was at the end of it. Staying seemed the easiest thing to do yet the least feasible.

"How far can we get without food?" Miho asked, and I assumed she meant east.

"I didn't say we are entirely without food," Abe said.

"I'm not going back in the mountain," Adam said, and there was a lining of panic in his voice. "I wish I could. I wish I could go back for the girl. But I don't have it in me." His words came out in short thrusts.

Miho shook her head sympathetically.

"Honestly?" I said. "I don't think I could do it either."

"So we just leave her over there?" Miho asked.

"She fell into the river," I replied. "Under the ice."

"So we just leave her over there?" Miho repeated, her voice swelling.

Our words at a deadlock, we looked to Abe.

"This is what I think," he said gently, shifting his tone. "This is what I would like to see. I would like the four of us to rest here today, tonight, maybe one more day, until you're ready. Then I'd like to pack up the food we have and any supplies that might be helpful, and head east."

Miho started speaking again but, uncharacteristically, Abe held up his hand to stop her. "I will bear responsibility for Lucia. I will make sure that anything that can be done will be done."

"What's that supposed to mean?" Miho said, and it was the harshest tone I'd ever heard her use with Abe.

He looked her full in the face, and there was nothing but love in his eyes. He said it again, this time somehow both quieter and firmer. "I will bear responsibility for Lucia."

I started to speak, to say that wasn't fair, that Lucia's fate was my responsibility. I wanted to argue with him, to

302

tell him they should all go on while I went back for her. But I didn't have the strength. I had to let him assume that burden, and I had to admit, it was a relief. When he said those words, it was the closest I'd felt to free in a long, long time.

Miho stood up and paced back and forth. She stopped beside Adam and put her hand on his shoulder. "Abe's right," she admitted.

Was she talking to Adam? To me? To all of us? I couldn't tell. But in that moment, it was decided. The air in the house held still. Outside, the wind stopped and the snow on the plains glittered. I felt an aching sense of relief now that the burden of those lies had been scattered.

We would go east.

I DON'T KNOW who decided that we should keep track of how many trees we passed, but at some point between the fourth and fifth tree, it was decided that I should use the charred end of a piece of kindling and mark one tally inside the front cover of the only book I had brought with me. I had pulled it from the shelves before we left and looked at Miho. "Not for firewood," I had said, not even knowing what was behind my need to say it. Was it to make her feel guilty for all the volumes she had burned? Was it an attempt at humor? Whatever the case, she had given me a sad smile as I nestled the book in the knapsack that Sarah and Karon had given me.

Would I find them again sometime in the east? Or had

they vanished into some in-between place in the canyon or here on the plains?

I took the book out, clumsily held the crooked stick with the black end, and marked five long straight lines on the page inside the hardback book. I blew the black dust away and stared at those five lines for an extra moment before putting everything back in the knapsack and following Abe, Adam, and Miho. Their forms were almost indiscernible, wrapped as they were in the bulky garments of other people's clothes, so many layers that their appendages were unnaturally short and plump compared to the hulk of their wrapped bodies. We were like astronauts.

They forged ahead in the snow, and already it had become shallower the farther we walked from the remains of our village. I did not hurry to catch up, content to place my feet where theirs had gone and watch from a distance.

At every tree, we changed out the leader, and it was slow going. At the sixth tree, I made the mark in the book and then took the lead for the second time. On the first day, we only made it to tree number nine, but we hadn't left until well after dawn, and we stopped while the light was still bright in the gray-white sky.

We hollowed out a place in the snow, piling it up around us as a shelter from the wind that occasionally rose. There were plenty of fallen limbs under each tree we had passed now that we were so far from town, though they were covered in snow and challenging to light. But with enough care and attention, we were able to start an anemic, smoking fire. We huddled close.

Miho seemed to be further inside of herself than usual.

Adam, on the other hand, was coming alive, gaining health, and eager to help in any way that required movement or action. Abe seemed always to have a small smile on his face, as if he had finally received a long-sought-after gift.

I felt like a clumsy butterfly only recently emerged from my chrysalis. Wings still bent and folded over. Walking with uncertainty and a kind of vague knowledge that there was another way. Confession had broken me free, but navigating the pain I had caused was no easy thing. And I sensed that whatever had existed between Miho and me could not be recovered.

Although we were all close together, she seemed to always lean toward Adam. I felt a peace with this. It seemed a deserved, almost welcome penance for the lies I had hidden behind. I wanted to pay for what I had done. This seemed fair enough.

"Any guesses on how many trees until the next mountain?" Adam asked as we huddled together in the dark.

"One hundred and seventy-nine," Miho said, and we all grinned. Adam groaned.

"Did Lucia ever say how many?" I asked. As soon as I said her name, I could feel a heaviness descend on the group, and I wished I could retrieve those words and put them away.

"No," Abe replied.

After a long period of silence, Adam ventured again. "Any other guesses? Closest one wins the prize."

"I'll take two hundred," Abe said. The fire grew in the midst of us, bringing with it a sense of home and comfort even though we were surrounded by snow and the dying evening light.

"Two hundred and one," I said, and Miho burst out a kind of one-syllable laugh, punching me in the shoulder.

We sat there for so long, leaning against one another, that I thought everyone but me had fallen asleep. But then I heard Miho whisper, "What's the prize?"

No one answered. The cloudy shape of her words rose along with smoke from the dying fire. I reached into my knapsack, took out the book with the marks in it, and threw it onto the embers.

WE STARTED PASSING other villages at about the thirtieth tree, which I found interesting. It meant people had left our village beside the mountain and, after walking for some time, decided to stop and create a new life in the plains. But every village was empty, and we found few supplies to gather up and take along with us.

A few weeks later, our habit hadn't changed. Wake with the light. Eat a small amount of our food, the supply dwindling. Walk east, changing leaders as we passed each tree, although since the shallow snow no longer required forging a path through drifts, the shift changes were mostly unnecessary and done out of habit. I no longer counted the trees.

Abe was in the lead, moving ahead at his slow but steady pace, when he stopped. We nearly bumped into each other, so unaccustomed were we to stopping between trees.

"What?" Miho asked.

The snow was not deep, only a few inches, and the air was warmer. I had shed a few layers that morning before leaving the last tree, laying my clothes at the base of it like an offering.

"Look," Abe said, and we peered around him, shading our eyes from the glare coming off the grass.

There was a large crowd of people walking toward us, coming from the next tree—coming from the east.

29 THE OTHER MOUNTAIN

"HOWDY, FRIENDS," ABE said as the group stopped a few yards away from us.

The leader was a man with a short beard, small eyes, and a mouth that wore a frown as its neutral position. He grunted some kind of a response.

"Where're you headed?" Abe asked in a nonchalant voice.

"Back," the man said, curiosity and skepticism making his tiny eyes even beadier.

"Huh," Abe said, as if the man's response concerned him but he didn't want to say why. "Mind if I ask where you're coming from?"

"The east."

"I can see that," Abe said, nearly letting out a chuckle.

"The mountain in the east," the man replied. I could tell by the tone of his voice he didn't enjoy being laughed at. But if his first response had amused Abe, his second answer brought the seriousness back.

"The mountain?" Abe asked, now in earnest. "The far mountain?"

The man nodded, looking satisfied that he had finally said something that apparently wouldn't be mocked.

"So, it's there." Miho let her words out in a quiet wave of

relief. Adam leaned closer to her, and she whispered something to him before speaking to the newcomers. "How far?"

"Maybe twenty trees," the man said. "Maybe less."

We were so close. I could feel the weight lift from my shoulders, but almost immediately it returned. Why were these people leaving the far mountain? It was supposed to be a good destination.

Abe was thinking along the same lines. "What's waiting for you in the west that you would go back?"

The man hesitated, seemed unsure of himself, or perhaps didn't know if he wanted to answer. "Nothing special about the east," he mumbled.

"Nothing special?" Abe said, not trying to hide his disbelief. "Did you even go up the mountain?"

The man shrugged. It was clear he had not. A few of the people behind him sat down on the wet ground. I was ready to do the same, wondering how long Abe and this man would keep talking.

Abe took a few steps toward the man and held out his hand. "Abe," he said. "You?"

The man paused. "Jed."

"Jed," Abe echoed. "Jed. Forgive me if I keep coming back to this. I just find it hard to believe someone would walk all the way to the mountain in the east and then turn around."

"She told us the truth," a voice shouted from the back of the pack.

"She?" Abe asked, his eyes narrowing.

"Black-haired woman," Jed said. "She explained what was actually waiting for us up in the mountain. Nothing better or worse than what we've always had. She said the old place was cleaned out and ready for anyone who wanted to return."

"We've come from back there," I blurted out. "Look at me. Does it look to you like a good place to be?"

I could feel their eyes on me, feasting on me, taking in my gaunt frame, my scabbed face. I could feel Miho look at me.

"Snow gets deeper too." Adam shrugged, acting as if he didn't care whether or not they believed him. "You can go if you want. Gets pretty cold over that way. You'll need something to get through the snow. And warmer clothes than what you've got on."

"And our village is burned," Abe said. "Yours might be too."

"What?" Jed asked, looking confused, doubting us.

"She did it," I said. "That woman. She's destroyed everything. And now she's trying to get you to go back."

We all stood there in the silence, taking each other in. Beyond them, I could see the next tree. Beyond that, on the horizon, a narrow purple strip the width of a thread. Was that an illusion? Or the eastern mountain range?

"Is that the mountain?" I asked. "Can you see it from here?"

Jed turned around, moving so that he could see through the crowd behind him. He looked at me again, and I could tell he was weighing my appearance with the promises Kathy must have made about how good it was back there.

"If you can see it from here," he said, "you've got good eyes."

I turned to the others. "You all ready? I'm not going back. Not for anything in the world."

Miho nodded, and for the first time I felt a softening in her toward me. Adam, too, seemed inspired by my action.

"Fair enough," Abe said. "Wait a minute."

I had already taken a few steps forward, so now I was even with Abe, could see his face, and it emanated peace and goodwill.

"Don't believe her," Abe said to Jed. "Come back with us. I'll show you the way into the mountain. Please." He finished by nodding a kind sort of greeting, something he gave each and every person who made eye contact with him as we made our way through their midst.

"Abe?" I heard someone ask. "Did he say his name is Abe? Is that Abe from the first village?"

Soon the crowd was behind us, and still we walked on, now with a clear view of the tree. Thinking about them going back into the old mountain nearly had me in tears. The dust. The bog. The cold. I wished I could tell them. I wished they would believe me, but I knew the way Kathy's words could whisper to you.

I tried not to look back, but after two or three minutes, I couldn't help it. I glanced over my shoulder.

Every single one of them was following us.

They weren't the last group we met. In between nearly every one of those final trees, we crossed paths with a group that had been persuaded, always by Kathy, to leave and go back. Sometimes the groups were large, hundreds of people. At other times they came in twos and threes.

And every single time, we were able to convince them to turn around.

So it was that we finally arrived at the last tree, in plain view of the eastern mountain, with a crowd behind us that numbered in the thousands. As we got closer to the mountain,

I could sense the difference between it and the range we had left behind. There was something calming about it, welcoming. It was bathed in a purplish hue as the light faded, and the trees were of every kind. There were maples and sycamores, oaks and birches. Farther up the mountain, where the rocky outcroppings became more dominant, evergreens swept the stone with their graceful boughs. And everywhere, flowers.

At the base of the mountain, I saw a woman standing beside a fire.

When we got closer I noticed that the mountainside was teeming with people. Soon the glow of a thousand fires lit the mountainside. There were more people there than I could have counted. The fires were like stars in the night sky.

We walked up to the woman. It was Kathy.

Abe turned to those behind us. "Go ahead," he said. "Make your way up. We'll join you soon."

It took a long, long time for all of them to file past. I could hear the sounds of reunifications on the mountainside, people calling out in loving surprise to returning friends or family. Names cried out with tears in their voices. Hugs. The pounding of backs. The rustling as people made more room around a fire.

It was the sound of coming home.

"You all go ahead as well," Abe said solemnly to the three of us.

"What? No," Miho said. "We're with you, Abe."

Abe looked at me when he spoke. "Thank you, Miho, but I have some unfinished business with Kathy. You all make your way up the mountain. I'll sort it out."

We turned to walk away, and I heard his voice again. "Dan."

He held out his hand, the same way he would have reached for me if I was falling. "I'll need that key to make sure everything goes back where it belongs."

I walked over to him and dug deep in the knapsack. I pulled out the key and laid it in his palm.

He nodded.

That was it. We walked up into the trees, into the smell of a thousand fires, and I felt emotion clogging my throat.

30 AND WE BEGIN OUR DESCENT

MIHO AND I remain at the back of the crowd, walking slowly through the trees, always farther up the mountain, farther in.

We hike during the day, sleep on the warm ground at night. We walk for a long time, maybe weeks? Could it be months? It's hard to say. But it's very slow going. It didn't take many days for the others from our village to find us, and now we walk together, a small cluster at the very back of this rustling sea of humanity. The old crew. We keep our distance from the rest, the way my house was always separated a bit from the rest of the town. John and Po, Miss B, Circe, and Misha. Miho and Adam. Me. Even Mary St. Clair. Together again. Everyone except Abe.

He went back for her. A sob catches in my throat.

No one walks at night, and at first it bothered me. I kept looking in the shadows, wondering if Kathy had somehow managed to trap Abe inside the mountain. If she did, I know she'll come for us, and I don't know if we have the fortitude to resist her without him. So I keep my eyes open most nights, as long as I can, waiting for her to emerge. What will

I do if I see her? What will I do if she walks into camp and starts filling our heads with nonsense about the old mountain range, how things are better there? I don't know. But if she does come back, I want to know the moment she arrives, so I keep my eyes open.

It is night, and we are all sitting around the fire. John gathers wood and makes a large pile. He will sit there and tend the fire all night. It's what he does. Po sits at the edge of the light, carving something, humming to himself. Our eyes meet through the dancing shadows, and his gaze is softer than I remember. There is nothing there but acceptance. He nearly smiles, then looks back at his carving. Adam sits beside him, watching, occasionally asking questions about all this time between what happened before and now. Miho comes over and sits beside him.

"The air is thin," Miho says.

"And dry," Adam replies.

"We're close to the top," I say. Soon we'll have to decide if we're going to cross over the mountain without Abe and Lucia. On the one hand, this feels like a silly concern. On the other hand, crossing to the other side of the mountain feels like something monumental, something that should only be done with serious consideration.

I look over to where Circe and Misha sit with Mary. The three of them whisper to each other, not because they are trying to keep secrets but because it is a quiet dusk that calls for gentle voices. It is cool, but perfectly so, without a chill. If this night is like the last few, everyone will sleep on the ground without blankets. I try to stay awake as long as I can, on the lookout for Kathy, but most nights I fall asleep staring up through the forest canopy, at the stars that have become visible ever since we started climbing, wondering if I could have brought Lucia back with me. What if I had kept the knapsack? What if I had gone to retrieve it? I remember Adam kneeling on the rock island and, after that, Lucia running back to me. I remember her disappearing. It is something I see in my sleep, her sudden dropping, the entirety of her vanishing.

We scavenged for mushrooms and berries during our walk that day, and there is always plenty for everyone. Wild fruit trees can be found standing in the open places, and we help ourselves to apples and cherries. The path is not treacherous. But it does sometimes feel long and winding.

"Where are we going?" Misha asks the group, and we gather closer to the fire, the darkness growing deeper behind us like a steadily filling pool.

"Only a little farther," I say, although I can't know for sure. "We're nearly at the top."

John smiles. "Now this reminds me of the village." He shrugs as if to preemptively ward off questions about why he's thinking about the village. But I was thinking the same thing. And no matter how far up the mountain we walk, there is still a part of me that longs for the old days. Is it because Abe is gone? I can't tell. I can't sort these things out in my mind. Any thought of Abe leads to my eyes welling up, my throat aching.

"Up front," Mary says, "before I came back looking for you all, I heard people say there's a city on the other side of the mountain."

"Like the village?" Miss B asks.

316

"Maybe," Mary says. "Maybe better, without that old mountain looking over our shoulder all the time."

Miss B shudders and moves closer to the fire. I look at her. She seems younger now.

"Do you think she'll try again?" Circe asks. "Do you think she'll try to take us back?"

There is a pause. No one wants to answer.

"I'm not going back," Adam says. "No matter what she tells me, I'm not going back." His is the voice of a child, convinced he has learned how to fly.

"What do you miss the most?" Circe asks.

"You're full of questions," Po replies, but good-heartedly, with a grin. A few of us snicker.

"No, really!" Circe smiles. "What do you miss? You first, Po."

Po raises his eyebrows in mock surprise. "Me? I don't miss anything."

Po is a changed man. We are all changed. When we first met up as a group, soon after I stared out from the rocky out-cropping, everyone eyed Adam with suspicion. They seemed to evaluate his every move, his every step, his every word. And that first night, when we all stayed together around one fire, an awkward silence fell among the dancing shadows.

That was when someone started talking, and it was the person I least expected.

Po.

He looked over at Adam and said in a firm voice, "I know what happened. I've asked around. We've compared stories. And I want you to know that I, that all of us"—he paused and looked at the group, received nods and sincere looks from everyone—"forgive you and your brother. That's all behind us now. We're ready to keep walking up this mountain." He stood up, walked over to where Adam sat, and shook his hand.

"Oh, c'mon, there has to be something," Circe insists now, staring at Po with laughter in her eyes.

He snorts, sighs, and stops carving. He stares into the fire, then looks around at each of us as he talks. "You know, I miss the plains. I miss the mornings, waking early with the light, and walking out into the high grass."

We all sit quietly in the wake of this unexpected revelation. He returns to his piece of wood, the knife peeling away shavings like butter.

"I miss the big sky," Mary whispers so that I can barely hear her.

"I miss the gardens," Miho says.

"They'll have gardens there," I say.

She looks at me with surprise, and it's the closest she has come to looking at me in that old way, back when we were friends. "How do you know?" she asks, giving me a curious smile.

"I don't know, I just do. Big gardens too, inside tall fences, and you can spend all the time you want in there, harvesting and pruning and planting. There are orchards there, and quiet corners."

"That sounds nice," Miho murmurs.

"And birds," I say, reaching out and patting my brother's knee. "All the birds you could ever want, singing and chirping. You can sit there and watch them all day if you want."

"I miss my oven," Miss B says in a sad voice.

"I miss your oven," Po says, and we all laugh.

A lightness moves in among us, binds us closer together, begins to heal these nameless things that have come between us. Circe, smiling, leans forward and throws a handful of dead leaves on the fire. They smolder and smoke.

There is a rustling in the woods down the hill from us, the sound a deer might have made if it was wandering up to see what the light was all about. But we have not seen any animals on the mountain. We all freeze.

"Anyone else hear that?" Mary asks, her voice a creaking door. A few of us nod. All of us stare into the darkness, and a shape emerges, the shape of a human being, standing at the edge of the firelight.

"Who are you?" Po asks, tensing up. John stands beside him.

The person falls to their knees, but they are now inside the light, and I get my first clear glimpse of who it is.

"Abe?" I stand, wanting to go to him but still holding back for the same reason that everyone else remains motionless. He is almost unrecognizable. His nose is broken and there is dried blood on his face. He holds up his wounded hands so that they do not touch the ground. His head is covered in deep scratches that have healed only partially. His clothes are mangled and torn.

But it is Abe, and we are all a rush of movement to get close to him. We bump into each other. Mary trips, picks herself up.

I'm there first. I stop, and everyone else stops with me. It's as if we cannot touch him, as if an invisible barrier is around him.

"Dear one," he says in a husky voice. He turns as if we're not even here, looks over his shoulder into the shadows, and gives out a weak call. "Come along."

A rustling sound in the leaves makes the hair stand up on the back of my neck. We all flinch at the sound, wanting to retreat back to the fire. But we are frozen there, congregating around Abe.

He sways and calls out again, "It's all right. Come out where they can see you." He coughs, a low, wheezing retch from the depths of his lungs, and lifts one of his hands. A wave. A beckoning.

I hear the rustling sound again—the sound of a squirrel dancing on dry leaves, or a bird flapping its feathers without leaving the ground. And then she emerges.

Lucia.

Abe passes out, collapsing face-first onto the forest floor.

We stare at Lucia, look at Abe, look back at Lucia again. They both look like they have come through a battle, but she has healed quickly or perhaps did not bear the brunt of it. She is wispy, as I remember her, and ready to run. But she looks around at us, and when she spots Adam at the fringe of our small group, she can't keep her voice from springing out of her.

"Daddy!"

A light rises in Adam's eyes, like the morning sun easing up over a mountain, and he just stands there. That's all he does. The two of them stare at each other in the darkness, the fire burning lower behind us. I can tell he is finally remembering everything. All of it. She takes a hesitant step toward us on her toes, and I can tell she's holding herself back, until Adam lets out a sound like a laughing cry and runs to her.

She vanishes in his embrace, and he is whispering to her over and over again. We watch, unable to look away. I feel like my heart might explode.

"Abe," Mary says. "We have to help Abe."

We take turns sitting with him through the night, and when it's my turn, I get on my knees and stare at his closed eyes. Circe and Misha took water from a nearby stream and washed him, so the Abe I am looking at is scarred and battered but no longer bloody. He appears to be sleeping. But I'm worried we might lose him. His breathing is so shallow. He seems so far away.

I reach over and take his hand. His weathered fingers are cracked and worn, and the wounds on his hands are wrapped in strips of torn clothes some of us donated to the cause. I want to say something. I want to say everything. But all I can say, with long pauses in between, is, "I'm sorry" and "Thank you."

John and Po rise early, when the fire has burned low, and build a makeshift stretcher out of poles long enough for eight of us to hold, four on each side, bearing the weight of our friend Abe. More than a friend.

And that is the day we come to the top of the mountain.

At first the trees clear, the sky growing large above us, the ground more rock than dirt. Then there is a flattening, and we realize we are crossing an open space. We do not even take a moment to look back. I can hear the people who have gone before us exclaiming and shouting to one another as they make their way down the far side of the eastern mountain, and there is joy in their voices. Astonishment.

We come to the edge where the path begins its descent, and we stand there for a moment, every single one of us. It is a vision to behold.

"You've got to see this, Abe," I say. Someone gives out a loud sob, but I can't see who it is through my own tears.

"C'mon," Adam says, his voice catching. He clears his throat and tries again. "C'mon. Let's take him down."

And we begin our descent.

AUTHOR NOTE

I HAVE ALWAYS found Dante's *Inferno* intriguing, and as soon as I imagined that it might be possible to escape from it, *These Nameless Things* was born. I thought about Dan and Adam for many years, from around 2011 until 2018, before being able to finally wrap my mind around the story.

If you have read the *Inferno*, doubtless you recognized things in this book: the signpost at the entrance to the mountain; the vision of the leopard, the lion, and the wolf; a few of the various circles, settings, and bodies of water; and some character names.

More importantly, I hope this book serves as a mirror to the *Inferno*, providing hope for those of us going through our own personal hell and leading us to ask questions about guilt, hope, and forgiveness.

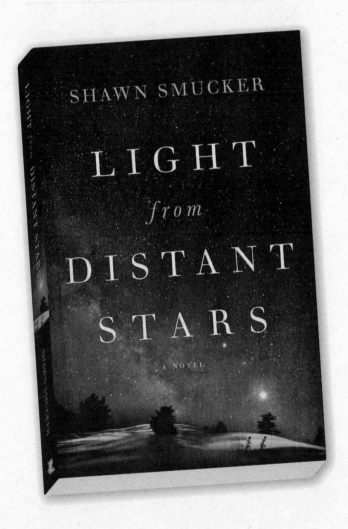

1 THE BODY

COHEN MARAH CLEARS his throat quietly, more out of discomfort than the presence of any particular thing that needs clearing, and attempts to step over the body for a second time. His heel no more than lightens its weight on the earth before he puts his foot back down and sighs. He tilts his head and purses his lips, as if preparing to give a talk to an unruly child. He does not take his hands out of his pockets, worried that he will taint the scene, which in the next moment he realizes is ridiculous. This is where he works. This is where he works with his father, Calvin. His fingerprints are everywhere.

He stares down at the body again, and sadness keeps him leaning to one side. It's the physical weight of emotion, and that weight is not centered inside of him but skewed, imbalanced. It is not his father's slightly opened eyes looking up at him from the floor that bring down the heaviness, and it is not his father's cleanly shaven cheeks, haggard and old. It is not the way the tangled arms rest on his chest, or the way his one leg is still bent and propped up against the examination table.

No, the thing that weighs Cohen down is the shiny baldness of his father's head, the way the light reflects from it the same way it did when he was alive. The light should dim, he thinks. It should flatten out, and the glare should fade. There should be no light, not anymore.

ACKNOWLEDGMENTS

DOES ANYONE RECOGNIZE the toll a book requires better than the family members of a working writer? Thank you to Maile, Cade, Lucy, Abra, Sam, Leo, and Poppy for loving me well, reading my words enthusiastically, and allowing the space for stories to thrive in our home and in our lives.

Shawn Smucker is the author of the award-winning novels *The Day the Angels Fell, The Edge of Over There,* and *Light from Distant Stars*. He has also written a memoir, *Once We Were Strangers*. He lives with his wife and six children in Lancaster, Pennsylvania. You can find him online at www.shawnsmucker.com.

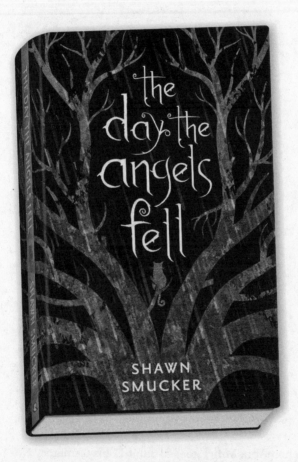